PERSONAL PRONOUNS

PERSONAL PRONOUNS

A Novel

David Allen Edmonds

Published by Snowbelt Publishing, Ltd.
Medina, Ohio

ISBN-13: 9780998546605
ISBN-10: 0998546607

Cover design: *Julie Bayer, State By Design*
Photo: *Judi Terrell Linden*
Editing: *Jeff Gabel*

This book,
as everything in my life,
is dedicated to
Marie

CHAPTER ONE

"I don't know how long it took for her to die. I already told you that." Joe dug the heels of his hands into his eyes. "Several times."

"Tell me again."

Joe Lehrer flicked his thumbnail with his index finger. Hastings demanded he bare his soul, while keeping the office light low and hiding in the shadows himself. Joe unlocked his jaw and began again.

"Three maybe four seconds? A minute? I don't know." Joe spoke quickly, the words running into one another, overlapping. Hastings nodded. "All I remember when I close my eyes are disconnected flashes. Never a pattern. Fragments. The time itself? Shit."

He forced himself to continue. "There was a thump, a crash, and she screamed. More a cough than a scream." Joe's voice broke. "Like she was gagging."

A few seconds passed, then Hastings prodded, "And?"

Joe squeezed his face with his hands, his voice now a bark. "And? What the hell do you think? That's when it smashed her face in, that's when, that's when--"

Hastings took a breath. "Tell me what you saw. Exactly."

Joe's voice came from someplace outside of him. Disconnected. Monotone. "Glass flying in...the thump...the glass whipping my face. In my mouth."

His eyes were unfocused. One hand gestured vaguely. "I can't do this anymore."

The light from the table lamp caught the edge of the scar on his forehead. Hastings wasn't sure how hard he should push. "When you're ready," he said in what he felt was his most reassuring voice.

Joe screamed and jumped to his feet. "When I'm ready? How the fuck can I be ready? For what, my wife to die?" Joe spun, looking for a way out. An animal trapped. His flailing arm caught the table lamp and smashed it to the floor. His head jerked to the sound, his shoulders sagged, and his arms slumped to his side.

Hastings was halfway to his feet before the man dropped back onto the sofa. He wanted both both to comfort Joe and to protect himself from him. His hand shook as he adjusted the lampshade on his desk.

Joe sobbed. The sound racking and tearing as it escaped. Hastings set the box of tissues onto the cushion beside Joe. He was surprised when Joe began to speak.

"The car kept going by itself. Right, then left, then right again. I don't know how. My hands weren't on the wheel. I was trying to reach her."

Hastings picked up his notebook.

Joe had curled himself into a ball, his face buried in his shoulder. "When the car stopped rolling I was above her. Hanging in the seatbelt."

Hastings kept his breathing steady and strained to hear.

Joe's voice bled into the air. "The whole thing was like an eclipse. Brilliant sunlight, then dark. The black came up the hood, crossed the windshield, hid her face."

"We were under an overpass. In the shadow. The car was on its side. I couldn't get out of the seatbelt." The ligaments in Joe's wrists and the muscles in his forearms stood out against his skin. His hands were balled like the rigid knobs of a burn victim. "I couldn't reach her because of the goddam seatbelt."

At that Joe's attention snapped to Hastings' pen. "And you're writing," he spat. "I'm talking and you're writing it down. That won't bring her back."

Hastings checked his growing frustration. "We're not trying to bring her back."

"Then why do I have to--" Joe let out a deep, tortured sigh, his arms now slack on his lap. The son of a bitch would not let up.

"She *died* in that shadow, Jerry. Two seconds. Two minutes. What difference does it make?" He bore his eyes into Hastings'. "Is that enough?"

Hastings willed himself not to respond to Joe's anger. After a pause he said, "I don't know. I wasn't there."

Joe spoke without thinking. "Just before, before it happened, she's happy. We both are. Together in the car. First weekend school is out. Sunroof open. Laughing. "

He paused as if hearing the word for the first time. "Laughing," he whispered.

"Sunlight on our faces. We spin out, roll over, end up in a ditch. She's dead."

"The last thing she says--" Joe spoke to himself as he faced Hastings. "The last thing, 'I might be pregnant'."

Hastings stifled a gasp with a cough. "You never told me that before."

Joe held his cupped hands so Hastings could see them. "I want to stop the bleeding. Her face is cut from her ear to, to her neck, the whole side of her face. At first it's a line, a smooth red line."

He looked from his hands to Hastings. "She's bleeding and I think I can stop it. Hold it back. The cut is a curve. Like a smile. I can hold it together if I can get both my hands on her. I can hold it together until--"

Hastings opened his mouth, frightened by this revelation, but Joe continued. "See, I have to hide her teeth. And her tongue. For when the ambulance gets there." Joe held his hands closer to Hastings. "I want to hold her together. I can see her teeth and her tongue through her neck.

"But the blood. At first it was just a line like I said." He nodded but kept his eyes on his hands in front of him. "But it starts to pump out. Once. Then twice. It spurts out, sprays into my face. Through my fingers. There's so much and I can't reach her. I can touch her, but I can't hold her. It gushes out of her neck. Her heart's pumping it. In bursts. Five, six times. I can't get enough pressure to stop it. Fucking seat belt. Blood in my eyes, I twist and reach for her. She gurgles, like speaking under water.

"Then it was quiet. No cars. No voices. Nothing. She saw me. I know she did, Jerry. For a second--just a second. I said 'I love you, Cathy, I love you.' Then she couldn't see me anymore. Her eyes were open. The blood had stopped. Her heart ran out. I couldn't help her." Joe's head slumped forward. "There's not a fucking mark on me."

"Very good, Joe." Hastings tried to loosen the muscles in his back and shoulders as he looked at the broken man on the sofa before him. He was horrified he had pushed him so hard. "You got through it all this time," he managed.

Joe's head suddenly snapped up. "So to answer your question, Jerry, what do you think? Seventeen seconds? Give or take?"

Joe Lehrer wiped his hands on the dish towel and turned away from the sink. The phone startled him as he passed the counter top between the kitchen and what would have been his family room. He snatched the phone from the end table, and choked the second ring.

"Joe? It's Bert. Just wanted to make sure you were up or see if you needed--"

"Yeah." He sighed and tossed the towel over his shoulder. It was the second call from Roberta Andrascik, who had reminded him the night before to set his alarm.

"--and with the weather so hot, I was worried that--"

"It does look like it's gonna be another hot one," Joe mumbled.

"--dunno, you were upset, and I thought--"

"Look, I'm sorry about that."

"--friends forever, and you can always--"

"I know, Bert. Thank you." He looked away from the two chairs on the patio outside and nodded as if she were in the room. "But I think I'll drive myself in today," he said quickly. He had shared an office with Bert for most of the twelve years they had worked at Stradford High School. He knew he had to interrupt her to speak. "No, really, I want to." A bird stood on the round glass table between the chairs and directed one small round eye at him.

"I'll be glad to drive you," Bert continued.

"Thanks, but a man's gotta do, what a man's gotta do," he said and stood up.

"You sound like Popeye, which would make me Olive Oyle."

His lips began to turn upward in a smile, then halted. "And neither of us is Bluto. See you there, Bert. Thanks." He dropped the phone into its charger and wondered if he was the last person in Stradford to still have a land-line.

No. I can do this myself. I need to do this myself.

Joe put his cup into the dishwasher and sponged the counter-top clean. He wiped his hands dry again and opened the cupboard beneath the sink. The waste container wasn't quite full, but it was better to empty it now than let it overflow like Cathy did.

Even the trash is a reminder, he thought as he fought the plastic trash bag through the screen door.

The bird had flown away leaving their chairs alone on the deck. The sky was already its late summer haze. Joe felt the warmth of the sun on his arms as he snapped the garbage can lid shut. He knew it would be stifling later, humidity trapped in a thermal inversion or whatever they called it. He returned to the quiet coolness inside.

The textbooks he needed were stacked on the dining room table with his laptop and several notebooks, one for each of his classes. As he straightened the pile he repeated to himself that Cathy was dead. He had meetings today, and the kids would be there tomorrow. It was time to get out of the house and back to work.

The phone rang again on his way to the stairs; he picked up in the small office where he kept the computer. "Joe," the voice boomed in his ear. "Why is six afraid of seven?"

I can't do jokes. Not today.

Joe leaned back into the computer chair and shook his head. Bob McCauley, his best friend, film buff, comedian wanna-be, amateur grief counselor. Like Roberta's, his phone call was not unexpected. Bob was either trying to cheer him up or giving him another chance to apologize.

"You're stalling, Joey, like you do when you don't know the punch line."

"It's not very punchy," Joe said into the guffawing on the phone.

"Okay, okay, seven, eight, nine. Get it? Seven 'ate' nine!"

Joe laughed in spite of himself. Bob and his wife had been with him the week of the funeral, Linda organizing the stream of well-wishers, Bob serving as unofficial Master of Ceremonies. They had cried together, and laughed, too, the emotions raw and indistinguishable. Joe didn't have much family of his own; Roberta, the McCauley's and others had taken it as their duty to get him through Cathy's death.

"Come on, you never heard it before," Bob said.

"Everybody's heard it."

"You could call me an asshole, like you do when I'm the funny one."

"You're an asshole, Bob" Joe said and laughed again..

"Close enough. OK. So what time should I pick you up?"

"You don't need to. I can drive myself."

"You think you should?"

"I'll drive myself." Joe drew his eyes away from the empty porch.

"It's no trouble. It's right on my--"

"--I'm fine, Bob, see you there. Thanks."

Upstairs Joe examined his face in the mirror and pulled his razor and shaving cream off the shelf. A tall man, he bent over to fit his entire image into the glass. He looked as he always had except for the eyes and the nearly faded scar on his forehead: a round face bordered with short, dark curls, a slightly crooked nose, and ears that seemed disproportionately small. The eyes, once a laughing dark brown, now seemed to have forgotten the joke. The flesh below them was saggy and dark, almost purple.

He left water on his face and spread white foam across his cheek. It wasn't that he didn't appreciate his friends' help. He wouldn't have survived the summer without it. But he felt he was always explaining how he felt. Defending his feelings. He stretched his chin side to side and ran the blade under warm water. They had called because they were worried about him, and he had told them he didn't need them.

Joe plowed a pink strip through the lather, rinsed the blade clean and shook it. He felt quarantined, locked in an isolation tent, observed from all sides. He had rarely been out of the house, never alone. Someone was always handing him a casserole, running the vacuum, arranging flowers. Carnations. They had always reminded Cathy of a funeral home.

He tightened the skin at the corner of his mouth by pressing against it with his tongue. He caught his eye in the glass.

They shared my pain. They hurt because I hurt. They cried for me.

He laid the razor to the side and braced his hands on the slick white surface.

I returned their concern with stubbornness, their love with arrogance. Instead of admitting I needed them, I told them to leave me alone.

The face in the mirror disagreed.

They'll forgive you because they're your friends. Bob and Roberta already have.

He rinsed the dabs of shaving cream with his wet hands, and followed with the towel. His fingers found the places on his face that burned and he rubbed moisturizer into them. It was like what his friends had tried to do for him at the wake, at the church, at the cemetery:

'I know how you feel.'

'Here's what you need to do.'

'When my mother died--'

They think I can't do anything by myself.

'Eat this, you'll feel better.'

'It's okay to cry.'

'Don't let it get you down.'

They mean well, but shit. It's patronizing. Contradictory.

'Forget about it. Go out and do something fun.'

'You'll find another woman.'

No, I won't.

He shook his head at the man on the other side of the sink and wiped his hands on the towel.

It's time to forget all the noise and get back to work. Get started on year number thirteen with the kids.

Vikki slowed her walk to reduce the sound her heels made on the brightly polished marble in the lobby of the Marriott. She told herself she didn't need to hurry, this was, after all, a regular and she was on time. She just needed to blend in with the guests, like Karl always told her, and not call attention to herself.

Juan made eye contact and quickly broke it as she passed the registration desk; the day shift manager knew his place. The stream of businessmen descending from the conference rooms on the mezzanine parted, and she stepped through them into an empty elevator. She slid her card into the slot for the top floor and checked her face in the mirror she kept in her tiny purse. The part in her blonde hair was straight and her lipstick was clean. She wiggled to adjust her breasts in the tube top, and noticed the reflection of her navel ring in the panel surrounding the floor numbers. The '8' lit up.

Her four-inch strapless heels sunk into the maroon carpet when she stepped off, and she thought again how it was always so quiet up here. She stopped in front of 833 and checked her breath in her palm. She rapped lightly on the door and called "Special Delivery."

"Right on time," the man said as he opened the door. "I like that."

"Your order, sir," Vikki said, and made a slow pirouette.

He ran his eyes over her as he always did, pausing at the ring, lingering at her breasts. He breathed in and nodded. "Black Opium."

"Just like you ordered." She kept her eyes on his as she stepped into the room and out of her shoes.

"I appreciate the punctuality," he said.

She looked down from his face and grinned, "Looks like you've already started." She sloughed off her skirt and followed him to the lounge chair by the window.

He adjusted himself on the leather and spread his knees apart.

Vikki pulled her top over her head, shook her hair free and knelt down in front of him. She closed her eyes and thought about the money.

⟩⟨+⟩⟨

Stradford looked to Joe like it always had: a farming community morphed into a generic outer-ring suburb. Strip malls sprawled unchecked down both sides of Cleveland Ave. Chandler Creek had once crossed under a bridge here. Now it was invisible, encased in a tunnel that ran beneath the white concrete. The rolling hills had been leveled, the shallow basins filled in, and the farms carpeted over with thick green sod. Wendy's and Taco Bell competed behind a row of identical, white-banded trees lining the storefronts of Chandler Meadows.

But something felt different to him. It's because I haven't been out much, he told himself as he stopped at the next light and looked around. It wasn't the traffic. Cleveland's five lanes carried the same constant stream it had before, and the lights still weren't computer controlled.

Maybe it's me.

Farther south on his right the strip of stores was broken. The sidewalk ended beyond the Jiffy Lube and became a dusty path that wound crookedly through tufts of stunted grass. A seven foot high fence loomed upwards, gnarled trunks of brownish gray wood connected by strands of rusted wire. Behind and through the fence, a jungle of tall weeds and small trees competed for light. Reddish pieces of farm machinery reached above the greenery, like dinosaurs lording over their domain. The remains of several cars, a big John Deere and a once blue school bus, its windows broken out, filled the space behind the fence. This was the last vestige of old Stradford, Oskar Brummelberger's farm-turned-junkyard.

Joe shook his head. It wasn't the rape of the pristine farming life that was bothering him. It was the politics. Ten minutes into my first class, lunch time at the latest, someone'll see I'm back and expect me to get involved in their *cris de jour.* You're the hero Joe, solve my problem for me. He bounced the ball of his fist on the steering wheel.

The light changed to green. He looked both ways before cautiously pulling through the intersection. Beyond Oskar's place the strands of fence wire pivoted around a thick, stunted tree, and the green sod returned. Joe stopped and signaled for a right turn.

I can't be their hero. I got problems of my own.

Karl knew to slow down when he turned into Oskar's. But he still wasn't prepared for the lurching jolt as he traded concrete for the rutted dirt of the path that led to the once white barn. The roofline of the enormous, slope-shouldered structure slumped toward the center above an open hayloft. Half a door dangled from the upper hinge. From the gaping hole a conveyor belt pointed down at a heap of washing machines, a striped beach umbrella and a trailer that read "Honey Covered Funnel Cakes."

I enjoy individual style, Karl thought, I do, but this is beyond the Pale. He brought the car to a complete stop, then drove slowly onto the grass. If he bitches about his lawn, I'll blow his fucking head off. After he pays for the new shocks.

Karl was tall and broad shouldered with a cat-like gait. Perhaps a little past his prime, he used racquetball at the Stradford Athletic Club to keep his body in shape and his contacts in the community current. Despite the white hair, he was still athletic enough to win or lose as needed. He carefully closed the car door, adjusted his sport coat and tried to keep the dust off his slacks as he walked toward the barn.

"You said we was jake," the fat man said as Karl entered what passed for an office inside the barn. "You said if I did that job you wouldn't be coming round here no more."

Karl could see well enough in the bad light to catch the fear in the slits that were Brummelberger's eyes. He did his best to hide it, glancing from the computer screen to the desk top before returning to Karl, but the fat man was scared. "First of all, Oskar, I have never used the word jake in that context. Nobody has used it for twenty years. Try *copacetic*."

Confusion competed with fear across Oskar's face. "I'm legit, a businessman," he managed, "uh, uh job creator."

Karl moderated his stare. "We all are. Which makes Stradford the optimal business location in Northeast Ohio."

"Yeah, and I'm tight with Alfie. He's the mayor."

"You are. He is. I digress." The man's obtuseness is legend. "Oskar, I gave you a job and you botched--"

"I didn't botch nothin'. I did just like Pedro told me."

Karl shook his head at the man's stupidity. "You killed the wrong person, Oskar. That is classified as a botch."

The fat man blanched and took a step back. "That was months ago, it, it was hard to aim, I--"

Karl bore his gaze into the fat face. "You're a lucky man. Only reason you're not dead is it somehow seems to be working. The poor schlepp is so broken up he's not making any trouble for us."

Oskar dragged a dirty hand across his sweaty brow. "Thank you, thank you--"

"Temporarily." Karl pursed his lips. "How can I put this? As long as he's quiet, you're alive."

Oskar's whiny voice sounded like it was being squeezed from his eyes. "There must be something I can do for you. Something else--"

Karl's mouth smiled. "Now that's the right attitude."

"What I got to do?"

Karl stepped around the table and closed on Oskar, forcing him to step back. "We'll get back to you."

Oskar straightened up and blurted, "I'm not sticking my neck out for you or nobody else." Hearing his words in the dim light, he clamped his mouth shut and took another step backwards.

Karl nodded. "You will, or you're dead."

Oskar deflated like a week old balloon. "I got no choice."

"You don't. And to reprise an oldie, we know where you live." Karl rapped the top of the computer two times then strode to the door. He turned back and said, "We know where your daughter lives, too."

Joe turned the corner and drove down the black asphalt of Stradford Way. Two clean, yellow lines led him toward the turn into the high school. He bounced over the pothole in front of Teeple's house, and waited in line for the oncoming traffic to clear.

Like the line at the wake, he thought. The whole building will be staring at me. Giving me that pity look. Have a doughnut, Joe, you'll feel better.

He checked the mirror but the sun blinded him. He flicked on the left turn signal. Stradford High School lay beyond a row of scraggly trees. A flat horizontal building, it spread from the auditorium on the left, to the two-storied addition on the right. The rest was one floor of cinder block faced with beige brick, a dark brown strip of metal running along the roof.

He checked the oncoming traffic and told himself what would happen inside. They'll try to cheer me up. They'll remember me blubbering at the funeral home, at the church, at the cemetery. They'll try to make me laugh. Fucking Bob. Here, have a joke, you'll feel better.

Parking lots filled the area from the creek bed beneath the trees to the brown aluminum doors, interrupted only by several islands of trees. If the grass and trees had been better maintained, the school would have looked like one of the strip malls along Cleveland Ave. The car rocked suddenly in the wake of an 18-wheeler and he jerked awake. He let out a breath and tried to relax.

It's always the politics. Usually the losing politics of us against the Board of Education, but after the strike last spring, even after winning, the weight will be back on me. They'll want me to be President of the Association.

He turned behind the truck into the faculty parking lot. No, we've got a new contract, it'll be a levy. That's it. The District is broke again. If we don't pass a levy, class sizes will explode and we'll all lose our jobs.

Joe, do something for us. You'll feel better.

The lot near his office was full; he found a place near the main entrance. He gathered the texts, his notebooks and his laptop bag from the passenger seat and yanked the handle. The seatbelt buckle clanged off the window. The door held for an instant, then fell back onto his shin. He shoved it open again and kicked his foot out to catch the rebound. "Piece of shit rice bucket!" he said out loud. He stepped away and slammed the door. It made a hollow, tinny thunk that pissed him off more. It wasn't his Audi.

"Need a hand there, Mr. Sunshine?"

"No, thanks Bob, I got everything under control." Joe stopped walking when he heard the clapping. "You may be more annoying in person than you are on the phone."

"It's a gift." Bob McCauley was a thick 6'0", a Tom Selleck mustache set in his round Irish face. "Or a talent, I get those mixed up."

"A pain in the ass is what it is," Joe said as he swung him the shoulder bag.

"Got it. You can put the rest of your crap in my office."

Joe didn't have the energy to ask why, and followed him out of the lot and through the glass doors into the front hall of the school. They threaded their way through the security gates by the main office, and up the three steps to the north hallway.

"Do not look at certain parts of the stallion." Bob grinned and hooked his thumb at the fifteen foot sculpture of the rearing school mascot.

"I am not in the mood," Joe said.

Bob shook his head and led him out of the noise into the Guidance reception area. Inside his office he closed the door and looked at him closely.

"So why am I in your office instead of mine?" Joe said.

Bob's eyes narrowed. "You okay?"

"I'm fine." Joe exhaled and looked away.

"Come on, you didn't joke about the studless stallion, and you look like shit."

"That's how I feel."

"Your face is pale and you're sweating. You don't have to be here."

"I can't stay home another day."

"Probably not," Bob said. "I just wanted to warn you that your old buddy Mel is in the building."

Joe turned to face Bob. "He doesn't work here anymore. They promoted him to the Board office."

"Mel always has an excuse. Been here almost every day of scheduling."

"Still mad about the strike."

"He is, but hey, we have cookies." Bob squinted at the cookie on a stick he was holding. "You know, Vlad the Impaler could have baked this."

Joe snorted as his friend bit into the gingerbread boy shape. "Thanks for the joke. And the warning, but I need to drop my stuff in the office."

Bob peeked his head through the doorway into the hall. "All clear, come on."

They navigated the hall to the Media Center and up the stairs to the Language Department. Bob stopped on the landing and gestured down into the library at several young teachers clustered around the copy machine.

"They get younger every year, don't they? Younger and nubiler. Whoa."

"Feeling old." Joe looked past him and nodded.

"Old and married." Bob turned his head quickly. "Wait, Joe, sorry, I--"

Arms suddenly encircled his neck. Joe dropped down a step and stiffened. "Oh, it's you Roberta," he said and hid his face in her neck.

"Joe, are you sure you should be back?" The French teacher appeared not to have noticed his reaction. "Wouldn't you be better off at home?"

"It's better to be here." He held her away and noticed her red eyes. Framed by straight brown hair. Swollen and full.

"It's too soon," she sniffed and turned her eyes away.

"The French never control their emotions." Zimmerman reached down from a higher step and shook Joe's hand.

"Good to see you, Zim. Thanks for the card."

"No problem." Zimmerman taught advanced math. He was a spare man, his alert, intelligent eyes bound by wire-framed glasses. "So what's better, being back where you belong or remembering we won the strike?"

When Joe didn't answer, Zimmerman looked a question at Bob. The guidance counselor shook his head.

"Well, we have you to thank for that anyway, Joe," Zimmerman said quickly.

Joe shook his head and continued watching the dozens of conversations in the noisy room below, his back to them. "No."

"Heard something interesting at the hairdressers yesterday," Roberta said brightly.

"See, Joe, it's all about gossip." Bob nudged him with his elbow.

"It's a good one." She waited till the three men met her gaze. "Kimberly Horvath is resigning from the Board."

Zimmerman nodded to Joe. "Another one bites the dust."

"Not quite," Roberta said. "She's running for Mayor."

Joe felt like an island in a sea of smiling, open faces. From school politics to city politics.

"Against her brother?" Bob asked. "No way."

"She'll get him to resign," Zimmerman said. "They keep it in the family. Sort of like how the Association does it."

He turned his sharp nose to Joe. "I checked the By-laws, and you can be President and serve on the Negotiations Team in the same year."

"Leave him alone." Roberta laid a hand on Joe's arm. "He's done enough for the union."

"So he's going to quit the Attendance Committee, the Negotiations Team and not run for office?" Zimmerman snapped. "Come on, we only got a one-year contract."

"I know," Joe said, "I was there." Sure, I got all the free time in the world, he thought. My wife's dead.

"I'll take the Attendance spot," Bob said. "It's about time I did something around here." He searched their faces for a laugh. They didn't.

"So who can we get to run for President? We can't let someone like--" Zimmerman wanted to say more but caught Bob's look and stopped.

"Maybe one of you," Joe said, his eyes again studying the faces in the library.

"We'll cover it, don't worry," Bob said. "We'll find somebody."

"Here, Joe, I got this for you." Roberta thrust a pink-frosted cookie on a stick toward him. "It's a little girl."

"See you guys later," he said and walked up the last flight of stairs. Another impaled cookie. At least it's not another green bean casserole.

The morning was taken up with the annual District meeting. Teachers from every building assembled in the high school auditorium to be welcomed by the School Board, oriented to new policies, and appraised of this year's goals. Joe didn't feel welcome, didn't find anything new in the policies and had one goal of his own: to get back to his classroom and his students. That would get his life back on track.

Now it was afternoon and the faculty was assembled for their high school specific meeting in the choir room. Bob looked around the half circle of chairs as Gale Stevens tried to quiet down his teachers and begin.

"You don't suppose he went home, do you?" Bob whispered.

"He wouldn't do that," Roberta said from behind the printed agenda.

"I don't know, he hasn't been out of his house this long all summer. Looked like hell today. Jumpy, nervous."

"Give him a break, Bob." Roberta gestured with the agenda to the doorway. "Oh, wait, there he is." Joe stepped into the room like a man entering a pool of cold water.

"Now the earlier we get started, people," Stevens was saying in his indoor voice, "the sooner we can leave." He cast what for him was a withering look at Joe, as he worked his way between the rows to the free seat between his friends.

"There now," the Principal continued, "everybody is here. Joe, Mr. Lehrer, it is good to see you again, and I want you--"

Bob and Roberta started to clap before Stevens could say something stupid, and the faculty joined in. Joe stood half way up and raised a hand to them in thanks.

"--and as I was saying, I want you all to have a cookie-on-a-stick, there on the table by the door. They're Cookie's Cookies from our current Board President, Kimberly, um,

Horvath. Be sure to take one on your way out." He grinned. "We don't want to mess up Mr. Boswell's music room."

As Stevens droned on about schedules and Homecoming and permission forms for showing movies in class, Joe looked around the semicircular rows of chairs. For the most part the teachers had grouped themselves according to departments, though Bob was sitting with the language people, not with his colleagues from guidance. The part-time French teacher sat next to Roberta, and in the row in front of him were Nancy Turner and her gaggle of Spanish teachers, including one he didn't recognize.

He rolled the muscles in his shoulders and forced out a breath. He had known it would be about politics. It was crazy to think this year would be any different than the last dozen. He hadn't thought it through: school politics, city politics, office politics. The Board and the Union. Republicans and Democrats. Spanish teachers and German teachers. The whole thing was politics. This wasn't an auditorium full of individuals, it was a room full of tribes. Joe balled up the agenda and threw it against the seat in front of him.

At the podium, Stevens was introducing his new Assistant Principal. "--and as I said we never had the opportunity to really get to know Mr. Weigel at the morning meetings, so I thought we'd take a few minutes this afternoon. You probably do know, he will supervise grades 11 and 12 discipline and be our go-to guy for technology." Stevens gestured broadly to the teachers and said, "Peter, the high school staff."

Stevens shook the hand of a slight man who was also wearing a dark suit. Weigel adjusted the microphone and peered into the audience through Buddy Holly glasses. Thin blondish hair lay across his head from left to right.

"Thank you, Mr. Stevens and faculty. I am grateful for the opportunity to work in the Stradford City Schools."

All these groups. All tangentially involved in education. Joe squeezed his eyes tight. All different. Colleagues. Office mates. Departments. Boards. Supervisors. Friends.

"I had other job offers," Weigel continued, "but Stradford is known throughout Ohio, and the entire Midwest, for its quality education. Its academics, the design of its educational delivery systems, the cohesive method it uses to impart learning on its young people. I observed this quality education from the outside, and wanted to be on the inside. I wanted to be a part of that team; I wanted to be a Stradford stallion."

Bob coughed, "Bullshit," into his hand. Joe looked away.

"My specific position on this team, in one word, is consistency. With the emphasis the Board has placed on consistent excellence, in terms of dollars and technology, it is my duty to take this building to the next level. We will raise the bar of quality through technology."

Several teachers applauded. Joe kicked the empty seat in front of him. All these words, and not one about children. Just like always. Don't they remember why we went on strike?

"This is not about replacing teachers with technology, it's about making your lives easier with technology. Now we will be able to keep track of all of our lesson plans, all of our attendance, all of our grades, as I said, consistently. For you out there, the word is easily. Everything will be computerized for your convenience."

"Why'd they move Gary Constantine to the Board office? I thought he was OK," Bob said. Joe shook his head.

"Maybe he wasn't techie enough," Roberta whispered. "This guy's a digital nerd."

Joe looked to her on his left and Bob on the other side. His friends had rallied around him as he had known they would. They were over the top about it, but they were there for him. He had to admit that.

"Even the traditional opening day staff forms," Weigel said. "You're all familiar with those?" He nodded at the scattered laughter and groans. "From now on you can file those on-line, from your office or from your home computer. Next semester we hope to be able to give you all a laptop of your own."

The faculty applauded. Joe wrapped his arms tighter around himself. Filing the Emergency Notification Form on-line or being called to the office to do it in person was all the same to him. He had no one to notify.

CHAPTER TWO

"I know about guilt, I do, all 2000 years of it. Original sin. 200,000 years, whatever." Joe's eyes darted around the rectory office, pausing only an instant on Fr. Hastings. "Everybody's flawed.

"I get the guilt part, OK?" His voice sped up as he continued. "No matter what I think, I'm not perfect. Far from it. I got issues. None of us is perfect. We don't always do the right thing. We need help. We need laws, and we need help from each other. We need help from above. I get it."

Hastings' eyebrows arched and the tip of his pen tapped the pad on his lap.

"But if all of us are flawed," Joe continued, "why do only some of us have to suffer? Like Cathy. Why did she have to die? What'd she do? She didn't do anything wrong. She made me better. And she's the one who dies?"

"That isn't the way you see it," Hastings said, "is it."

Joe's eyes finally settled on the priest. His voice slowed as if he were reciting from memory. "No, I get the imperfection part, and I get the free will part. I do. But Cathy didn't deserve this. No way. She wasn't even driving. I was the driver and I'm fine. I lost control of the car. She was just sitting there. One minute she's alive, the next she's dead. Wasn't doing anything, just sitting there. On the seat next to me."

"It doesn't make sense in human terms," the priest said.

"God moves in mysterious ways." Joe lifted both hands and wiggled his fingers. When he got no response, he said, "All these years and you still communicate like the Sphinx."

Hastings' bland face returned the look. He nodded.

"OK, OK, maybe Cathy had to die for something she did. I don't believe it. She was the best person I know. The best person I'll ever know. And what about the baby? Was the baby at fault, too? What could an unborn baby have possibly done to deserve to die? How in hell would that be fair?"

"That's really Old Testament, Joe, even for you."

"Yeah, I'm Joe, not Job," he snapped, his eyes again flitting around the small room. "Good and evil I can handle. It's a struggle. I don't always make the best choice. I admit that. But I'm hanging in there. I'm trying. Big picture. It's hard, and we need each other. We have to help each other. Cathy was my help."

Hastings held himself still as Joe ran his hand across the scar on his forehead. The man's breathing was rapid, more like panting.

"So where's the pattern in all this?" Joe demanded. "The big master plan? God's plan. Now that you mention it, where the hell is God in all this? How could this be part of the plan? Anybody's plan, let alone God's plan? How does it work that an innocent person, a good person dies?"

The priest swallowed and tilted his pen at Joe. "Are you sure you want to go there?"

"That's one of the problems I have with the Church, Jerry." Joe's voice gained speed again and he leaned forward on the sofa. "If he's God, if he can do the whole thing in heaven and on earth, and he did this. Then he planned for her to die. She died as part of his plan. He wanted her to die."

"You know that isn't--"

"Yeah, it is," Joe said. "God damn God."

＊＊＊

The words still burned in Hastings' mind after Joe slammed the door. The priest knelt now before the crucifix. It had been like holding a drunk's head and watching him retch. He knew his job was to lead Joe through the process: administering the syrup of Ipecac was a big part of it. But vomit was still vomit, and the words still hateful.

A little more of it is out, he thought. Maybe that's progress.

＊＊＊

"Do you mind?" Nancy Turner hissed as Joe entered the Language Department. "We're trying to have a conversation here." She spun her face from his and found Lexan Warner's eyes still locked onto hers. Joe crossed to his desk between the head Spanish teacher and the new-hire, and muttered something that neither woman heard.

"Nancy," Lexan said again, "my kids didn't do well enough on the last quiz. They need more time before they take the chapter test."

Nancy shook her head. "No. We have to stay on schedule. Your sections didn't do very well, but other sections did." She gestured with the sheaf of papers in her hand. "The numbers are here."

"But mine didn't understand the concept," Lexan said. "They need more time."

Nancy adjusted her blazer, summer peach, her eyes never leaving the younger woman's. "You need to keep up with the other sections. If you take extra days now, it will snowball and you won't be ready for the final exam."

Lexan let out a sharp breath. "If they don't understand the basics, they won't be prepared for the final exam."

"If you must, give them extra homework. We have plenty of sources." Nancy's finger jabbed at the wall of workbooks behind her, then returned to its primary function of finding lint on her skirt.

Lexan's voice sped up. "They're overwhelmed now. They have three quizzes a week, the paragraphs to write, the workbook, the CD's. They're spinning their wheels."

Snicker-doodle. Joe slammed the top drawer of his file cabinet shut, the sound like a gunshot in the high-ceilinged room. First it's cookies on a stick, now the new one smells like Cathy's favorite dessert.

Nancy shot him another look and lowered her voice. "Then you need to be more efficient."

"It's not about me." Lexan put her hands on her hips and matched her mentor's harsh whisper. "The kids aren't getting the material. It makes no sense to pile more work on them. I need to slow down for them."

Nancy waited a beat. When she continued her words were precise and condescending. "You can't slow down, Lexan, the chapter test is Friday."

"What happens if I move the test back till next week?" she shot back.

"That's the kind of thing he would do." Nancy's eyes stayed on Lexan as she jerked her head at Joe. "You never want to let the students control your teaching." Nancy stood up, smoothed her skirt. "Keep your classes on schedule. The test is Friday."

Lexan watched her march out of the office, then slapped her hand onto the desk top and flopped down into her desk chair. This wasn't why she had become a teacher.

⇒⊦⊣⇐

"TJ, Bobby, time to leave," Ellen Teeple called. "You'll be late!"

"I don't want to walk," her older son said, slowly pulling his backpack over his shoulder. "Why don't you drive us?"

"Let me see what you two are wearing." The boys mechanically pirouetted before her and she nodded at their collared shirts and cuffed pants.

"It's right across the street, maybe two blocks, TJ, and I don't have time today, you know that." She pushed him gently toward the door. "Bobby, your lunch."

The fifth grader snatched the brown bag from her hand and pushed past his brother to the porch. "Come on, stink-breath, I'll race you!"

The adolescent turned to his mother. "See how he is, Mom?"

"TJ, I know it's not cool to have to walk to school with the little kids, but you'll be driving soon enough."

"I will?"

"If you keep your grades up, now scoot."

She watched the boys race across the lawn to the sidewalk, TJ pushing in front of his brother. She turned around at the tug of a small hand on her skirt. "What about you, DeeDee? You want to go to school too? You want to be a big girl?"

She reached down to the upraised arms and hoisted the little girl up. "Don't you grow up, too," she said and snuggled into her damp neck. "You just stay little."

The girl hugged her then turned at the sound of feet on the stairs. "Daddy!" she screeched and held out her hands.

"Keep hold of her, would you El?" Terry Teeple said. "I just got this cleaned."

"Daddy, I want a hug!"

Terry stepped carefully toward her and quickly kissed her on the forehead. "No hugs now, rugrat." He avoided the sticky hands and pecked his wife on the cheek. "Gotta run, hon. Busy day."

Ellen spun to let him pass. "Say bye-bye, little girl."

"Bye-bye, Daddy. I'm big."

"Yes you are," he said. "I'll be a little late tonight."

"Hold supper?"

"I'll grab something at the office."

"Fine," she said. They stood on the porch and waved as he pulled away.

"I'm hungry," DeeDee said squirming in her mother's arms.

"Well, let's get you something to eat, little girl, oops, big girl." She set the girl on the ground. Hand in hand they walked into the house.

⚒

"Grammar is not a disease," Joe said to his German II class. He was comfortable in his classroom walking between the rows and talking to his students. Far from a disease, grammar had a pattern, a form, something he could get his mind around. Unlike the rest of his life, grammar had answers. He hoped it would help.

"If you guys could hear German 24/7, I wouldn't have to make a big deal about grammar. You'd just pick it up without even knowing it. Chuck, I'd like to get going." He stopped moving as the lumpy sophomore rummaged frantically through his backpack.

"It looks like we need a pen here." He spoke calmly, with no trace of sarcasm. Knucklehead never had a pen.

A wide smile covered Chuck's face as a BiC appeared on his desk. "*Danke,*" Joe said to TJ Teeple seated at Chuck's left.

"But we can't. We only have these five hours a week for German," Joe continued.

"It seems like more than that, doesn't it?" He encouraged their collective groan with his arms as he continued to the board. "But because we really don't have much time,

I have to abstract the language and teach the rules first. This isn't the way you and I learned English. We learned to understand it, and to speak it, years before we learned any rules. Most of the eyes met his and several pairs appeared to be understanding him.

"Chuck, you with me?"

"Uh, yes sir." His big face brightened. "*Ja!*" The class laughed.

"That's it," Lehrer said. "A German response in context. Way to go."

"See, when little Chucky here really was little, lying on his back in the crib, what he was doing--" He stopped and shook his head. "That's a picture isn't it, Chuck as an infant?" The class laughed along with the two-hundred-pounder.

I can still make them laugh, he thought. Not bad.

Joe smiled. "Well, one of the things he was doing was learning the English language. No books, no school, no teachers, certainly no grammar rules. His goo-goos and gaa-gaas were attempts to practice the language." He stopped as assorted baby noises filled the room.

"Unlike the school model, what we're trying to do here, OK, that's enough." He waited for quiet. He nodded and spread his gaze across their faces. "Unlike what usually happens in school, what happens when a baby actually says a word we can understand? When he says 'Dada' the first time? Do we criticize his grammar?

"No, we don't. The opposite. We go nuts. Get the camera, roll tape, call the grandparents. FaceTime! Right, we love it when the baby speaks. Jodi?"

"My parents have a video of my first word. They show it every Christmas."

Hands shot up and several voices spoke. "As you can see," Lehrer said, "we all have stories like that, don't we? It's a big deal. It is." He returned their smiles.

Like I never missed a day, he told himself.

"The problem is," he said as they settled back down. "We can't do it like that anymore. We don't have the time. We do it backwards, and frankly, you guys are getting a little old for language acquisition. It works much better at a younger age." He returned to the front of the room.

"Irwin?" He nodded at a boy in a seat by the narrow window.

"Yes, I was five when we came to America. I didn't speak English at all."

"But you picked it up quickly, didn't you."

"I did, but not my parents."

"His mother still doesn't speak good," Jodi said. "When you talk to Mrs. Kasagawa on the phone."

"Doesn't speak 'well', Jodi, not 'good'."

"Whatever." Jodi rolled her eyes.

"So here we are in school," Lehrer said on his way back to the board, "it's time to talk about grammar."

"We're starting today with pronouns." The marker squeaked as he wrote the word. "Can anybody tell me what a pronoun is? One of the eight parts of speech. Pronoun."

"A noun that gets paid?" TJ offered. The sophomores paused, then two or three laughed.

"There's one in every good class," Lehrer said.

I must be getting better, they actually got the joke.

Joe looked around the room. "Professional, Chuck, like a professional noun."

"I got it, I know."

"Sure you did. There's more to it, class. Ketul?"

"Isn't a pronoun a word that takes the place of a noun?" The boy spoke softly.

"Exactly. Examples?"

"It, he, her, she, us, words like that."

"Notes, people," Lehrer said. "If I write stuff down or if you think it's important, get it in your notebooks." His hand passed over 'he', 'she' and 'us' on the white board, and circled 'it' in blue.

"Good place to start. 'It' replaces any noun we mean. Maybe 'it' means the house or the car, or the lunch we just ate in the cafeteria, or the cafeteria itself. A pronoun is a convenience. A replacement. A substitute."

Their eyes dropped to their notebooks and he tried not to substitute 'she' for Cathy.

"So," he coughed. "So, we don't have to repeat the noun over and over. We love the cafeteria. The cafeteria is a wonderful place to eat. The cafeteria is filled with friendly people. That would get boring. We can use 'it' instead. It has great food. It is a wonderful place to eat.

"The problem is of course, we can't just randomly go around using 'it' and expect anybody to understand us. If I say, 'It is great,' what am I talking about? What is it that's so great? What is 'it'?

"Irwin?"

"We have to replace nouns with pronouns, right?"

"That will be tonight's homework. Replacing the nouns with pronouns."

"But we can't just use any pronoun."

"Nope, that would be too easy. This isn't Spanish." He encouraged the laugh. Chuck dropped the pen onto his notebook. "Man, this is hard."

"No, Chuck," Jodi said. "The pronouns look like the *der, die, das* thingies."

Joe stopped passing out the homework sheets and smiled at her. "Did you catch what she said? The articles or 'thingies' look like the pronouns. Just match them up. Good work, Fraeulein Fenster."

"And all of you, thanks, it was a good class today. On this sheet you replace the nouns and their modifiers with the appropriate pronouns. Folks, it's gonna get harder, but take it one step at a time. We aren't trying to do everything at once. Remember--"

He hung on the last word until they looked up at him. "You can trust me. I'm a trained professional."

Sure I am. As long as I don't have to replace *her*.

"Don't forget your backpack, DeeDee," Ellen Teeple called up the stairs, before turning back to the mirror on the foyer wall. She pursed her lips, then pressed them against each other. She dabbed a bit more lipstick to the edge of her mouth and said, "You don't want to be late for play group."

"Not play group, Mommy," her little girl said. She clutched the rail with one hand and carefully descended the stairs one at a time. "After lunch school."

"Big girl school, you're right. How could I forget?" She crouched and reached out both her hands as the backpack bumped the girl's leg and she tottered on the bottom step. "I can do it, Mommy," she said.

"That's right, you're so big." She snatched her daughter from the last step and hugged her. "Almost all grown up."

The girl burrowed her small face into her mother's neck, then arched her back and wiggled her arms and legs to get down. "We have to go now, Mommy." She turned at the door and said clearly, "Teacher says don't be late for school."

"That's right."

Ellen smiled at the reflection of her daughter in the rear view mirror of the SUV. Her chin resting on the top of the backpack and her arms clutching it to her chest, the little girl surveyed the passing world from her car seat with serious, adult eyes. "Why are you smiling, Mommy?" DeeDee demanded.

"Nothing, honey," her mother said as the cell phone tweedled. She looked away and thumbed it on.

DeeDee reached for the end of the dry cleaning bag on the seat and pulled it from the window to see the gazebo in the square in front of city hall. Baskets of red and pink flowers swung in the light breeze beneath the white gingerbread trim.

"Room 622," her mother said into the phone. "OK, I got it. Yes, Karl."

The Lexus sped across Cleveland Avenue and moments later lurched into the drop-off lane in front of Raub Elementary. On the sidewalk Ellen crouched in front of her daughter and tugged her dress straight. "Now be good for your teacher," she said. "I'll be back to pick you up after I run my errands."

"OK, Mommy," the little girl said and raced to join the line of kids entering the building. Ellen watched her until the door swung shut.

⋈

Joe released the bail on the lawn mower and rubbed the sweat out of his eye with his shoulder. The engine sputtered and died, he took a long breath. The lawn looked pretty good, even and smooth, and it felt good to be a little winded. He rolled the red Craftsman up the drive and into its spot in the garage. He wiped his hands on a rag and looked at the front yard again.

The lawns on Stag Thicket Trace were much like the houses, varying only slightly in shade. Grass ran along the somewhat curved street as far as he could see in both directions, skipping only the driveways and sidewalks, as if one roll of carpet had been laid over the subdivision and pieces cut out for the concrete. His lawn now fit in.

The houses seemed also to have been made by the same hand. They were in fact all built by Western Reserve Homes, Inc. All were two stories with sharply peaked roofs and brick chimneys. All had two-car garages that faced the street and front porches with railings that ended in a knobbed newel at the top step. In the rear, wooden decks led through French doors to family rooms. Ranging from off whites to muted pastels, they varied only slightly more in color than the lawns.

He looked up at the sound of a car horn to see Doug Eck's long arm wave at him from the window of a white Land Rover. He waved back and it occurred to him that all in all it had been a pretty good day. Doug and the seniors were voluntarily speaking German to each other, and their excitement over the spring trip to Germany was keeping them on task. The Media Center hadn't screwed up his copies too badly. The sophomores were sophomores, but he had fired the first shot in the grammar campaign and it had gone pretty well. He nodded and tossed the rag onto the shelf next to the gasoline can.

Instead of walking into the house through the garage, he crossed behind the car to the front porch. He flicked a bug off the pink knock-out rose bush and sat down on the top step. It had been a decent day, one of the better ones. His thoughts ran to Lexan. Maybe she wasn't a complete Nancy clone.

He told himself he was making progress. He had felt alive in the classroom. In control. Like his life mattered. He stood and leaned over the rose bush, using his thumbnail to cut off a dead bloom.

The orange red sun was setting behind the houses across the street. The third week in September was still warm, and it felt good to be sweaty and tired from working. He waved to a little girl on skates as she wobbled past, and pulled open the screen door.

He peeled the wrapper off a Lean Cuisine and keyed the microwave before trotting up the stairs. He knew the shower would last longer than the chicken cooked, but he wanted it to be ready when he was finished. His usual routine was to shower in the morning, but this had been a pretty good day. He sat down on the bed and picked up the picture from his bedside table. It was last June, in the Board office parking lot during the strike. He smiled as he remembered.

In some ways the scene had looked to them exactly as they had envisioned it, a Family Picnic. From where he sat on a lawn chair next to Cathy, they could see families eating hot dogs at picnic tables, and kids running between tents and camping trailers. Dads stood over smoking grills in several places, and moms were cutting watermelons and passing out slices on bending paper plates. A group of teachers played badminton off to his left. Joe laughed as Bob fell to his knees trying to block a spike.

"If you look at it a certain way," he said to his wife, "it sorta looks like a Kincaid family reunion."

She pulled a strand of brown hair off her cheek and smiled. "We've got the sunset, the noise, the running around, but I don't see Uncle John teaching the kids to fish."

"Or one of your nephews lighting firecrackers to see if the car alarms will go off."

They both smiled at that remembered scene, then Joe looked away from the campers in the Board of Education parking lot to the winding line of teachers still marching up and down the street in front of the building. And the police cars. And the television crews. And the crowd of on-lookers still standing across Cleveland Avenue in front of the library.

Now it was nearly quiet and relatively peaceful. It had been loud and disruptive. Early on the teachers had tried to keep the buses from leaving their garage behind the board offices. Then they tried to limit access to the board and the middle school behind it when the SUVs arrived and the filled buses returned from their routes. Most of all, the picketers wanted the incoming cars to read their signs and listen to their chanting, so their intent was not to seal off the traffic, but to slow it down. The signs had been hand-painted in cheerful primary colors last night at the Association office. They read *Bargaining Rights for Teachers, Recognize our Association, We love Stradford Students,* and *Let's all work together for your Kids!*

They might as well have read *We Want More Money, Stradford Sucks* and *We are Commie Rat Bastards!* for the reactions they caused. Some parents got out of cars to yell at the teachers, others stared straight ahead and lifted middle fingers. Other parents and most of the high school kids tooted their horns in support. Many of the kids in the buses waved when they recognized their own teachers. The police made sure a lane was left open and limited the number of pickets at each entrance. Matt Stanton and an elementary teacher Joe didn't know had been questioned inside a police cruiser for a few minutes and released.

Since the school day had ended several hours ago, the Stradford Education Association was holding its 'First Annual Family Picnic' in the Board parking lot, and withholding the students' final exam grades. The Board members were holed up in the offices on the third floor, overlooking the teacher campsite below.

Joe felt Cathy's hand on his arm. "Where'd you go off to there?" she asked, smiling. "I thought I lost you."

"We were pretty lucky this morning. Most everything worked the way we planned." He reached for her hand and held it. "Gene's idea to hold the finals was brilliant.

Commencement's in a few days and they need the exams to compute the final grades. Otherwise, they could have closed the school year and waited for us to go away."

She laced her fingers through his and squeezed gently. "It wasn't all his idea, Joe. I'm proud of you."

He lost himself, truly now, as he always did when he looked at her.

"Joe, hey Joe, committee meeting!" an obnoxious voice said behind him.

He held her hand tighter and tried to keep himself locked deep inside her smile as the voice grated in his ears.

"Joe, come on, we--" Bob stopped. "Hey, Cathy. I'd tell you two to get a room, but all the tents seem to be taken. Maybe I can find you a pop-up trailer or something."

Joe pulled back, their spell broken. Giving her hand a final squeeze, he said, "Hold that thought, I'll be right back."

"He probably won't," Bob said, "this could be a long one."

Cathy crossed her legs and pulled a book from the bag at her feet. "Take your time, boys, I'll be right here."

⊷⊶

Joe turned off the shower and left the stall door ajar so it would dry. Towel over his shoulder in front of his closet, he smelled Cathy's scent and turned around, expecting to see her at the mirror, arms up over her head, asking him to help her with the clasp of her necklace. The silver one, the Irish knot with the tricky clasp.

His heart pounded as blood raced. Sweat sprang from the pores in his face. He spun again to the mirror.

"She's not here, you idiot! She's not here!" His voice was ragged, loud, more of a sob than a scream.

He slammed his fist against the closet door. The hollow surface boomed and cracked, leaving a half circle indentation. "God damn it!"

He hurled the wet towel at the mirror and took two steps forward, one back, spinning first left then right, his eyes darting to the bathroom, the closet, the bedroom. "God fucking damn it!"

He yanked open the door to her closet. Her clothes on the rack. Her shoes in boxes and on the floor where she had left them. Sweaters folded neatly on the shelves to the right. Purses and her tennis racket on the top. Wrapping paper wedged in the corner.

It smelled like Cathy.

Winter clothes at the far end, summer ones closer. The gray suit she wore on interviews. Her pants for heels. Her pants for flats. The running shoes. The black anniversary dress.

It all smelled like Cathy.

He slammed the door shut, scraping the skin from the top of his toe. He stamped his foot onto the carpet and spun around. "God damn it!" He slumped against the closet and forced his mouth open. His panting rasped through his throat, slowed, and his fists opened. He took two more breaths and swallowed, his throat now dry and constricted. He pulled on a pair of shorts, went down to the kitchen and returned with a box of black plastic trash bags.

⇥⊹⊹⇤

"Thank you, Vikki," the man said and dropped the bills onto the night stand. "We should do this again some time." He added another. She was a pretty good fuck.

Ellen gave him her number two smile. The john wasn't worth any more than that, and it was nearly time for school to let out. "Call the number. I'll see if I can fit you into my schedule."

He took a step toward the bed and she pulled her knees up to her chin. "Once is enough, Mister." She fixed the smile and looked past him to the door of 622. Karl should be in the hall.

The man stopped and raised his open hands. "A deal's a deal, that's my motto." He looked at the same door and grinned weakly. "Another time then."

"Works for me," Ellen said as he left. She stretched and rolled off the bed, catching the time as she did so. Inside the shower stall, she pulled the faucet on and banded her hair behind her head. Still on schedule, she thought. I'll have time to finish my errands.

CHAPTER THREE

"I think I can accept that it wasn't an accident," Joe said. He had leaned back in the sofa, his legs splayed. Exhausted. Fr. Hastings sat in the recliner. Late afternoon sun spilled into the rectory. "What's an accident really? There's a plan for everything, we just can't see it. It's not God's fault."

Hastings nodded, kept his expression bland, and wrote in his notebook. It had been a struggle to get him to this point.

"How could it be God's fault?" Joe continued. "God wasn't driving the car, I was. My hands on the wheel. I should have seen it and swerved away. I was there. God wasn't."

"This is quite a reversal from our last session. And the way this one started."

"No, it's me. It's all me. I had the chance. Missed it." Joe massaged his fingers as he spoke. "I should sack up and take the blame. You're right. Only way I'm gonna get over this. Can't get back at God. It's time for me to take a look at myself. It's fall, the school year has started. I mean, here we are, they're paying me to work. I'm there every day doing my thing. Helping the kids."

"Do you think you can help others after what you've been through?"

"I think I actually am making some progress." Joe's brow furrowed and he inflected the last word nearly as a question. "Sleeping OK, pretty much so. Some days I just sort of pass out. Fall into a complete fog and wake up drooly with stuff caked on my chin." Joe looked at him for a response.

The priest nodded to continue.

"But the sleepless nights, when I can't close my eyes because I'll see it again. Those are pretty much gone now. Once a week I get nothing but the car rolling over and Cathy bleeding and I can't stop it. The bleeding or the dream. Maybe only three times in two weeks. Better than it was."

"You could take something for that."

"I don't want to take anything." Joe rubbed the base of his right thumb. "I'm afraid I'll take too much. No, I tried a couple times. Benzodiazepine or something. I mean, I slept. Slept like a dead man. But that's the thing you know? I can do it by myself. Yeah, I'd rather have seven or eight bad nights a month. Not worth it otherwise."

"Probably not." Hastings wrote on his pad.

"No, I got so fogged up in class the next day. I couldn't tell what the kids were asking me or anything. I got through my classes on autopilot. I have to do better than that. The kids deserve that.

"I am making progress though, really. I'm pretty sharp some days. Back to my old self, the old Herr. Most days. But I can't do anything more than teach. No politics. Don't care about school finance. Don't care who the Mayor is."

Joe kept his hand from touching the scar on his forehead, and focused on Jerry's eyes as the priest said, "You shouldn't expect everything to fall back into place at the same time."

Joe nodded several times. "Right. It's a process like you said. Not quite there yet. Getting there. Doing my job. In school every day. Just not quite." Now Joe looked away, uncrossing and re-crossing his legs.

"So I hear you saying, and I agree, you're getting better. You're out of the house. Especially so in class. And you recognize that it's not going to be smooth sailing. Maybe this was a setback along--"

Joe's head snapped up. "This wasn't a 'setback,' Jerry." Joe quoted the word with his fingers and fixed him with his eyes. "This wasn't just a 'bump in the road'."

Hastings was startled by the vehemence in Joe's voice. "Maybe you need to look at it that way." He dropped his pad onto the table beside him.

Joe flinched at the soft sound. "I don't need to look at it your way, or the right way, or any way." He poked his finger at the priest with each phrase. "I need to stop seeing it, period. That's what I need."

"You can control how you look at it. You can manage it. It doesn't have to--"

Joe swiped furiously at his forehead and his voice raced. "God damn it, you know what it means. I told you three times tonight. I trashed Cathy. Literally. I took all her clothes out to the curb, and I threw it all fucking away. All her stuff. All of it. The shoes, the coats, the dresses. The stuff in her drawers. The shirts, the, the blouses. Everything. I dumped it out, all of it, this big fucking pile in the middle of our fucking bedroom. This heap of her stuff. Just took it and stuffed it. Stuffed her for God's sake. Into bags. Black, plastic, garbage bags. Seventeen hundred of them. To the landfill--" He gasped and slapped at the spittle on the edge of his mouth.

Hastings waited for Joe's breathing to slow, then said softly, "Yet, in your own words, you are making progress. You know you are. I agree."

"Progress." Joe snorted a cursing laugh and wiped the tears from his eyes. "Yeah, that's great. Now I can't even smell her anymore."

—›‹—

Bob McCauley swiveled from the computer screen to the printer and removed a pile of pages from the tray. Sensing someone in the room with him, he swiveled again. The thin figure of Gale Stevens stood just outside his office door, and entered after catching his eye. You're the Principal, Bob thought, why don't you just walk in?

"This picture, it's dreadful. Awful." Stevens held the Monday edition of the *Stradford Star* with the tips of his fingers.

McCauley squared the papers on his desk blotter and gestured for him to sit down. "Saw it at home this morning. I can't imagine how fast she must have been going."

"Police estimate the car was traveling well over sixty miles per hour when it struck the tree," Stevens read in his reedy, faculty meeting voice.

"You can't even make out what kind of car it was."

"A Honda Civic."

"I know, but look at the picture." Bob pointed at the news photo and shook his head. "The whole front end is shoved back into the seat. She didn't have a chance."

"Did you know her? I heard she was a nice girl." Stevens sat down on the office chair. "Amber Larkin."

"She wasn't one of mine, she was in Carrie's part of the alphabet. She'd stop in the office sometimes. Great personality, a pretty young lady."

"A Flagbearer and in the Show Choir," Stevens said. "Honor Roll, too."

"She wasn't a Flagbearer this year, she dropped band." Stevens raised his eyebrows, and Bob wondered if he didn't know that you had to be in the band in order to be a Flagbearer. "But yeah, she had been."

"So where are we on this? I just got off the phone with Mr. Radburn."

McCauley handed him the stack of papers. "It's all here in the Crisis Protocol, that we discussed last summer. There's a before-school faculty meeting," he glanced at the desk clock, "in twenty minutes. I've called the Crisis Management Coordinating Team, and they'll have extra counselors in the building by 8:00. Clergy, too."

"Rev. Patterson got me out of bed at 5:00. He'll be here."

"School Board member and a minister."

Stevens fingered through the papers. "Do we really need to do all this?"

Bob shook his head. We were at the same meeting, he thought. "The tears will be falling, Boss."

Stevens grimaced. "Can't we, you know, do something about that, keep it under control? It's all so, I don't know. Like that suicide several years ago--"

"--when you were at the Junior High," finished Bob. "Look, for most of these kids it's the first dead person they've known. At least the first dead person their own age."

"I know, I know." The Principal waved his hand. "But the noise, the disruption. Mr. Radburn was saying, oh, I don't know."

"They're grieving, Mr. Stevens. They need time to process the whole thing."

"But the drama, the wailing. It's disruptive to the education. They'll decorate the lockers, they won't go to class--"

Bob waited for the administrator to look at him. "It's a part of their education. They're learning how to deal with death." Stevens' eyes darted away. "It's not a lesson we want to teach, but they need it." Bob kept his eyes locked on him. "We need to do this for them."

"I suppose we'll have to loosen the tardy pass policy."

Bob wondered again how a man could be so out of touch. "We have to give them time, Gale. That's one of the things the extra counselors are here for. Don't worry, I'll make sure they have plenty of hall passes."

Stevens looked relieved. "Good. We need to keep track of who's where."

"Yeah," Bob said with a sigh. "We'll keep that vital base covered."

"What about the parents, the Larkins. Should I call them?"

"Not today. You'll probably see them at the wake tonight. Talk to them then."

The Principal sniffed. "Now about the lockers, decorating the decedent's locker."

"She's not 'the decedent,' she's Amber Marie Larkin."

"Yes, of course." He adjusted his cuff inside his suit coat. "Now then, Mr. Radburn said that we'd get cards and stuffed animals, flowers, all kinds of things, spilling into the hallway, across the neighboring lockers. He said it would be a mess, we should--"

"Mel's gone," Bob said. Stevens' eyes flickered back and forth. "You're in charge now."

"But he said the disruption, and with the state tests coming up, we--"

"No," Bob said sharply, and the other's tiny eyes landed on his. "The locker decoration or shrine, whatever they happen to do, is part of the process. It's concrete and tangible. Something they all can see and be a part of."

"So you're saying we shouldn't prevent them from doing it."

The man is completely oblivious. "Not a good idea, no."

"We can limit it then. To a week. Through this Friday."

"We can re-visit the time frame later."

"Good." Stevens nodded. "Now, about the cause of death. Drinking was involved."

"They can't be sure of that. It's too early."

"Alcohol was found at the scene, in the car." Stevens pointed his finger at the newspaper on his lap.

"They don't know if alcohol was in her body." Bob nodded. "Maybe."

"What should our position be?" Stevens looked up from the paper. "On that part of it."

"Our position? We're against underage drinking. It's illegal." McCauley's brow furrowed and he opened his palms. "What else could our position be?"

"V is-à-vis Students Against Driving Drunk," the principal said.

"SADD? I'm sure they feel terrible about it. I know Matt does. I'll bet some of his kids feel responsible for it in some way. They'll have to grieve, too."

"Yes, yes I'm sure you're right." He poked the Tiger Woods bobble-head on Bob's desk. "It's just that we never had a DUI death during the regular school year before."

"Yeah, we haven't. The ones we've lost have had the good sense to die in the summer or wait till they'd graduated."

Stevens nodded. "Yes, right, but that's not what I meant."

"You can't mean that this is somehow SADD's fault?"

Stevens' eyes blinked several times. "No, no of course not. I do think however, that this club deals with this issue, and we may need to examine what Mr. Stanton and his club really do. In hopes of not having to deal with this again," he added quickly.

Bob watched him sit up straighter in the chair and looked at Stevens. Sure, now you feel better, he thought, you have someone you can blame. "We will always have to deal with this. Drinking is part of their culture. At least they think it is."

"To be clear," Stevens said, "it's not that I want to blame SADD."

"No, of course you don't." Bob looked away. "You just feel helpless."

"Yes, that's it exactly," Stevens said intently. "I want to do something about it. I want to stop it."

"We all do, Mr. Stevens."

Kimberly Hellauer Horvath looked down through the window behind her desk at the first building she had ever owned. She'd rented at the corner of Cleveland and Center and renovated it herself before she had the capital to buy. She smiled as she thought about how hard she had worked on the cinder blocks with a wire brush before she could get the paint to stick. Tom had helped when he could, he had been just starting his practice then, and those sweaty, dirty hours had been some of the happiest of their marriage. She looked away from the shoe box shaped building, now the serif of an enormous L extending down Cleveland at the corner of her complex. It was covered with a peaked roof of cedar shakes like the others, and she wondered if anyone else remembered it used to be the old Phillips 76 station.

"The room is full, Kimberly, it's time to start."

"Thanks Eleanor, just daydreaming." She gave the older woman a small smile and followed her through the door into the conference room.

The council chamber of the old city hall was indeed full, rows of chairs covering the carpeted space from her office in the rear to the raised dais in front of the large Romanesque window. Eleanor Mindrivan walked through the crowd beneath the high, hump-backed ceiling, and up onto the rostrum next to Amy Michalik, the police chief's wife and Kimberly's secretary. Several women turned around in their seats.

Eleanor stepped to the lectern and said formally, "We are assembled here to elect the next mayor of Stradford, Kimberly Hellauer Horvath!"

The three dozen supporters applauded loudly and jumped to their feet as Kimberly walked swiftly down the aisle. They were mostly women, a few older men scattered among them. From his post at the rear door Karl unfolded his arms and joined the ovation. His expression didn't change and his eyes didn't stop moving.

Eleanor raised her hands over her head as Kimberly stepped up beside her. "I see you already knew that, didn't you?"

The crowd laughed, then quieted. Mindrivan's white, curly hair framed a nearly cherubic face. A short woman, she seemed somehow larger. Her face and her whole body, alive and energetic. She spoke rapidly, vigorously, clearly.

"That's why you're not here to listen to me." She returned their laughter. "But I do want to say thank you for taking time from your busy days to come out and support our Kimberly." She smiled broadly at them. "We know how valuable your time is, and we appreciate your volunteering to help our campaign. Sincerely, thank you." She joined the applause until Kimberly embraced her.

"All these smiling faces," Kimberly said into the microphone. "I'm overwhelmed." She pulled a cookie from the podium shelf and held it next to her face. "To think it all started with a cookie, a happy face cookie on a stick just like this one. Some of you remember when I was baking them in my kitchen, driving them all over town in my old Caravan.

Remember that? My trusty old Dodge?" She looked at the faces in the seats and the yellow-faced cookie in her hand. "That was a long time ago, before we renovated this old place and built all those buildings. Before some of you joined us." She noticed that Karl had moved to the opposite corner.

"That was a good time, and because of your help and the support of many, many others, this cookie has brought me, brought us, some success. I am proud of that success and I am proud of you." She smiled at the applause and bit the cookie.

"And I am proud to say that we still make one fine cookie!" In the third row Ellen Teeple turned to her friends, and laughed.

"We will continue, you and I, to bake and market these cookies." Kimberly laid the happy face on the podium and dabbed the corner of her mouth with a Kleenex. "We are going to build on our success. We are going to move our success into a larger arena. We are going to transform Stradford into a great community.

"This is not a political takeover, as I have heard murmured around town. This is not some dark and devious plot. This is not the overthrow of an inept dictator or the breakup of the old boy network. Alfie is my big brother!" She paused for the inevitable laugh.

"My brother has given many years of his life to turn a sleepy, bedroom community into a vibrant, modern city. My desire to become mayor is in no way a contradiction or refutation of anything Alfred has done, but a desire to continue the fine work he has begun.

"Then why am I running for mayor? Why am I asking you to support me in this cause? " She made smiling eye contact around the room. "It's not that Alfie is too old; I'm sure he'll learn how to operate a smart phone someday." The ladies laughed with her again.

"It's very simple: my brother has done enough for Stradford. It is time for me to do the heavy lifting and time for him to ease off a little bit. With your help, we can continue to run this city the way he has and make Stradford even better!

"But I am still his little sister and we don't want him to feel that we don't need him anymore." Knowing smiles from the audience, a small nod from Karl. "He has agreed to accept the position of Service Director in my administration. That will give him the opportunity to do what he really likes, playing with trucks and police cars."

As the clapping died she said, "This is my plan for Stradford and it is a good plan. But as I have found in my career, a plan is no good at all without the support of people like you. People to do the campaigning, people who believe in our goal.

"People like Eleanor Mindrivan who has worked at my side on the School Board for many, many years. People like entrepreneur Pamela Holmgren."

Ellen and others in the crowd turned toward the dignified, gray-haired woman in the back row. "That's the cosmetics lady, PamLeeCo," she whispered to Patti.

"My sister-in-law, Ursula Hellauer. New friends like Amy Michalik, and all those who have supported me and my work in so very many ways. People like you!" Kimberly

Hellauer Horvath spread her arms wide to take them all in. "And you most of all, the people of Stradford!"

"If it's not the computers," Joe yelled, "it's the goddamned phone!"

Lexan looked up from her stack of Spanish II tests. "Sounds like you can use some help."

"You digitally literate?"

"I am, but I don't think the Generalissima would want me to share with anyone in the German Department."

When Joe smiled, she looked down and said quickly, "I am so sorry about your wife. For your loss."

"All I want to do-- Thank you, that's very kind." He looked at her closely. The girl's brow was furrowed seriously, and she was still looking at her hands. "All I want is to post one message on the Homework Hotline and stop getting nasty notes from Weigel."

"That's the last thing Mrs. Turner wants. We post the homework once a week, so they know what to do if they miss class."

"How do you know on Monday what they need to do on Friday?"

"Every Spanish II class is on the same page every day."

"What if one class goes faster than another? Or slower?" She must have taught somewhere else before Stradford, he thought. She can't be as young as she looks. "Same material, same course, same day, different kids."

"There are extra days built in," she said. "Hey, you were listening to our 'discussion' the other day."

"Not the first time I heard it."

"Nancy told me not to teach like you do." Lexan rolled her chair closer to his desk. "Maybe she knows what she's talking about; she's been doing this a long time."

"Doesn't mean it's the only way to do it."

"You've been here for a while, too, haven't you," she said and narrowed her eyes. They were gray or blue under dark brows. Intelligent, lively. "But If I give the test on a different day, the answers would get out. The kids would cheat."

"So change the test." Joe was pushing buttons on the phone as he spoke. "Hard to cheat on an oral test. Hard to fake a writing sample."

"We don't give those," she began. "That's stupid. Then you end up with different tests and it's all the same course."

"Different kids, different methods," he said. "Sometimes I don't even give the book test. I make up my own."

She listened to his harsh whisper and waited for him to look at her. "But you're the only person teaching level II aren't you, and we have to give all the sections the same final."

"Yup." He straightened up and folded his arms across his chest. A younger, blonder version of Nancy. Just what the world needs.

"Maybe she was right about you." She looked him straight in the eye, a slight flush in her cheeks.

"She was."

When he didn't say anything more, she looked at the phone and said, "OK, so what do you want on your message?"

"Sure it won't get you in trouble?"

Lexan smiled without thinking and shook her head no. The curls around her face bounced back and forth. He looked away and rubbed his chin with his thumb.

"Here's the message. 'Come to class and do your assignments. Send me an e-mail if you need help, or call my cell'."

"What? You give out your e-mail and your phone number? You'll get spammed!"

"Hasn't happened yet. Maybe the German keeps them from doing that."

"You want the message in German?"

"I sure as hell don't want it in Spanish."

Her eyes flashed at him like they had at Nancy.

"I give them credit for using the language." He tried to soften his tone. "When they call me, at least they have something to talk about."

"But--"

Joe held up his hand. "You're going to say, how can I control the content. You're afraid they'll try to use words they don't know."

Her face screwed tight and her head jerked as if shocked. "How did you--"

"It's not about controlling them, it's about enabling them."

Lexan shook her head. "They'll get frustrated if they make too many mistakes."

"They get frustrated when it's Chapter Two and all they're allowed to talk about is *La tienda de ultramarinos.*"

When she didn't respond, he gestured with the hand set. "So what do I do?"

She started to speak, didn't, then reached over and jabbed the key pad. "Your code?"

He looked flustered and opened his palm. She reached for a salmon sheet of paper from a pile on his desk, and entered the digits. "Get ready. When I nod, you speak. Now."

He spoke slowly into the phone, then raised his eyebrows at her. For an instant he felt several years younger.

Lexan jabbed the pound key. "That's it. All set."

"OK, what's my next crisis?" Joe pushed back from the desk and his eyes left hers. "Oh, yeah, I got to see how badly the Media Center screwed up my copies." He stood up and looked at his watch. "Thanks, Lexan. I'm not always such an ass."

"It's OK," she said to his back as he disappeared into the hall. "Any time." She wondered how much of what Nancy had told her about him was true. Or if any of it was.

Karl turned away as if to leave, spun around on the balls of his feet, and drove his fist deep into Oskar's stomach. The force of the blow and the crashing of the desk satisfied him, knocking the fat man onto his back, where, eyes bulging, he tried to catch his breath and rise.

Karl had timed and spaced the punch perfectly. He exhaled as he examined his knuckles, but he only had a minute or so until the slob was on his feet and he would have to hit him again. He tried to move efficiently through the mess in the barn to the door, and made sure it was locked. Not that he worried that anybody would interrupt him; barely any Stradford shoppers frequented Brummelberger's Salvage.

Oskar had levered himself onto his hands and knees next to the table now puking onto the floorboards. Karl adjusted his weight and swung the heel of his shoe into the man's right kidney. Oskar cried out again dropping into his spew.

Karl didn't think anyone could be this stupid. He shook his head as he removed his suit coat and threaded the ends of his tie inside his shirt. This must be how it is to be a parent. You tell them, you warn them, you promise them, and you still end up having to readjust their attitude. He reached to his rear pocket for the handle of the leather-clad weapon.

Oskar was making a wet noise as he tried to breath. Karl worked his left wrist through the strap and hefted the sap in his right palm. The leather made a thick, slapping sound, the weight of the lead filings reassuring as always.

"I told you to scare her, Oskar, not kill her. People notice a dead kid." The fat man's eyes widened and his wailing increased. "Don't even think of blaming Pedro, this is all you." He set the computer and keyboard onto the chair and rolled it out of the way.

One quick blow to the back of the head stunned Oskar, and Karl rolled him onto the door that served as a desktop. He hoisted the door and the body onto the sawhorses, one end at a time. Oskar mumbled something, but lay on his stomach like a big fish, his mouth gasping open, his arms dangling down.

Methodically moving from his shoulders to his thighs, Karl beat Brummelberger's back. The pace rapid, staccato almost, whap, whap, whap. The sap never more than a foot above the skin. The blows landing neatly in rows, top to bottom, left to right. Karl didn't need to see inside the fat man's clothing to know that he was bruising, turning blue, but his skin holding.

Oskar tried to roll over, a vain attempt to protect himself. Karl silenced him with another blow to the head and resumed his task. It was after all, just that. A part of his job. Something that had to be done. He called it tenderizing, joking to colleagues that he could find work anywhere as a master butcher. After several minutes he switched hands, the whap, whap, whap now administered from his right.

The task completed, Karl released a long breath and stretched the muscles in his lower back. The desktop was nearly the perfect height, but not quite. He wiped the now warm sap with his handkerchief and returned it to his pocket. He took several more cleansing breaths then passed to the small bathroom in the back. He splashed water on his face, pulled the tie out of his shirt, and re-buttoned the cuffs. Returning to the office, he rolled the chair with the computer closer to the desk, removed a business card from his wallet, and stood it in the keyboard where Oskar would be sure to see it. He leaned down to check the man's breathing, patted his head and left through the rear exit.

⚔

The DiBello-Blaha Funeral Home was on a tree-lined block of Cleveland near the Square in the oldest part of Stradford. A white Victorian that had been expanded several times, it sat on a low rise amid the trees, removed somewhat from the traffic on the city's main street. Now the parking lots around it and the spillover lot across Harding Street were filled, and the traffic itself was slowed by the steady stream of cars.

The line of mourners extended out the double doors under the porte-cochere and into the lot itself. Many of them were teenagers, friends and classmates of Amber Larkin. The girls in dresses and the boys in dress slacks, ties hanging awkwardly from their necks, they spoke incessantly, their high pitched voices audible from a distance. They touched each other, consciously hugging their friends or unconsciously bumping them, reminding themselves of their vitality.

Several of the adults among them, parents mostly, some with younger children, were not as well dressed. One man wore a t-shirt and shorts, a woman a low-cut tank top. They appeared disinterested, as if they had done this before or if they would rather be elsewhere.

Not so the adolescents. Gathered around the death of a contemporary, they were alive, defiantly so, even while crying. Despite make-up smearing and bravado cracking. Children admitted to this most adult experience, they were both attracted to and repulsed by the death of their friend.

Joe turned from signing the memorial book as Bob and Linda McCauley entered the building. Nancy and Roberta followed behind them with their husbands.

"I didn't think I'd see you here," Roberta said quickly and touched his arm.

"Amber's sister is in my class," Joe said and gave her hand a squeeze. "I'm fine."

"Chelsea, the kids call her Sea. She's a Goth," Bob said.

"Goths, I know all about them." Joe turned as Nancy's husband explained, "They wear all black, fingernails, hair, the whole nine yards. Wear dog collars, can you believe it? Anti everything. Losers if you ask me."

"You don't have to tell him, Norm," Nancy said. "What I want to know is why parents insist on bringing young children here. A wake is no place to have little kids running around under foot. It's not the place for it."

Joe nodded as he wiped the perspiration from his forehead. They're fighting for attention. Maybe Nancy is so aggressive at work because she has to fight to get a word in at home.

"I'm glad we didn't bring our kids," Bob winked at Joe. "She'd be yelling at me."

"Some parents want to have their children with them," Roberta offered.

Nancy's husband pushed further into the group. "What I don't understand about parents is how they can turn a blind eye to drinking. They know their kids are doing it, yet it keeps going on." He gestured at the overfilled room. "This shouldn't happen. The parents are to blame."

"The police, too," Nancy said with an assertive thrust of her head. "They know where the parties are. If they don't, they should."

When Joe returned her look with a small shrug, Nancy increased her voice and continued. "Every Monday morning the kids in my classes talk about the parties they went to on the weekends. Who was there, who was drunk. Every weekend it happens. Everybody knows, and no one does anything about it. Am I right?" She looked around the group as if expecting a fight.

"I hear you," Bob said. "It even filters down to the Guidance Department."

"If you all know it's happening," her husband said, "why don't you do something about it?"

Joe pulled his collar away from his sweaty neck and wondered which one would back down if they were at home instead of in public. He had never seen Nancy retreat.

"Everyone knows about it and that includes the kids," Roberta said. "We've told them at school. It's all over the media. They know it's wrong."

"Then the laws need to be tougher," Norm said raising his voice. "Take away their damn licenses."

Nancy noticed heads turning to look at them. She took her husband's hand and he stopped. "Let's move along," she said.

The group turned from the hallway into a large room under a steepled ceiling. At the peak an arched window added light to the muted sconces along the walls and floor lamps in the corners. The line serpentined to the casket in the opposite corner. They paused at an easel with pictures of Amber.

Bob looked away from a picture of Amber making jazz hands in her blue-sequined Show Choir gown and said under his breath to Roberta, "How you think he's doing? It's barely been three months."

"It must be hard," Roberta said. "He keeps looking over his shoulder. Like he's looking for someone."

Bob saw her hand clasped in her husband's, and his wife Linda at the easel next to Nancy. He sighed. "Last thing he needs is another death."

"Here she is in the National Honor Society with most of my Spanish IV class," Nancy announced pointing to the easel.

Bob took Joe's elbow and pulled him away from the others. "So how are things going in the old Department office, huh? That new girl, Lexy whatever her name is, got everybody all riled up, I hear. A civil war, a Spanish Civil War I guess you'd say, huh?"

Joe allowed himself to follow. He loved Bob for trying, but Joe knew it was his own mess. He would have to handle it himself.

"You on her side or Nancy's?" Bob said, his eyes twinkling in his round Irish face. "She came into my office and told me you and her have the same teaching styles. I didn't even know you had a style, and she says she's not like Nancy, but Nancy's always telling her what to do and how to teach, and--"

"Stop." Joe looked at his friend. "Bob. You don't have to do anything. I'm fine."

"What?" Bob dropped his eyes and shuffled his feet. "Thought things were getting a little heavy."

"Amber's dead. That's why we're here, OK?" He patted Bob's shoulder and stepped around him to hug Nancy and Roberta. "Thanks for the conversation, but I have to deal with this."

Joe shook hands with their two husbands and moved forward ahead of them as a gap opened in the line. On a table to their left stood framed pictures of Amber: on a rocking horse, with an older couple in front of a flowering bush, in a maroon cap wielding a baseball bat. Joe wiped his handkerchief across his face and forced himself to breathe. He moved closer to the casket.

Other adults hovered behind Chelsea and Mrs. Larkin. An aunt, a shorter version of the girls' mother, her face red and swollen. She squeezed a cloth in one hand and rested the other on her sister's shoulder. An older man, a grandfather, stood stiffly behind them, his eyes unfocused, elsewhere. Daniel Larkin stood several feet away from his family, a hard, angry line etched into the skin between his eyes. His mouth a deeper, horizontal slit.

Joe fumbled between shaking Daniel's hand and hugging him, surprised at the ferocity in the man's grip. He reached around the dead girl's mother and felt her damp face against his cheek. He said something to her and she responded, but he didn't know what it was beyond "I'm so sorry and thank you for coming."

Inside the heavy black mascara Sea Larkin's eyes were red-lined and wet. Her chin quivered as she said, "*Guten Abend, Herr Lehrer,*" the words strained but clear.

"Chelsea, I am so sorry," he said as his voice broke. He hugged her and breathed through his mouth to keep from crying. He felt the girl's hands on his shoulder.

"Hey, I'm supposed to be comforting you." He stepped back and forced a smile. "What are you doing speaking German at a time like this?"

"My teacher says I have to practice."

"Listen, if there's anything--" His throat closed before he could finish.

"Thank you." She patted his arm.

He turned away and wiped a hand across his eyes. His fingers cold against his skin. A photo of Amber stood on her coffin, the blue of her dress and yellow hair running together in his watery eyes. He made the sign of the cross and dropped to the kneeler.

When he finished the prayer, his breathing was closer to normal and his eyes clearer. He looked back for his friends. They stood in the line with their spouses, comforting and being comforted. Nancy leaned against her husband's chest, the competition over.

"May I have your attention, please?" The room hushed as a gray-haired man in a black suit raised his hands over his head and slowly rotated.

Joe turned away from his friends and walked directly to the several rows of folding wooden chairs in the far corner.

As the Larkin family seated themselves on upholstered chairs to his left, Mr. DiBello adjusted the lamp on the small stand in front of the chairs and said, "Officiating this evening's service is the pastor of Holy Angels Church, Fr. Gerald Hastings." He stepped aside as the tall, florid man took his place. Hastings' light blonde hair receded from a smooth round face. He removed a pair of reading glasses and spoke in a deep, confident tone.

"The time allotted to Amber Larkin is at an end. Tragically and too short, her time on earth is now over. What are we who are left behind to do? How can we manage without her? How can we cope?"

Joe slipped the knot of his tie lower and undid the button. He dabbed the sweat from the sides of his nose and his upper lip. He tried to control the trembling in his hands by counting slowly as he inhaled and exhaled.

"It is a trap to think about the whys and wherefores of Amber's death. To discuss how it happened, where it happened, and to assess blame. If we bury ourselves in the facts of her death, we indeed bury ourselves. These details are the little pieces of God's plan that we can see. We cannot understand the depth and breadth of His plan and it is very easy, it is too easy, to get caught in the question that bothers us the most: why did Amber Larkin have to die?"

In the hallway a door slammed shut. Joe jolted in his seat and spun around. As he turned back to the priest, he saw Bob shaking his head.

"*Why* is a question for humans, not a question for God. The facts of Amber's death, and worse, the responsibility for her death, are questions we cannot answer. Questions that will ravage and torment us, for they are unanswerable in our limited, human terms."

Joe looked at the casket behind the priest and saw another one. Shiny, dark wood. Brass handrails. Cathy's body inside.

"What are we humans to do? We are left with a huge hole in our lives. We are left with the pain of having to face life without Amber. What can we do?" He slowly scanned the faces before him.

"We can do what Christ told us to do. Simply and completely, we can follow Jesus' message. We can love one another, and in this time of torment we must. No questions, no blame, no crime scene investigation. We simply love one another. That's how we fill the void, that's how we live our lives. We follow His words. We love one another."

Joe rocked slowly back and forth on the hard wooden chair. Head pounding. Shirt damp with sweat. Face chalk-white. Pupils dilated. Breath coming in gasps. He fled from the room and the crowded heat, to the open night air outside.

"Look around the room," Fr. Hastings continued, "at your family and your friends. They are the ones who need your love. They have life and they are in need of your love and your care. As Jesus said, 'Go now and love one another'."

⚔

"I didn't say that it wasn't a good speech or that she messed it all up." Eleanor Mindrivan mashed the cigarette into the tray on Kimberly's desk and reached into her purse for the pack. "I said neither of those things."

"I thought the audience reaction was very good." Amy Michalik nodded as she spoke. "We got a dozen new volunteers."

"No, it wasn't a disaster." Eleanor whisked the blue smoke away from her face.

Pamela Holmgren noted Kimberly's glum expression behind the desk and said, "It wasn't, but we needed more."

"It seemed fine to me, Kim, but as you know, I wasn't at the earlier meetings."

With a look at Amy that agreed more strongly than the tone of her voice, Eleanor said, "Everything you said was fine, but you should have addressed the part that could hurt us."

"Aren't we causing the trouble ourselves if we keep bringing it up?" Ursula Hellauer, Kimberly's sister-in-law and wife of the current mayor, was a heavy set woman in a flowered dress and thick-soled shoes. "Alfred always says the less people know, the better."

"Ursula, we have to get it behind us. You're right. We want the noise to stop, but we have to be the ones to stop it." Eleanor laid the cigarette down and opened the folder on her lap. "We had it in the notes, here. We told her what to say and she didn't."

Kimberly waved at the smoke. "*She* is sitting right here, Eleanor, and *she* didn't forget. *She* didn't want to keep bringing it up."

"I agree, we should let it die," Ursula said.

"As you said before," Eleanor said, "but the candidate has to distance herself from the strike last spring. Either she fixed it or was not involved in any way. We decided she should say how she brought both sides together and ended it before it could get out of hand. She saved the city from further embarrassment. We had it all written out for her."

"But the more times we mention it--"

"I know, we all know, Ursula, the real estate values, the school report card. We know that," Eleanor said. "But we have to take the initiative. If we wait for a charge that she failed to lead or that she let it happen, we're in a defensive posture. We're reacting. We should be pro-active."

"We still have time," Pamela said. "Kane hasn't said anything about it."

Eleanor looked from her to Amy. "That's not the only problem, is it?"

"No, it's all over town," Amy replied. "Steven says the men on the force are hearing things. It's hard for him to keep them quiet."

"The mayor can keep the police department under control," Ursula said to Kimberly. "You'll be their boss."

"Too many people were involved last spring," Eleanor said. "Too many petitions and too many meetings. Even the damn newspaper. If we hadn't stopped it after the long weekend, people would still be talking about it. That's why we have to get it behind us."

"So keep quiet about it. That's what I think."

"Duly noted, Uschi. Again. There are worse things than public outrage."

"I think that's an adequate summary of both positions." Kimberly nodded first to Eleanor then the other three in front of her desk. "Thank you. That'll be all for today."

"So what are we going to do? I think we should settle--"

Kimberly stopped Ursula with a look, and steered her and the others out of the office. She let out a breath and dropped down in her chair.

"Pretty feisty group you got there, boss," a voice said from behind the partition of the work station in the rear of the room. "Not a bad thing from a democracy standpoint."

"Thank you, Karl." She motioned for him to sit. "I suppose you think it's a sign of how much they care."

"That, or an overly active imagination." Karl adjusted the cuffs under his suit coat.

Kimberly waited a moment. "You heard both sides. What should I do?"

"I've taught you better than this, Kimmy."

Her face began to flush as she watched him fiddle with the red-stoned cufflinks in his shirt. Nobody wears French cuffs anymore.

Karl sighed without looking up. "What is Rule Number One?"

"Let sleeping dogs lie," she said. "You agree with Ursula."

"It's not Uschi I agree with, or your brother Alfie for that matter," Karl said. "This is Stradford. We like it quiet. Besides..."

The mayoral candidate looked at him when he stopped. His eyes in the low light of the desk lamp were a lifeless gray. "We can always put the dogs to sleep."

"In this case bitches," she replied. "Rule Number Two."

Karl nodded.

CHAPTER FOUR

"I just don't understand what all the fuss is about," Eleanor Mindrivan was saying, "they have jobs. They should be happy. I know many people who are out of work." She nodded at the others around the table in the Board of Education work room. They returned her nods in proportion to their professional experience with education.

The Rev. J. Humphrie Patterson was very much in agreement. "They are public employees. We are their statutory employers. We shouldn't even have to discuss this." His right hand thumped down on the table, reminding Mindrivan of his hand striking the pulpit in church. "Or any other issue for that matter."

Mel Radburn, the business manager of the school system, checked Superintendent Karen Metcalf's expression first, then nodded vigorously. "While I agree with you wholeheartedly, Reverend, I believe that ship has sailed."

He nodded again to his boss at the end of the conference table and continued. "Unfortunately, we have a contract with the teachers, and they are allowed to discuss working conditions."

"That's not how it was when my Brian worked here," Mindrivan said. "When he or the Superintendent spoke, those teachers went back into their classrooms and shut their mouths. That's all there was to it."

"Those were easier times," Metcalf said.

"I don't like it," the Reverend said. "The inmates are running the asylum. You're the Superintendent, what you say should go."

Five of the six heads around the table nodded sympathetically. The sixth, Gary Constantine, said without looking at the administrator on his right or his left, "On the other hand, the teaching staff does spend their days with our children. Maybe they're not completely out of line. In this case."

No one responded verbally. Metcalf looked past him to Radburn. Radburn jabbed his elbow into the former high school assistant principal's rib and covered it by coughing into his handkerchief. Patterson raised his eyebrows and focused his deep, black eyes on him. Mindrivan came closest to speaking, releasing a long, nearly painful sigh. They held those poses for several seconds until Constantine gave up looking for agreement and dropped his gaze to the shiny surface of the table.

Finally Eric Tuttle cleared his throat. "That is why you hired Chevalier, Edelmann and Tuttle, ladies and gentlemen. I will speak during the negotiating sessions. You will take notes and listen." He looked around the table, finishing with Metcalf at the opposite end. "The young man here is free to speak in this room, that's fine, but let me do the talking out there." He gestured to the door, then drew his arm toward his face and checked his TAG Heuer. "It's time to go back in."

As the Stradford Board of Education Negotiating Team filed out, the lawyer put his arm around Constantine's shoulder and whispered in his ear. Radburn bent down to hear what Metcalf was saying, and Patterson said to Mindrivan, "Eleanor, my friend, I fear we must part ways. I leap into the breach, and you-- I don't know exactly what it is you do out here."

Mindrivan pointed to the binders and sheaves of paper in front of her and the open laptop. "I have plenty to do here, Humpfrie, don't worry about me." She smiled to him as he followed the others out, then reached for her phone and punched a number.

"They're going back to the table. That's right." She nodded again. "I will, Kimberly."

⇌⇋

The present-day Board of Education building was once the entire Stradford school system. Every student attended classes there, from kindergarten through twelfth grade. Joe had seen grainy, black and white pictures of those early years, girls in long dresses, boys in knickers, a line of dour-faced women teachers and one man, the Principal, in a black suit.

Negotiations were held in the room the Board used for its regular meetings. Across the long rectangular table five large, leather chairs faced Joe, three-sided nameplates, water glasses and yellow pads in front of each. Behind him were two sections of folding metal chairs, seven or eight in each and perhaps ten rows. He and the rest of the Stradford Education Association negotiations team sat at the large table on the same short metal seats. He wondered for the third time if he had made a mistake in re-joining the team.

Ken Prusnek, the Ohio Education Association representative, sat to Joe's left. On Joe's right sat Georgia Campbell, the white-haired music teacher from the junior high. She was one of the founding members of the association and this was her fourth time at the table. Zimmerman sat to Prusnek's left, a stack of papers and open laptop at hand. Beyond him was the youngest member of the team, Emily Kander, a primary teacher at Raub Elementary. Joe didn't know her as well as the others, but she seemed tougher than her doe-eyed expression. He hoped so at least.

"With the way things went last spring," Zimmerman was saying to the OEA rep, "I'm thinking this might be an easy one."

"We've only agreed on the simple issues, and they're only tentative agreements at that," Prusnek replied. "We'll have to see."

"Nothing happens till we talk about money." Georgia tapped the table with the end of a yellow pencil. "That's how it always is. That's how it'll be this year."

Joe nodded to Georgia. It's only negotiating, he told himself. At least I won't have to worry about the Attendance Committee or being President.

The negotiator pursed his lips. "The money will work itself out. They have it or they don't."

"Or they have it, and they say they don't," Georgia said.

"Well, sure, they'll try that," Prusneck said, "but we have ways of finding out. Boards have to file certain documents with the state, and the state association in Columbus has access to that data. It's not perfect, but funds are a lot harder to hide than it used to be."

"So why the long face?" Zimmerman's voice, even when not upset or angry, sounded like he was.

"They haven't presented their whole package. What we've seen has been reasonable, nothing really surprising. But the money issues they've held back, and I have the feeling there's something--" He turned and fell silent as the door opened.

Tuttle sat down across from Prusnek, and Joe shot Zimmerman a look as Radburn seated himself opposite Joe. They had made a bet on which of them would be graced by the presence of their former principal; Joe had clearly lost. Georgia nodded to Rev. Patterson as she opened her notebook, the same book she had been taking notes in for years.

"It's time to talk about money," Tuttle said placing a stack of papers on the table in front of him. "It is going to be a very short conversation, because, frankly, we don't have very much. Clearly not enough to fund your proposal."

"What are we to do?" Prusnek asked. Zimmerman jabbed a finger at the computer screen. The OEA rep glanced at it and nodded.

"Unless that was a rhetorical question, you should rethink your salary proposal," Tuttle said. "There is no way we can approach those numbers."

"Show us your books," Prusnek countered. "We have reason to believe there is more than you are telling us."

"You know we can't--"

"--or won't."

"Play word games all you want, Ken, but you can't squeeze blood from a rutabaga."

That brought a laugh from Georgia and a quickly fading grin from Patterson.

Joe settled back to watch the two men spar about the numbers. Several times he wanted to speak, but he knew he should keep himself in check and wrote notes on his pad instead. The others at the table alternated between bored and scornful expressions, but kept silent as well.

Finally Tuttle tapped the stack of papers in front of him and said, "We could do this all night, and these good folks are paying me by the hour, but the Board has a new proposal. Something we've never done before. We hope you like it, because at the end of the day, we have the best interests of the staff and the children of Stradford in mind."

Joe kept his eyes down and wrote *and we don't?* in his notebook.

"We need to be more efficient," Tuttle continued and held up his hand. "Before you even start, no, we're not talking about cutting staff."

Radburn stared across the table at Joe, his eyes hard, empty. That can't be the issue, Joe thought. We're a growing school district. Two or three new families a week move into the district. We can't keep up with the growth as it is. Radburn looked expectantly at Metcalf, then Constantine, but they kept silent, and Constantine lowered his eyes.

Prusnek said, "We have population figures that show--"

"--we have figures too," Tuttle said and shook his head. "It is customary for the side presenting a proposal to speak without interruption until finished. Then there is a discussion phase, as you well know, in which you all may participate."

With effort Joe carefully placed his pencil on the lined yellow pad and let out a careful breath.

"Now, returning to our proposal," Tuttle gestured theatrically. "The district needs to be more efficient, to handle our present situation and the foreseeable future." He passed the paper-clipped pages to both sides of the table. The teacher team read along as he continued.

"As you all know, the largest single expenditure for a school district, any school district, is the cost of personnel, variously estimated at between 83% and 89%."

"The actual figure I believe is something closer to 90%," Radburn said.

"Give or take," Tuttle said. "The point being, it is an enormous part of the budget."

Patterson whistled softly at the numbers. Joe ground his teeth and let out a slow breath when he felt Georgia pat his arm.

"Most people solve the problem of growth by simply throwing money at it: buy more teachers. But then the teachers get tenure, their salaries go up, hospitalization and other benefits increase, the population boom slows or changes, and the district is stuck with an aging and expensive staff. We can't fire them because they have tenure.

Joe underlined 'aging' and 'expensive' in his notebook. The room seemed suddenly too hot, the air smothering. He pulled his collar away from his neck and tried again to slow his breathing.

Tuttle continued, "So instead of following a path we believe leads to financial ruin, and is therefore untenable, we propose a more efficient route. In a few words, we will solve the budget crunch by using technology. Cutting edge, 21st century technology. We will be more efficient, leaner, and we will produce children equipped to function in the future, not in the past." Tuttle patted the papers in front of him and rested his head on the high back of the chair. His eyes scanned the team opposite him.

"If I read this correctly, the Board is proposing a 'blended' classroom?" Prusnek said. Tuttle nodded. "So a teacher, Mr. Zimmerman here or Ms. Kander, they would teach a different group of kids every other day."

Tuttle nodded. "Clearly more efficient."

"So in ten days, a teacher would teach one class five days, and a different class five days."

Joe snapped the point of his pencil. Tuttle's head reacted to the sound, then continued. Georgia handed Joe another pencil.

"Two classes for the price of one. The district can handle the numbers now and well into the future."

"What happens to one group when the teacher is with the other group?"

"In a word, computers." Tuttle smiled. "Kids love computers." Radburn nodded and Patterson bobbed his head enthusiastically.

Joe had heard it before. Robo classes. Access to the internet. Packets of information. Tech heaven. Clickety clack. Cooperating with the machine. Ignoring each other. No unifying spirit. No need for eye contact, inflection or tone. Dots and dashes. Zeroes and ones.

He looked Tuttle in the eye and said, "Who is with the children when they're with their computer and their teacher is with the other group?"

"Teacher aides."

Joe laid the pencil next to his pad and began to clap his hands slowly, his eyes on Tuttle. When he could feel all their eyes, he said, "Aides who work for minimum wage. Way to go, save a few bucks on salary and use an electronic babysitter." Metcalf tried to catch his eye, but Joe kept his eyes directly on the lawyer.

Tuttle glared at Prusnek who waved an open palm to Joe.

"I said they would be with an aide," Tuttle said

"With a teaching certificate?"

The lawyer glanced at his notes. "No."

"With educational experience?" Joe's voice increased in speed and pitch.

"Perhaps."

"With a college degree?" Joe could feel his face reddening.

Tuttle glanced to Radburn who shrugged. "Perhaps."

"Part time?"

"Certainly, that's where the real savings come in. Para-professionals. Educational para-professionals."

"So you don't have to pay them benefits," Joe said, "like you did to the tutors last year."

Patterson looked as if he hadn't known about the tutors, or was confused by the concept.

"That's where the savings are," Tuttle said as if explaining a difficult concept to a child. "It's not just about the difference in salary between part-time and full, it's--"

"--Save me the lecture," Joe said and turned to the Superintendent. "Tell me, Dr. Metcalf, in your time here, how many teachers have you hired who have neither a college degree, nor a teaching certificate?"

Metcalf looked to Tuttle, then said to Lehrer, "None. All our teachers have both, and many years experience, in fact--"

Tuttle held up his hand to stop her, and turned to Joe. "What is your point?"

Joe dropped his hands to the table in frustration. "Don't you people see? One of the reasons we have good schools is because we have good teachers. With your plan the children will be with non-certificated aides half the time. This effectively lowers the quality of the people working with your children."

"Perhaps you don't understand," Tuttle said. "These aides are simply there to--"

"--baby-sit," Joe snapped. "They don't know the subject matter. Could one of them explain calculus to Zim's kids, or sing with Georgia's?"

Tuttle's brow furrowed. He glared at Prusnek who shrugged slightly, then aimed his glare at Joe. "The education will come from the computers, not from the aides. They are there to maintain discipline and to make sure the machines work."

"Their educators will be human on Monday and machines on Tuesday, is that it?"

"The computers will allow the teachers to expand what they can do for the children."

"But not *with* the children. We would only see them every other day. What happens when little Johnny is absent on a human day? Two days in a row without seeing his teacher? Three?"

Tuttle nodded. "Like I said, the best districts, the Hudsons and the Medinas, are utilizing more and more technology, and Stradford doesn't want to be left behind. Like Cleveland."

"Comparing Stradford to Cleveland? Really?" Joe paused. "Your plan is to store our children in a room with a computer and a person who doesn't know the subject matter. That is half-assed at best."

Patterson raised his hand. "Your language offends me, sir. Do you speak that way in the classroom? If you do, I--"

Tuttle feigned shock and looked to Radburn and Metcalf. "Reverend Patterson, thank you for your concern. Mr. Lehrer, there is no need--"

"--who was your favorite teacher, Mr. Tuttle when you were in school? Or you, Reverend? Dr. Metcalf? Was it a machine? An IBM? A Trash-80? The photo-copier? The overhead projector?"

Prusnek put a warning hand on Joe's arm. He pushed it away. "No it wasn't, it was real person. A human being. Probably a professional teacher. Someone who went beyond the subject matter. Who lit that spark of interest inside you. Who helped you with just plain growing up. Who saw you for who you really are. Who helped you become better." Joe dropped his eyes and shook his head.

Get a grip, he told himself. Don't lose this in anger.

Joe took a deep breath, tapped the pencil on the pad and said, "What happens between a teacher and a student should be the heart of a school." He was speaking calmly now, his voice measured and sure. "I cherish that interaction, as Zim and Georgia and Emily do. That's why we teach. The connection between the teacher and the student is based on our ability to relate to the child as an individual. On the trust we establish with them."

He scanned the other side of the table, his eyebrows up and his face open. "Kids are not all the same. You know that, we all know that, and we want the teacher to make a connection with each kid. We can't do that in a large group, the kids get lost. The loud ones drown out the quiet ones and we can't meet their most basic needs: to be heard, to be understood, to be appreciated. Large classes prevent that. We need smaller classes, and seeing the kids half as many days would hinder that interaction."

He slumped back into the metal chair. "Our kids don't need less human contact, they need more."

Seconds passed quietly. Tuttle said, "That was quite a speech, Mr. Lehrer, heartfelt words, I am sure." He paused as if to gather strength from those on his side of the table. "But Stradford exists in the real world. We just can't afford it."

"Then you need to pass a levy," Joe said. You need to get your head out of your ass, he thought.

CHAPTER FIVE

"I assume you were saving this for me," Bob said squeezing into the chair between Joe and Roberta.

"As you assumed we couldn't have a conversation without you," Joe said.

"Or go more than three weeks without a faculty meeting." Bob put his arms around both of them. "But it is great to be together again, the three amigos."

"I don't know if it's more miserable with him or without him," Roberta said, struggling out from under his arm.

"I kinda like it," Joe said and snuggled into Bob's hug.

"Whoa," Bob said leaping to his feet. "Keep your hands to yourself."

"You started it, big boy, sit down and get some sugar." Joe gave him a broad wink and patted the empty seat. It did feel great to be back with his amigos.

At the portable lectern in the Choir Room, Principal Stevens cleared his throat and thunked the microphone. "We'd like to get started here, people."

Bob wedged himself back into the chair, slapping Joe's hand as he did so. Stevens glared at the sound. "Mr. McCauley, if you please."

"Now you got me in trouble," he whispered.

"You're blushing," Roberta said.

"Our first order of business tonight, people, is the upcoming election." Stevens waited as latecomers found seats. "Thank you. We want to keep this brief tonight as you know because of the Parent Conference Meetings we have scheduled."

"Longest day of the year," Bob said out of the corner of his mouth. "We get a couple hours off between school and the conferences, and he has to fill them with a meeting."

"As you undoubtedly have heard, Kimberly Horvath has resigned from the Board of Education. "The Cookie Lady has done much for the school system, the senior high in particular, and will be missed." From the way she had acted during the strike, Joe found her to be shallow and self-serving. "I am sure however," Stevens continued, "that she will bring credit to her future endeavors as our city's mayor."

"Is she running against anyone, Mr. Stevens," Joe said quickly. "Or has her brother simply anointed her?"

Stevens looked at Joe as if something was caught in his throat. "Uh, of course, she, there will be--"

"He's back!" Bob pumped his fist.

Joe nodded to his friend. "So there will in fact be an election. Somebody is actually running against her."

"She, Mrs. Horvath is of course, she is--"

"Thank you, Mr. Stevens," Joe said and sat back down. Someone in the row behind him patted his shoulder.

Stevens shuffled the papers on the lectern as red crept up his cheeks. "Our next order of business, also pursuant to the November election, here, next month, the Superintendent, Dr. Metcalf, Karen Metcalf, your, our superintendent." Metcalf reached past him and adjusted the microphone with a skreek.

"Of more specific concern to the school district than local politics," she said looking directly at Joe, "is the operating levy the Board has placed on the ballot.

"7.5 mills, renewable, this money directly affects us." She used her eyes to dampen the noise coming from the teachers. "All of us. In this building and throughout the district. We need to pass this levy or we will be forced to consider budget cuts.

"There are two major factors putting us in this position, three if you consider the constant growth of the district. First of course are the concessions the Board made as a result of the strike last spring."

She looked directly at Joe again and said, "At this point that is water under the dam, and no, I am not taking questions or comments about that."

She paused, then pulled her stare off him. "Secondly, if you are aware of the financial situation in Columbus, you know that the funding formula is flawed." She stepped out from behind the lectern. Her severely cut black suit accentuated her shoulders and narrowed her waist. "Old news. Nothing we can do about it." She nodded to a raised hand.

"Is there a definite correlation between the passing the levy and staff cuts?"

She shook her head. "Not 100%, Mr. Zimmerman. But if I were a betting woman, that's what I would bet. We've already cut where we could, and we've reduced the amount we're asking for. There is only so far we can back up.

"We can get through this school year without making any additional cuts. The problem is, if we don't pass the levy this calendar year, we can't collect the revenue before the start of the next school year."

"Dr. Metcalf can't take any more questions now," Stevens said to the several raised hands.

"Yes, I do have to speak at the other buildings, but I will say one last thing." The room fell silent. "The parents you meet tonight are voters. As you well know, if every parent in the district votes for our issue, it will pass. Please bear that in mind."

"Enough said." Stevens pulled the mic toward himself. "Let's thank the Superintendent for speaking to us today." He clapped and nodded for the others to join him. Metcalf looked at him strangely, waved curtly to the staff, and strode from the room.

"Before we get to out next agenda item," Stevens said, "I want to remind you to be positive with the parents." He glanced at the closed door. "What Dr. Metcalf wanted me to stress to you is we, er, you, didn't make a lot of friends with the strike last spring--"

The teachers' reaction burst against the podium like a wave. Stevens waited for it to pass. "I am sorry, but there is no way around it. There are a lot of irritated folks out there, and they may just vote against the levy because of that."

"It wasn't our fault!" Teri Dieken shouted.

"We're beyond that now, Ms. Dieken. We have to deal with it."

Bob nudged Joe. "Mr. Milktoast is showing some spine here."

"We can lose our jobs, but he won't."

"It's not all doom and gloom around here, you know," Stevens continued. "As an example, you could mention that our sports teams are doing well."

Teri let out a disgusted syllable and sat back down.

"Or on a more serious note, not that sports are not serious." Stevens fumbled with his notes and reddened. "Here it is. The state report card is due out in a matter of weeks. Hopefully, before the election. It would certainly improve our chances of passage if we could tell the community that the state has rated us 'Excellent' or even 'Excellent with Distinction'. I believe that what we do here is in fact excellent, but we're awaiting the results of the proficiency tests, and then we'll know.

"Lastly, I have asked Assistant Principal Weigel to speak to us for a few minutes, just a few, people, on the doings of our Attendance Committee. Peter?"

Weigel stepped from behind the Principal to a cart with a lap top and projector. The screen lowered and the lights dimmed. "My thanks to Mr. McCauley and the other members of the Committee.

"We are in the information gathering phase of our work, assembling the data we need to produce an effective new policy." He fingered the clicker and the committee names fled across the screen to the right. "These are the categories of student absences," he said as a list popped in behind frowny-face bullets.

"No Mas," Bob said. Joe shook his head.

"We need you teachers," Weigel continued, "to categorize the student absences as you record them. In other words, don't just mark them absent, but tell us if they are medical, field trip or other school-related, legally mandated, or whatever.

"This last category is of course, the unexcused absence. If there is no other reason the young person is not in your class, you record that as a cut." He turned from the screen and nodded at one of the raised hands.

Stevens touched his arm. "Mr. Weigel, we don't have time to take questions."

Weigel jerked his arm away and shot him a look. He might have said something too, for Stevens backed away, but in the darkened room Joe couldn't see clearly. "We have time," Weigel said, and turned again to the teachers.

"What will become of all the data?" Matt Stanton asked.

"This data will help determine how many classes may be missed per semester," Weigel said. He glared quickly at Stevens again, and took the next question.

"Does that change any policy we have in place now?" Wosniak demanded.

The balding man keyed the next slide. "After any five missed classes, emails will be sent home to the parents. So, no, this is not a change of procedure. Next?"

"We'll have to send the emails. More busy work for us." This from Zimmerman, and several conversations broke out at once. Stevens stepped forward and opened his mouth. Weigel held his arm across the Principal's chest and continued, "Do you have a question?"

"With the Board membership changing," Paul Stewart asked in his slow, deliberate tone. "What if we correlate all these data and the new Board decides to drop the whole thing? That happened before."

Weigel stepped into the light of the projector and waited for the room to quiet. "It could happen again, I'm not going to lie to you. But there is only one new seat and it will be appointed." He looked at Joe. "The remaining members will probably pick someone they can work with. Not someone with wildly disparate views. They should anyway."

Joe kept his eyes on him and raised his hand. "Last question. Mr. Lehrer?"

"I'd like to ask an educational question, not a procedural one." Joe stood up. "From a teaching point of view, does it matter why a student is not in class? If they miss the class, they miss what happened. Whatever the reason."

Stevens wrung his hands, but before he could speak, Weigel said, "As a former member of this Committee, Mr. Lehrer, I am sure you are aware of our mandate. The Board wants to know how often the children are in class and why they are not in class."

"So you're saying, your record keeping is more important than our teaching."

Weigel's eyes bored into Joe's face. "Your words, not mine."

"It will come down to what's a good reason to miss and what is not a good reason, is that correct?"

Weigel took half a step forward. "You were on the Committee."

"I was, and I know that this is all about make-up work. If somebody likes the excuse, the child will be allowed to make up the work missed. That means we will be allowed to re-teach the activities that were missed."

Weigel snapped off the computer, and his voice rose in the dark. "There are classes in this building where a kid can miss 20 days and get a "B!""

"Then deal with--" Joe began.

"No more questions!"

The lights flashed on and Stevens stepped to the center of the room. "Thank you, Mr. Weigel, for that presentation, and all of you for our, um, discussion. We will dismiss now, so you have time to return for Parent Conference Night, which begins at 5:00 pm." He turned to face Weigel as the staff filed out.

"Neither his father nor I have had German, Mr. Lehrer, and we just can't help him. I don't know why he took it. We both took Spanish and we could have helped him, but German. We are so frustrated."

Joe nodded and looked away from TJ Teeple's mother, distracted by the noise in the gymnasium. Parent Conferences were held here and in the adjoining Cafeteria. Round tables were set in rows, the teachers assigned alphabetically. Lines of molded plastic chairs wound among the tables where parents, mothers with a sprinkling of fathers, waited nervously or impatiently. In other years, parents followed their child's schedule and met the teacher in a quiet classroom. The din of a hundred simultaneous conversations now replaced that privacy.

"It's good that you and your husband want to help TJ," Joe said. "I wish that all my parents were as interested." Ellen Teeple's thick blond hair was pulled back in a long pony tail and framed an open face. Her eyes, wide set above a sharp nose, twinkled, and she seemed ready to speak, but smiled demurely instead. She wore a dark blue jogging suit with pink trim and bright white running shoes. An attractive woman.

"It's important that he does well. We think so anyway." She looked directly at Joe and smiled again. He flipped open the gradebook and tapped a small calculator. "He's fine, Mrs. Teeple. If he keeps this up, he'll be right in there."

"What exactly is his grade?" She had opened a Franklin Covey notebook and unscrewed a silver pen. Light twinkled on the stones of a tennis bracelet. "Call me Ellen."

"80 or 81 percent."

"That's a C," she said and wrinkled her nose. "That's not good enough."

"It's a high C or a low B, I haven't drawn the line yet. He's OK."

She wrote something in the notebook then twirled the pen back and forth between her fingers. The polish on her fingertips made pink dots in the silver blur. "What seems to be his problem?"

"In the big picture, nothing. He's an adolescent male," Joe said. "I'm happy with his attention in class, and he's respectful. It looks like he wants to learn."

"But his grade is a C."

"Even if he gets a C, it's a first quarter grade. That grade is only in my gradebook; it never appears on a transcript."

"Terry, TJ's father, will not be happy," she said. She frowned theatrically, her mouth a pouty rosebud. "What can we do about this?"

"TJ's problem, like many in the class, is the grammar. He doesn't know how to approach the structure of the language."

"Is there anything we can buy, CDs or computer games? He loves computers."

"Once he gets the basics, those kinds of things would help."

"Didn't he learn the basics in German I, last year?"

McCauley mouthed something to him from behind her head. Joe waved him away. "Sure he did. Frau Beitel tells me he did quite well. But somewhere along the line, we have to teach the grammar, and that's my job."

"He really wants to talk German. Probably so I won't know what he's saying."

"That's the fun part." Joe nodded encouragingly. "But there's only so far you can go without controlling the grammar."

"If he gets that far."

"What do you mean, Mrs. Teeple?"

"He only needs two years for an Honors diploma, and if his grade isn't better than a C, we won't let him go on. His grade point average can't take it."

"That would be a shame. He's a good boy."

"But good doesn't get it done, does it?" She inserted the pen into the leather ring in her book. "With what college costs, we need a scholarship. The right schools won't look at C's."

"It's still early and we have a chapter test coming up next week. If he does well on that, he has a B." Joe closed the gradebook. "There are a lot of very good state schools in Ohio."

"Most of the students here go to Kent or Bowling Green or Miami, don't they, Mr. Lehrer? That's fine for them." She nodded. "But not for my son." She thrust her open hand at the crowded gymnasium. "We're getting him away from these people."

The plastic chair stuck on the heavy canvas covering the basketball floor, and Joe had to stand and move it back to get enough room to cross his legs. Finally he sat down and rubbed the heels of his hands into his eyes.

"So how many have you had?"

"More than you, Robert, that's a safe bet."

McCauley rotated the yellow pad and ran his finger down the list. "Nine and it's not even dinner time. Hmm, several MILFs, too, I see."

"Pig."

"Oink-oink, but you can't say that Teeple woman for example is not scalding hot."

"Whereas I am a professional educator--"

"--not a blind professional educator." Bob dropped down into the chair.

"So while I am concentrating on why Johnny can't read German, or English for that matter, I don't even notice the things you fixate on."

"Now you're lying."

"Maybe a little." Joe's grin faded. "Do you know her?"

"I'm not going there," Bob giggled. "No, I really don't. Seen her around a lot."

"Looks the part. Involved. But there's something about her." Joe slapped the table top lightly. "I don't know."

"OK, I got a story," Bob said and pulled his chair closer. Joe nodded. "You do have a gift."

"Sure, like Rainman. Or Einstein."

"The idiot part you got down cold. The savant part--" Joe leaned back and opened his hands. "This had better be good."

"It is," Bob whispered. "Or it are, I got two things. Same topic though."

"I'm starting to fall asleep."

"OK, OK. Stevens comes over and starts talking about your new little colleague, Lexan. Funny name, it doesn't rhyme with 'Texan'. Should spell it Lex-Anne. And isn't Lexan the stuff they make football helmets out of?"

"Get to the point, Bob, if you have one."

"Anyway, she's getting good reviews from parents, and the kids love her. Sounds to him you were right. She teaches more like you than Nancy. She thinks of you as her mentor."

"I guess that's a compliment." Joe narrowed his eyes. "You said two things."

Bob dropped his voice. "But the same topic. Lexan. Seems like there really is bad blood between her and Nancy."

"She stood up to her. First week of school," Joe said. "But how does Stevens even know about that? Did she complain to the Principal about Nancy?"

"No, that's the funny part. Stevens had Lexan in his office for a conference and she mentioned some stuff, but it wasn't really a complaint. He said it felt like she was sizing him up. Seeing if he could help her. Like she was lining up his vote."

"She's playing politics."

"Yeah, a veteran move. Stevens said he didn't buy it, told her to relax and wait until she had tenure. Nancy's not doing anything she hasn't been doing for years."

"So the cute little girl thing is an act?"

Bob looked at him closely. "You think she's cute?"

"Asshole."

"I do, too." Bob smirked. "I was thinking, maybe there's an iron fist inside that cute little velvet glove."

Joe shook his head. "Would you have had the balls to take on your supervisor the first month on a job?"

"Hell, no. My first year I never opened my mouth."

"Right," Joe said. "So are you done yet?"

"Yeah, I guess, no, not really." Bob tapped his pen on the table several times and looked away before saying to him, "I was thinking that if she's that devious, and she likes you, shit." He looked away again.

"Likes me? You said she teaches like me." The last thing I need, he thought.

"I don't know, I, uh--"

"What, you think she's trying to play me?"

"I don't know. It sounded better in my head. But with Cathy gone--"

Joe released a loud laugh; people at nearby tables turned and looked. "That's great! Think maybe she'll hit on me?"

Bob reddened. "I'm sorry, hey."

After a moment Joe sighed.

"The way you stood up to Stevens and Weigel at the faculty meeting, you do seem, I don't know, better."

"I don't know if I'm better, but the last negotiations session got me fired up." Joe released another bark of laughter. "You're saying a 109 pound blonde girl is going to, what, take advantage of me?"

Bob stood up from the table. "I don't know, Joe, I just think there's more to her than meets the eye."

"Maybe there is, Mom. I'll be careful."

Joe watched him make his way through the gym, stopping every couple of tables to chat and wreak his jolly chaos. There was usually a nugget of truth beneath his friend's apparently carefree surface, but he found it hard to believe he was actually worried about him getting involved with Lexan Warner. Joe chuckled to himself as Bob high-fived a white-haired lady talking to Zimmerman. But Bob was rarely wrong about people; he had pegged Mel Radburn before Joe caught on, and had been right about Supt. Metcalf, too. He needed to think about this.

"Mrs. Kasagawa, Irwin is doing his usual masterful job. There is no need to worry."

"I'm not worried. I want to know what I can do to help him do better."

Joe pulled two folders from the file boxes stacked on the metal cart. "This is his writing folder and this one is for his reading. His compositions are clipped together, the drafts and final copies. You can see how good the grades are."

"This one is an A-. Oh, and here, this one is a B."

"These are his writings from the last two years. This B is a year old; he got an A on the report card."

"There are so many red marks, so many mistakes." Patty Kasagawa sadly shook her head.

"Irwin is a brilliant student. Sometimes I have to struggle to find things wrong."

"But the red marks--"

"These are things I hadn't taught. He tried to do something he didn't quite know yet." Joe rotated the paper towards himself. "This is not really a mistake."

"But it is incorrect, Mr. Lehrer. It is marked in red."

"Yes, but it is passive voice. I haven't taught it yet to the class, and it's pretty much correct. These marks here are me explaining how to do it."

"And his reading?" She closed one folder and opened the other.

"His reading is beyond what most of the class can do. I grade his book reports harder to keep him in line. You won't be able to tell from the titles, but he is reading texts that are much harder than what most of the kids do. This is excellent work."

She closed the folder. "We want to help him, Mr. Lehrer."

"He is doing well, Mrs. Kasagawa, very well."

"We don't speak German. We don't know what to do for him."

"You don't need to help him, he is doing it himself."

"We haven't seen him do much German work at home. Physics he does all the time and Calculus."

"He has time to work in class, and the quality of what he is doing is excellent." Joe tapped the folders with his pen.

"He needs to do more homework."

"I think he is balancing his work load very well. He has several Honors classes; he's playing tennis and doing all the music. He'll test out of a lot of hours in college. He's fine. In fact the only problem--"

He paused at her horrified look. "--only problem is, I will miss him when he graduates. He is so good to work with." Joe nodded. "I will."

══╬═▶

"Ms. Warner," Joe said. "I don't have an appointment, but can we talk about little Johnny?"

Lexan finished the smiley face on the paper she was correcting, and ran a finger down her schedule of appointments. "I guess that would be OK," she said and raised her eyes to Joe. "Hey, you're not a real person."

"What am I?" Joe sat down across from her. "A figment of your imagination?"

"You're not little Johnny's father, that's for sure."

"No, I'm just a war correspondent. Call me Hemingway."

"Pardon me?"

"Everybody's talking about the Spanish Civil War. You teach Spanish, I assumed you would know."

"Oh, my little skirmish with Nancy? Fine, thank you for asking."

"You're not getting off the hook that easily. What are the latest casualty figures?"

"If she keeps wearing those old fashioned suits, no one will know if she has a figure or not."

"That's better," Joe said. "How about the body count?"

"Like the song says, 'Four dead in O-hi-o'."

"You and Nancy are two, who am I missing? Roberta? Me?"

"Some people don't even know when they're dead."

"Ouch. Any collateral damage?"

"Apparently to my reputation," she smiled. "But it was from friendly fire."

God, she's quick, Joe thought.

He held up his hands. "OK, OK, you're too good at this. I surrender."

"I don't like to lose. That's always been my problem."

"Not a bad thing," Joe said. "To be fair, I've heard some good things about your work. Really."

"The faculty grapevine is not just for bad news?" Lexan furrowed her brows. "Nice to know."

"It's not like everyone is watching all the time, but you are the new kid. And you're not exactly shy. Apparently you're doing a good job."

"Is that why you dropped by?" Her dark eyebrows lifted.

"That's one of the reasons." Lexan was looking at him closely, her gray eyes intent under her bouncy yellow curls.

Joe thought maybe Bob was right about her.

He said, "Another reason is to tell you not to pick a fight you can't win. Close the door and fight inside the classroom. You can win that one, you are, and that's the important one. You can't win the office politics."

She trained her intelligent, lively eyes on him, and for a moment looked older.

"Welcome to the 'Ford, Lex." He put on a broad smile and paused. "So how's the rest of your day been? I've had eleven conferences already."

She let out a breath and a small grin. "I've had let's see, thirteen. I win. Sorry, it's that competitive thing again."

"Fair and square. I owe you a drink."

"Bob mentioned something about 'grading papers'." Joe noticed a smudge of blue ink on her cheek, several curly rings askew above it.

"That's his code for drinks at the bar in the Marriott. Sounds more professional." He pushed the chair away from the table. "See you there?"

"Sounds good. Listen, there is something else." She looked away again. "This is weird. You're going to think I'm even weirder."

"You can't be any weirder." He grinned at her expression. "But I owe you one for helping me with the Homework Hotline."

"OK. You may not believe this. I'm not sure I do."

Joe watched Lexan's eyes flicker again, to her hands, the table next to her, the paper she was grading, the grated clock on the gymnasium wall. "Either tell me or don't, whatever you want."

Her eyes darted to his. In a low voice she said, "I think Amber Larkin was murdered."

"That's ridiculous," Joe blurted.

"I knew you'd say that." She slapped a palm on her lap. "I knew it."

"There were beer cans all over, the picture in the paper."

"Amber didn't drink."

"They all drink." His voice came out in a harsh whisper.

"Not Amber, that's not what I heard."

Lexan's eyes were steady now and Joe could again see something inside their neutral color. Inside or behind them, something glowing, intense. He couldn't tell what it was. "Did you know her?"

"No, I talked to her sister Chelsea. She's friends with some girls in my class."

"She's in my II class. I know for sure Amber was a drinker. They suspended her from flag team for it when she was a sophomore. Before you got here."

"That's the last time she drank."

Joe looked away. Several women sat nearby pretending not to listen. "You've got people waiting."

"You don't believe me." Lexan nodded and straightened the stack of compositions on the table. "That's OK."

"Whether I do or don't, we can't talk about it here." He stood up.

"I'm not crazy."

"Then you're a crazy magnet."

A half smile beneath the glowing eyes. "Maybe I am," she said.

"Mrs. Saylor," Joe said. "I think you're trying to bribe me."

"Open it." Joe took the envelope from her and she smiled.

"But if someone sees it, and it's a bribe--" Joe hunched his shoulders and looked left and right.

"Like you're afraid of Big Brother." A dark-haired woman, slightly overweight, her grin covered the entire lower half of her face.

"I am a big supporter of legitimate authority," he said and ripped the beige paper. "A gift certificate for Morton's Steak House." He met her eyes. "This is too much."

"Lindsay and I have been worried about you. Not eating."

"No, really."

"You have to eat."

"I can't, this is so nice of you."

"You can and you should. We want you to have it."

"I don't know what to say." He swallowed. "Thank you very much."

"Just wait," Mrs. Saylor said and held up her hand. "Now before you tell me how you don't deserve it and all that nonsense, just let me say."

"I don't--"

"My husband and I and Lindsay of course, just wanted to thank you for everything you've done for us. No, you just listen."

Joe closed his mouth and smiled.

"Junior high was not a good time for Lindsay. She was tall and gawky and didn't have many friends."

Joe nodded. "And she spoke like an adult,"

"It was hard for her. She read a lot and didn't, I don't know what you call it, 'hang out' with kids all the time. She enjoyed spending time with us."

"The kiss of adolescent death," Joe said. "Now she's up for homecoming court."

"We have you to thank."

"Me? I didn't do anything. She came into her own. She got involved in theater and now she's popular." Joe leaned back in his chair and opened his hands.

"It all started with being on the stage crew, Mr. Lehrer, and I think you had something to do with that."

"I was just looking for someone responsible to help build sets, and she ran with it. One year she's painting scenery, the next she has the lead in the fall play. I didn't do anything special. Not to deserve this." He slid the envelope across the table toward her.

"It was special to our family." She put her hand on his arm. "Please keep it."

Joe picked up the envelope and tapped it against his palm. "Thank you. Lindsay's such a great kid. She's no work at all."

"That's because she likes you. You should see her at home." Mrs. Saylor smiled. "She is so excited about the Germany trip."

"Me too, I wish you could come with us."

"And leave the rest of those hooligans at home?" she laughed. Then seriously, "Is there a chance they'll cancel the trip because of the levy?"

"No, they don't give us any money for it, so I think we're safe."

"That's good." She looked around furtively.

"Now you look guilty."

"What about Mrs. Horvath?" she whispered.

"Our future mayor? Nothing."

"Did you hear she had to resign?"

"I didn't hear that." He shook his head. "What did she do?"

"I don't know." Mrs. Saylor bobbed her head several times. "But it was bad. Why else would she leave? She has a job already. She was the Board president."

"Stradford, who knows?"

"Where there's smoke there's fire." She wagged a finger at him.

"But you don't have any evidence or a story even."

"I see things," she said and winked. "You just wait." She patted his arm and quickly stood up.

"You drop a bombshell and leave?"

"My other children aren't as gifted as this one. I have to get to the junior high."

"Let me know when you want to sit down and talk about college," Joe said. "We'll see what we can do. Thanks again for the dinner."

"You deserve it."

Joe leaned back from the table to stretch and get a look at the clock. A couple minutes to 8:00 and the gym was nearly empty. A pretty typical round of conferences. The parents of kids with problems didn't show, and he'd have to call them. Those who did come in, worry too much about the wrong things. Stradford had only two kinds of parents, the ones who don't care at all and the helicopters.

He checked his appointment sheet, hoping he was right and no more conferences were scheduled. He collected the papers he had spread over the table and put them back in his gradebook. He dropped it and the pens that had accumulated into his bag and laid it on top of the metal cart.

"You're like a homeless old lady, Lehrer, pushing your shopping cart around town."

"Zimmerman, you're an ass, and that's not a simile."

"Here's one more for your collection." Zimmerman put an empty Nestea can on the corner of the cart. "Hey, nice job at the faculty meeting. You're on a roll."

"Good to be back," Joe said. "You can buy me a drink."

"You coming? That's great."

"Gotta drop my stuff in the office first. I'll be right behind you."

Joe rolled the cart down the hallway over the smooth terrazzo. He passed several teachers hurrying out and a couple of lost parents. In the office Nancy and Roberta held the door and assured him they would be joining the group. He arranged the reading and writing crates on the bookshelf, decided to leave his bag on the desk and turned to leave.

"The Conference Sign-in Sheet is due in the Main Office before you leave."

Joe flinched at the sound. "Mel, nice to see you." The former principal leaned against the partition, his bulk obscuring the hallway beyond.

"Hope I didn't startle you."

Joe noticed the smirk on the man's jowly face. "It's in my bag, I'll drop it on the way out." Without breaking eye contact, Joe slid his hand through the strap and shouldered it up.

"Thought you were parked out there." Radburn unfolded an arm and thrust a fat finger toward the teacher lot. "The Office is over there." Like an elephant's trunk the finger swung the opposite way.

Joe tightened his lips. Doesn't even work here and he wants to bust my balls. "A chance to get some exercise." he said. "Sitting all day."

"Good idea. Another is to turn in the appropriate paper work in a timely fashion."

"I'm on it." Joe took a step toward the doorway. Radburn didn't move. "Do you have anything constructive to say about how my students are doing in class?"

"Your lesson plans, Mr. Lehrer. Are they properly formatted and submitted?"

"Like clockwork. Every kid in AP passed the test last spring."

"Clockwork." Radburn levered himself vertical and filled the doorway completely. "As I recall, that was not always the case."

"Under your expert guidance I learned." Joe shifted the strap on his shoulder. "When they pass the AP test, they get college credit. That's money in their pocket. As Business Manager you should like that."

"I was generous to you, Mr. Lehrer, extremely generous. I often overlooked your tardy paperwork and your other numerous, shall we say, indiscretions."

"For which I am internally grateful, Mel. Listen, I'm in kind of a hurry."

He raised the elephantine finger again. "Don't take advantage of Mr. Stevens. He is not as kind as I was."

"It's hard to follow a legend," Joe said.

The grin faded, the finger remained outstretched. "This is not a suggestion. You have made enough waves around here."

"My paperwork isn't your concern anymore, it's Gale's." Joe avoided the finger and locked his eyes on Radburn's massive face.

"Your lack of attention to paperwork was an embarrassment to this school, but an internal embarrassment. Your activities during the strike and now at the bargaining table are an embarrassment to the entire community."

The rest of it now fell into place. "Give it up, Mel. The Board caved in the spring and now it's up to the voters."

"If this levy fails because of the negative actions of your teachers, it will be on you."

"My teachers?"

"You were the poster boy, Mr. Lehrer. It was your face on the TV every night."

"Sorry, Mel, the Board wouldn't talk to us, so we talked to the press."

"Your people acted without class. Barricading drive-ways, catcalling, waving signs. A disgrace." He leaned his massive head closer. "Some of your members got arrested! You didn't control them."

"No, I trusted them." Joe dropped the bag back onto his desk. "Stop me if I'm wrong, Boss, but all the charges were dropped."

Radburn's face was by now bright red. Before he could speak again, Joe said, "Listen, what I really want to know is why the Board caved so fast. They barely put up a fight."

The other looked as if he had swallowed some bad fish. "Money," he rasped and held a closed fist over his mouth. "It's always about the money." Seconds passed. Radburn burped again and backed into the darkened hall.

Joe turned off his desk lamp and brushed past the former Principal. Several steps down the stairway, Radburn said to his back, "Don't think this is over, Mr. Lehrer. It's not."

Joe kept walking and extended a hand over his head. "No, Mel, you're wrong about that, too."

CHAPTER SIX

J oe looked closely at the miniature Fokker above him trying to shoot down the Spad to see if the German pilot
looked anything like Mel. The tiny figure's face in the open
cockpit was obscured by his flying goggles, but the barrel of
his machine gun jabbed at his enemy like Radburn's finger.

"Mel busted you about paperwork?" Bob said again and
gestured with his drink. "The strike or negotiations I can
understand, but lesson plans? That's old news."

"Yeah, and it's not like he enjoys being a bully or anything," Zimmerman said.

The lounge in the Marriott was called the Flying Circus.
Decorated to resemble a WWI aerodrome, the front end of
a Sopwith Camel jutted out over the bar from the back wall,
its propeller wired to a bell the bartenders spun to acknowl-
edge a tip. The Stradford teachers were sitting in a circle
of campaign chairs beneath the tiny dogfight. Joe watched

Bob try to laugh, swallow and speak at the same time, and felt like smiling.

"Boys being boys," Nancy nodded at Roberta and Lexan for encouragement. "You boys get bigger and older, but you never leave the playground."

"I resemble that," Bob managed to choke out. Beside him Keith Boswell nearly spit out his drink.

"But it doesn't make sense," Roberta said. "What does Radburn care if Joe doesn't do paperwork anymore or not? He works in the Board office."

Joe saw Lexan's fingers digging for the cherry in the frosted glass of her Vodka Collins.

"It's not like Joe got him fired," Boswell said. "Bob's the one who caught him faking the attendance figures, and that was years ago. Besides, now he's got an easier job and makes a lot more money."

"I don't know if it's that much more," Roberta said, "but it has to be easier. It gets easier the farther you are from the kids."

Joe noticed that the Spad was not directly in front of the German bi-plane, but dipping down and away.

"What about the attendance figures?" Lexan asked. "That was before I got here."

"Bob, and Matt Stanton actually, found out a couple years ago that Mel was cooking the attendance books," Zimmerman said. "Making it look like Stradford had fewer students than we really did so we could do better on the state tests."

Lexan set down her drink. "Fewer kids? I don't get it."

"Money, Lexan." Nancy shook her head. "It's always money."

"State funding is based on how the school does on the tests," Bob said. "Mel didn't let the kids he thought would do poorly take the test, so our percentages were better, and we could get more money from Columbus."

"Then Bob did his thing," Bert said as the drinks arrived. "Got him replaced."

"Yet Mel hates Joe," Zimmerman said. "Go figure." He took the Bloody Mary from a waitress dressed like Florence Nightingale in a mini-skirt and handed it to Roberta. "Looks like O-Negative, must be yours."

"Blood typing didn't begin until the thirties, sir," the girl said. "Wrong war."

"Shot down in flames," Nancy smirked and pointed up. "How appropriate."

"Leggy and learned," Bob laughed as the girl left. "Like one of your Show Choir girls, Keith."

"There's nothing wrong with being nice looking," Boswell said. "But don't start on me about that again. The music department has its own problems."

"Problems!" Nancy said. She set her drink down so hard it sloshed over the side. "You have 13 different choirs so kids can sing whenever they want. We only have one class per grade level." She nodded to the other language teachers. "Kids drop Spanish all the time to take music."

"How many supplemental contracts do you have," Roberta demanded. "Five?"

"Yeah," Zimmerman said. "And you give private lessons during the school day?"

Boswell surrendered with his hands up. "Sorry, I didn't want to bring up all this old crap. But more than I ever have, kids are dropping music classes. I know how you guys feel, but when they drop your classes, at least it's for another class."

"Stradford kids are just like their parents," Nancy declared. "They want money for cars and clothes."

"Amber Larkin had a job." Lexan pulled her chair closer to Joe.

"The other thing is, Nancy, they get out of class all the time, too," Boswell said. "They're counted present in school, but they're not in my class."

"You're complaining about kids getting excused from class?" Roberta said. "Your music kids are always off somewhere, singing and tooting."

Boswell looked helplessly from Zimmerman to Bob. "Tooting?"

"Cheap shot, ladies, but funny," Bob said. "No, this is different. Maybe there is something more going on with Mel and Joe than we thought."

"There has to be," Joe said. "He really doesn't have a reason to be mad at me."

"I don't know," Bob continued, "but now kids can get a new kind of pass from the guidance department. Carrie Raymond excuses kids with a 'temporary,' work pass." Joe looked to Lexan as Bob bracketed the word with his fingers.

"Amber got out of my class all the time with one of those," Boswell said.

"Isn't this what they do for work/study kids?" Roberta said. "That's not new."

"This isn't a program for credit," Bob said. "They can miss class whenever it's convenient to the employer, with full administrative approval. And make-up work is allowed."

"Even my choir kids can miss concerts with one of those," Boswell said. "And it's an excused absence."

"It's not a cut to miss a performance? Where did this come from?" Nancy demanded.

"From the Attendance Committee, our future mayor and Mel," Joe said.

"Now that I think about it, it might have been Weigel's idea," Bob said. "It's limited to so many per semester, but it's basically a get-out-of-school-free pass. "

"This is so Stradford," Roberta said. "The kids don't have to be accountable. It undermines everything we do."

"The parents don't even have to lie," Bob said. "They get the employer to ask for the kid and the admin backs it up. It's a great plan."

"Especially if you think being in school isn't all that important," Joe said.

⚔

"I don't know why I'm surprised, Uschi," Alfred Hellauer said. He swirled the Glenlivet around the heavy crystal. "You've always taken her side."

Ursula Hellauer sighed and looked across their yard to the blue flowers on the hydrangea at the edge of the garden. She knew how to handle his moods, and waiting before she answered was important. She didn't know why the flowers were blue on one part of the bush but pinkish red on the other. "There is only one side," she said finally. "You're both on the same side."

"Then why is she trying to get rid of me? My own sister." He clanked the glass onto the wrought iron table between them. "Why is she doing that?"

Several of the softball shaped flowers were both blue and dusty pink, and some of the petals themselves were bi-colored. "Do you remember why you ran for Mayor in the first place? How many years ago was that?" Diversion was usually a good tactic.

"I never wanted to be Mayor in the first place. She talked me into it," he snorted. "All I wanted to do was mind the hardware store. Nothing the matter with that."

"How many years ago was it, dear?"

"Years? What, I don't know, eight, ten."

"Fourteen. That's plenty of time to give to the city."

"I never really wanted to do it, remember that." He pointed a gnarly finger at her.

She smiled at his expression. Kimberly had used that very pose, a younger version of it, on his first campaign poster. A younger Alfred, a determined man with more hair, darker hair, jabbing that finger at the world. But the same man, her husband.

"I just don't like all those women around her," Alfred said.

"What an old curmudgeon you sound like. Women work now, you know. Women have jobs outside the home."

"For one thing, there's too many of them. They're like a brood of old hens, clucking away at everything. It's a wonder any work ever gets done at all."

"Kimberly's advisers are not all women, Alfred. You hired Steven Michalik yourself. The police department was a mess before he cleaned it up."

"That was before he got married. Now he listens to that Amy."

She reached across the table and took his hand. The thick fingers were calloused and warm. "It's not a crime to listen to your wife, is it?"

He looked away and sighed, his breath a slow raspy hiss. "You think I can't do it anymore, don't you. You both do."

The strong features of his face seemed to be melting, the wrinkles drooping farther from his eyes, the lines deeper at his mouth. "Not at all, Alfred. You've done enough for Stradford. I think we should move south." Her voice increased in warmth and speed. "We could live year round in Naples, tear down the cottage and build a bigger place. Leave the cold weather and all the stress behind."

"The store, I can't just leave it." His face still in profile to her.

"Tony and Sue have been running it for years."

"Yes. They have," he conceded. A firefly blinked above a blue flower, disappeared, then blinked again near a pink one. "But it's like I'm running away from a job, Uschi," he said in a near whisper. "Quitting."

Her hand dwarfed by his, she squeezed his thumb tighter. "You feel like that because you care about Stradford." His face turned to hers as she knew it would.

"If you were a politician instead of the man you are, you would have run away to Florida years ago. That's not you, Alfie. You brought all those jobs here with Cookie's Cookies and PamLeeCo. Stradford's not a little hick town anymore, it's a city. We can leave here with our heads high."

He nodded at her words, his face firming, a smile forming. "It's not like I'm leaving it to some political hack, is it now?"

She stepped around the table and eased onto his lap. "Not at all. We have Kimberly to take care of everything." His heavy arms folded around her and both colors disappeared from the hydrangeas. All she could see in the garden now were the fireflies.

"No, thanks, I have to get home to the little woman." The ice cubes jangled in the glass as Zimmerman returned it to the table a little too hard. "I appreciate the offer though." He tossed several bills on the table and stood up. Boswell joined him.

"The long-suffering and strong-stomached Mrs. Zimmerman," Bob said. "Be sure and extend her my condolences and deepest sympathies. Keith, you, too."

"Joe, glad you came out tonight," Zimmerman said with a smile. "Been a long time. Good to have you around again." He shook Joe's hand, then gestured to the pile of money on the table. "Think that's enough?"

"We're good, thanks. See you tomorrow."

"Don't pay for it yourself, Joe," Roberta said and reached for her purse.

"I got it." Joe covered the money with his hand.

"I should be leaving, too," Nancy said. She wiped her lips with a napkin and looked questioningly at Roberta and Lexan. "It's a long day tomorrow."

"I'm going to finish my drink." The French teacher munched the celery stalk.

Nancy covered the purse in her lap with her hands and let out a long sigh. "Then I'll have to wait. I'm not walking out of a bar alone."

"You know, Joe," Bob said, "I have never fully appreciated how very difficult it is being a woman."

"OK, mister smarties, how would it look, me walking out of a hotel bar? People know me in Stradford." She shook her head. "We should have gone somewhere else."

Roberta sipped the Bloody Mary. "I'll be ready in a minute. Bernard can get along without me a little longer."

"Joe, you hear me? I said I'd buy another round," Bob said.

"Sure, now that most of us are gone," Joe laughed. "No, I'm fine."

"When did you switch to iced tea? You some kinda wuss?"

"I don't want to lose my edge. Besides, I wanted to talk to Lexan."

"You hound," Bob said looking from his friend to her empty chair.

"Come on. She mentioned something really strange during conferences," Joe said to Roberta. "I didn't want to get into it in the gym."

"Here she comes," Bob said loudly, "the lady of the hour."

Lexan examined their faces from behind her chair. "Put something in my drink?"

"It's fine. Sit down," Nancy said. Her left foot jiggled over her crossed knee.

"Then why are you all looking at me?"

"Nancy gets this way when it's close to her bedtime," Bob said. "OK, I won't buy. I'll accompany you ladies to your cars, lest something untoward befalls you. Hey, that was pretty good, wasn't it?"

"A silver-tongued devil," Joe said.

Nancy jutted her head at Joe while looking expectantly at Lexan. "So what did you want to talk to *him* about?"

"Nothing really, just about Amber Larkin and her sister."

"The one with all the black make-up." Nancy pushed away from the table. "That one."

Bob shook Joe's hand and winked. "See you tomorrow."

"You didn't tell her anything, did you?" Lexan said after they were alone. "You know how Nancy is." Her eyes shone in the semi-lit room. Her face was flushed.

"What could I tell her?" Joe said. "I don't know anything."

"Another round for you folks? An iced tea and let's see, a Vodka Collins?" The waitress pointed at them with a pen shaped like a thermometer.

"You don't believe me, do you." Lexan said flatly.

"I don't think so, no."

"You don't know anything about it or about me either."

"I don't know anything about a murder, but I know quite a bit about you."

"How could you? You hardly ever talk to me even." Her fingers fumbled as she took a cigarette from her purse.

"Please don't."

"It's a bar, I can still smoke in a bar." Lexan blew a cloud of smoke in the air. She took her drink from the waitress and held the cigarette away from the table.

Joe wished they hadn't ordered the drinks. "I know that women are great at covering things up, like how much they drink."

"You talking about me or Amber Larkin? I drink, Amber didn't."

"She did drink," Joe said. "Maybe she stopped, but it's hard to believe."

"All young people drink, that's what you said before."

Joe squeezed the lemon into his tea. "Most of them."

"But not you. You're some kind of saint."

"I know when to stop." His laugh turned into a cough. "Usually anyway."

"So you know all about Amber Larkin." Lexan stubbed out the cigarette. "What about me?"

"You, you're a whole different story."

"Go ahead, I'm all ears." She set the drink down and looked at him.

"OK, let's see. Good student. No, very good student. I haven't seen your transcript, but I'll bet there aren't more than two, maybe three B's on it.'

"Two," she said. "How did you know that?"

"And they're B pluses, right?" He raised his eyebrows.

A small smile. "Go ahead."

"So any problem you have in the classroom is not the subject matter; you got that cold. It's the explaining part," he said. "Explaining it to the dumb kids who don't get it."

"You talked to Nancy." She took another swallow and glared at him.

"I never talk to Nancy. It was easy for you. So easy, you don't know how you learned it. You just did. You don't know how to explain how you learned it."

"Maybe that makes sense to you."

"Think about it."

"What else, Mr. Know-it-all?"

"Moving on to your social life, kind of the same. Good looking and certainly interesting. Guys flock to you, but you don't have lasting relationships."

She sipped her drink and looked at him coolly.

"Do you have trouble getting guys to go out with you or not?"

"I'm not a slut!"

"Not what I said and not what I meant," he said calmly.

"What did you mean?"

Joe drank some tea and wondered why he had gotten into this.

"I meant that it's so easy for you to get guys, maybe you don't know what to do with them when you do."

"Thank you, that's quite a compliment."

"Alright, maybe I'm off track here. It's only a theory."

"Another theory you're wrong about," Lexan said. "Just like you're wrong about Amber Larkin. She was murdered."

The citrus and vodka on her breath competed with her cinnamon perfume. "Do you have any facts to back that up?" he said.

"Why do you need facts? You know everything." She looked at her empty glass and picked up her purse. "I gotta go."

"Wait a second. Do you know anything about her not drinking besides hearsay?"

"As a matter of fact I do. Her car. It was damaged in the rear."

"It flew off the road and landed in the trees. The front end was demolished."

"The back end, too. Somebody pushed her off the road."

Joe thought back to the picture in the paper. "If it's still in town, it'll be at fat Oskar's."

She looked at him dumbly.

"We could go to the junkyard and look at it," Joe blurted before he could stop himself.

"It's a date." She stumbled as she stood up and he reached for her. "I can do it."

"I'll drive you home."

"I can drive myself."

Joe stood up with her and added several more dollars to the pile. "Whatever. I'm going out to the parking lot anyway."

"Other people will help me, I don't need you."

He steered her through the tables and into the lobby. "Other people like who?"

"Like Mr. Weigel." She giggled. "He likes me."

Stevens wasn't the only one she'd been schmoozing, Joe thought. "A little louder, Lexy, not everyone can hear you." He waved to the people behind the check-in counter.

"That's what people call me, Lexy. Sexy Lexy." She whispered the last part.

The doors pssshed open and he stopped under the awning. "Where's your car?"

"I know where it is, over there."

He grabbed her before she could step in front of the passing airport van. "Let's go this way. So you told Mr. Weigel about Amber. What did he say?"

"Mr. Weigel likes me," she said again. "And he helps me."

"Sure he does."

"He does. Hey, this isn't my car."

"No, it's mine. Get in." He opened the passenger side door.

"I can so drive." She flopped down into the seat.

"Sure you can, but it's late."

He reached across her to fasten the seatbelt.

She pushed his arm away. "I know what you're up to."

She pointed suddenly at his head. "You got a scar."

Before he could answer, she sighed and her head lolled back onto the seat. He snapped the belt around her and got into the car.

Ellen Teeple reached across the console and turned the car radio off. "How can you concentrate with that filth blaring in your ear?"

"Mom," TJ said desperately and leaned toward the controls.

"Two hands on the wheel. Both hands." She forced herself to speak calmly.

The car lurched back into its lane. TJ opened his mouth, then sighed instead.

Ellen turned to the back seat. "Bobby, leave your sister alone."

"She started it."

"She's in her car seat. She can't reach you if you stay in yours."

"I don't have a car seat." Bobby poked his sister, then bounced back to his side.

"Mom, should I turn on the lights?"

"Your seatbelt, whatever. Put it back on."

Twin lines of red and white lights traced the lanes of the interstate. "Don't you have them on already?"

"The running lights are always on, Mom." He muttered more under his breath.

"It's dark enough for the real lights, TJ. DeeDee, quit the crying, you're all right."

"Which exit for the airport? There's two."

"The second one, I always get lost on the other," Ellen said slowly. "You're following too closely, slow down."

"Everyone's flying past me."

"Just slow down."

TJ tapped the brake and disengaged the cruise control.

"I told you not to use that thing. I don't like it. Put your blinker on."

The GX 460 drifted to the right and up the ramp to I-480. "Stay to the left here." Her cell phone tweedled.

"Quiet back there," she said and keyed the phone. "Fine, good, now keep to the right, slow down, baggage claim uh-huh, DeeDee I mean it, not so close, watch that car, no not you honey, TJ, two minutes, slow down, 'kay bye."

"Relax, Mom, I got it handled." The car swung into the airport entrance and jerked to a stop at the light.

"Ow, my neck. I got whiplash."

"Shut up, Bobby."

Ellen pulled down the visor and opened the mirror. She re-parted the hair on her forehead. "Follow the sign for arrivals, he's at door five."

"Duh," TJ said. "It is not like he's leaving or anything."

"Be careful, there's lots of idiots stopping and starting. Go slow."

"Mom. I got it, OK?"

"Bobby help us look for Continental. I think it's past Frontier. DeeDee, look out the window for Daddy."

"There he is, he's waving," Bobby said.

"Where? I don't see him," DeeDee said.

TJ cut in front of an airport limo and a black station wagon. A horn blared.

"TJ!" Ellen cried, then pursed her lips in the mirror.

"It's OK, here he comes."

"Daddy!" DeeDee cried.

"I'll drive, get in the back. Pop the hatch." His father appeared briefly at the driver side window.

"Dad, I need the hours." He turned to Ellen. "Mom."

"Honey." A voice from the cargo space, a horn sounding, then a thump.

"Daddy! Daddy!"

"Come on TJ, I'll get us out of here. The cop is coming."

His son slid out of the driver's seat, opened the rear door and climbed in. Terry climbed in to replace him, and leaned over to kiss Ellen.

He wove out of the congestion and onto the freeway. "So, how was everybody's week?" He put his hands on the top of the wheel and looked around.

Three voices responded at once from the back. "OK, OK, one at a time," he laughed. Ellen tracked the blinking lights of an airliner climbing into the black sky. She wished she were on it.

Ten minutes later he pulled the car up the ramp and onto the five-lane road in front of SouthWest Mall. At the light he turned to Ellen. "And now how about you? You look exhausted."

Before she could open her mouth, her daughter cried, "I can stay up late tonight, Daddy, I'm a big girl."

"Yes you are, DeeDee. You sure are."

Ellen patted his knee and smiled.

The car dipped and lurched as Joe pulled out of the parking lot of the Marriott. He looked quickly to see if Lexan was still asleep. Her head had slumped onto her shoulder toward him, her breath coming through her half-open mouth. He was glad she had stopped talking.

Joe glanced to his right to locate her purse. It lay on the floor between her feet. He shook his head and turned up the radio. Her snicker doodle scent was jumbled with the alcohol, and he cracked open both windows.

Lexan stirred and mumbled something about being able to drive herself.

"You couldn't even walk," he said to her sleeping face. He wondered to why he felt responsible for her.

He arched his back and felt the breeze on his face. There was little traffic on Cleveland Ave. North of Center, the main street was hillier and tree-lined, with small offices and houses replacing the strip malls. He made good time, soon passing Holy Angels Church, a beekeeper's hat silhouetted against the dark sky. After the entrance to the MetroPark he turned into the Brandywine apartments and felt her hand flop onto his knee.

"I'm not asleep," she whispered.

"And you weren't snoring either," he said and pushed her hand away. "Which building is yours?"

"I know why you wanted to drive me home."

"You couldn't walk. Which side of the street, Lex, left or right?"

"I'm fine, I could drive." Her hand again on his knee. "I let you take me."

"Sure you could, you're superwoman. Do I turn in here?"

"Right there. That way."

He ripped her hand away and pointed to the apartment clusters. "Damn it Lexan, I'm taking you home. That's all. Which one is it?"

She rapped her fist into his arm and the car jerked to a stop. "You lure me into your car and that's it? I'll get out here." She yanked the handle and shoved the door.

Joe hit the unlock button as she pulled a second time.

"Open this door!"

"Wait a second. Let go of the handle."

"I swear to god I'll scream!"

"Relax." Joe put the car in park. "I'll come around and help you out."

"I don't want your help." She folded her arms across her stomach.

He opened her door and reached inside for her hand. "There you go," he said.

She pushed past him and stomped erratically up the short walk. "I don't need any help from you."

Joe watched her stumble on the bottom step, catch herself, and nearly fall again. He picked up her purse and followed.

"Don't want your help. Don't need your help. Stay away from me," she was muttering to herself as he reached the top step.

"But you might need your key."

She snatched the purse from his hand. "Go to hell."

"Probably." He retreated down the steps.

Lexan fumbled through the purse and finally found the key. "I don't need anybody's help," she mumbled and jabbed it at the door.

The keys jangled in her hand and she lunged at the door again. She missed the slot, but the door fell open as she lurched into it.

Joe was putting his key into the ignition when he heard her scream. She screamed again as he ran up the steps.

She stood in the doorway, one hand over her mouth. Her eyes wide open and her face flushed red. Behind her Joe could see a small dining room, and to her right the living room. Pictures on the white walls, a TV, some plants on a bookcase.

"This isn't my apartment," she cried. "Everything's wrong!"

"What? Were you robbed?"

"No, everything's here, it's, it's all wrong." She spun at him. "Why are you here?"

"You screamed, I thought there was someone here, I thought, shit." He walked past her.

"I told you to leave."

"You called for help, but everything looks OK. Why did you scream?"

"You came back to help me?" Her chin quivered and a tear ran down her cheek.

"Yes, Ms. Moodswing I did. I thought you were being robbed or someone was here."

She wiped her hand across her face. "Someone was here."

"What did they take?" He spun around in the living room, his arms open.

"Nothing, but it's all different."

The furniture was neatly arranged. "Maybe it'll look better in the morning."

"You don't believe me. Again." Her face crumpled and her eyes filled.

He took a step toward her. "Just get out," she said and turned away.

"Look, if there's something wrong--"

Lexan dropped to the edge of the sofa and covered her face with her hands. "They moved everything."

"Nothing's missing, right? Or torn up or thrown on the floor. I don't get it."

"Everything's all moved around, in different places." Her arm flailed at the room.

Joe stopped at the door and saw her wrapped in a ball on the sofa. "Got any coffee in the kitchen, or tea?" She mumbled something he couldn't understand. "I'll bet the kitchen's right over here." He stepped between a small dining room table and a refinished tea cart into the narrow galley. He found tea bags in a canister shaped like a pumpkin; mugs were in the second cupboard he opened, on top of a stack of dinner plates. The kettle was in the dish drainer. He filled it and set it on the stove.

"It'll be ready in a minute." He turned a recliner to face her and sat down.

"You must really think I'm crazy."

"The thought crossed my mind."

"I think I'm crazy." She wiped her eyes again and sat up straighter. "If I were drunk, this would make more sense."

"Yeah, we can rule that out," he smiled.

She let out a long sigh. "The furniture has all been re-arranged."

"Or maybe you are drunk."

"Believe me or not," she shot back. "I don't care. It's not your problem."

He held up his hands palms out. " OK, OK. What exactly do you mean?"

"What do I mean?" She sprang to her feet and pointed. "When I left this morning, the sofa was over there, under the window. The bookcase was on that wall, and the chair you're sitting on faced the TV. Which was over there! So you could actually watch it."

Joe turned with her as she continued.

"That huge picture there, the landscape, was over the mantel, not squeezed into that little space. It doesn't fit."

A tiny 5" x 7" hung on the wall above the fireplace. "The dining room too?"

"The table is turned the long way, and the tea cart my mother gave me and the chest are reversed. See?"

He turned to find her on her hands and knees by the tea cart. "Look, in the carpet, you can see the feet marks from the chest." She rubbed her fingers across the carpet.

He leaned back on his haunches beside her. "I feel like Doubting Thomas."

"I'm not making this up." She pushed a handful of hair out of her eyes.

He looked at the chest on the other wall. "It would have fit there."

The tea kettle peeped from the kitchen and he got to his feet.

"See, the marks are this wide." She kept her hands apart and wobbled on her knees around the table to the chest. "They fit!"

"But all that means is the chest used to be there." Steam clouded out as he poured the hot water into the mugs.

"There are marks from the sofa, too," she said from the other room. "Look!"

He set the mugs on the coffee table and patted the seat next to him. "Tea's ready."

She held her cup in both hands and sipped. "Thank you."

He saw a scared little girl above the rim. "What do you think happened?"

"Somebody moved my stuff all around. Like I said."

"I hear you," he said patiently. "But why would some-body do that?"

"I was gone today, the whole day."

"Sure, they would have time to do it. But why? And a better question is who?"

"I don't know everything, I never said I did," she snapped. "Who, why? What difference does it make? My apartment is, is, I don't know what it is, it's just wrong!"

"You should call the police."

"No. I can handle it myself."

"The door was unlocked when you got here, right? You have to call them."

"And tell them what?" she snarled. "My apartment was redecorated?"

"That could be seen as an insult to the artistic sensibilities of the good citizens of Stradford," he said and set his tea on the table.

"What? That's stupid, that's--" She glared at him. "I know what you're doing."

"I'm trying to help you, Lexan, but man, I don't know. This is weird."

She held herself close and seemed to shrink into the sofa. "I'll be fine."

"But you can't stay here tonight, it's too dangerous."

She sat up straighter. "I'm not leaving my apartment. No."

"Then we have to call the police."

"You're trying to get me to stay at your place, aren't you?"

"Damn it, Lexan," Joe said and stood up. "What I'm trying to do is get you someplace safe. You can't stay here!"

Her eyes widened at his words. "Don't tell me what to do!" she shouted back.

"Either call the police or we're leaving, Lexan. It's your choice, but you're not staying here."

Her chin quivered as she started to speak, and her eyes filled. She covered her mouth with her hand and hurried from the room.

Joe took a step after her before realizing the bathroom must be down the hall. He put his hands in his pockets and turned in a small circle.

She screamed.

For a moment Joe considered not going to find out what was wrong. Her mood had changed three times the last several minutes, and it was too much like her first scream. He shook his head and followed her voice down the hall.

Her bed was covered with photographs. Snapshots, pictures in frames, some loose, dozens of them. "My pictures," she cried, "all my pictures." She was on the floor reaching across the bed, raking the pictures toward her, her fingers frantic on the quilt.

The pictures on the bed had been neatly laid in rows, in a grid, all facing the door way. He stepped around her to the foot and guessed the bed had been moved too. There were photographs on the floor and he stooped to pick them up. Family pictures, kids posing in front of a minivan, kids in a wading pool, families dressed up on the porch of an old colonial. "It's OK, Lex, I'll help you. We'll get them all picked up."

She slumped onto the floor next to him and sobbed, her face on the bed, her arms and fingers now still. "They're ruined. All my pictures."

He looked closely at the pictures in his hand and the ones still visible on the bed. A thick black X slashed the face of a little blonde girl in one, in many of them, all of them. An X through her face as she grew up: on a horse, in front of a roller coaster, in a marching band uniform, in a prom dress, wearing a sombrero, in a wedding party.

On her knees beside him, Lexan wept. An X across her face in all the pictures, her face only, two black Sharpie slashes. Lexan had been removed from her family pictures. He put an arm across her back.

"It's OK, Lex, you're safe," he murmured, his shirt soon wet. He patted her back and shoulders and looked across her head. Her body shook against his.

He saw Lexan in a large, framed painting leaning against the headboard and the pillows. She was in her graduation cap, a gold tassel hanging to one side and a bright yellow stole around her neck. At her throat a gold cross on a chain, now broken where the canvas had been cut. No black X. A knife had slashed the fabric, ripping open her face and her neck.

The canvas flopped forward, the pink pillow visible behind it. From the cheekbone to the chin, a second mouth. Down across her neck a gaping hole. No blood, only pink from the pillow case, not an X, only the slash. Two mouths now. Lexan had two mouths. The one, the bright red lipsticked mouth, the white teeth, the smile, the happy smile, the smile with the devil in the corners. The other, the horrible smile, the one that gaped forward, scored her cheek, opened her arteries.

He gasped and felt her turn toward him, her arms reaching for him. Their faces both wet with her tears. She clutched him to her as they fell to the floor.

Terry Teeple turned down the bedspread. "So how are you really?"

"It was a long week," she said. "I'm tired."

"Did you get the bills paid? I asked you to do them."

"All done."

"How'd you manage that?" The bed bounced as he got himself comfortable. "I thought we were going to be short."

"I'm efficient, Terry."

He looked at her and grinned. "You're the best. Are you really too tired?"

"Too tired for that." She pulled the covers up to her chin.

He looked at the mounds of her breasts under the blanket. "I had a long week and I'm not too tired." He snuggled closer to her.

Ellen turned onto her side away from him, pulling her arms and legs tight to her body. "Maybe tomorrow."

"That's OK. You do too much around here, you know." Terry rolled to his back.

"Who else is there to do it? You're gone all the time."

"Guy's gotta make a living."

"And the wife gets to do all the work around the house."

"I was working. What do you think I was doing?"

"So was I."

"I didn't say you weren't," he said. "We both were."

She waited a moment. "I hate it here."

"What do you mean? We got a great house. This is a great neighborhood, good schools, the mall's right here. What's the matter? Everybody likes Stradford."

"I don't know, it's not that, it's just--"

"You'll feel better in the morning. Get some sleep."

"There's so much to do all the time. No matter how hard we work, we never catch up."

"Wait till I get the regional director's job. Then things will be better. You've been running around all week, you need to rest."

"Maybe so."

"Night, hon." He rolled onto his side and turned off the light.

She lay there in the dark with her eyes open, the only sound his rhythmic breathing. Not everybody likes Stradford, she thought. I will get my children out of here somehow. Especially DeeDee.

Heart racing, Joe began to wake. Inside the crook of his arm, she burrowed closer. He cupped a hand over her breast, and took a long breath. She covered his hand with hers and snuggled tighter. She purred when his thumb found her nipple. He stiffened.

She slid a leg over his. Her tongue darted across his mouth. He moved his hands down her back. He kissed her and tasted cinnamon.

His eyes snapped open. Light through the blinds made film noir rhomboids across the ceiling and down the wall.

"What's the matter?" Her eyes as wide as his.

"Lexan!"

"You all right?" she extended her arms and laughed.

"We're on the floor, in your room."

"Don't you remember?" Lexan sat up and rubbed her eyes. "The pictures, my furniture--" Her voice faded as she turned away.

He looked at the snapshots and the framed pictures scattered across the floor. The large portrait was face down in a pool of light and he could see the carpet through the gash.

"You fell asleep. I didn't want to wake you, so I pulled the pillows and the blanket off the bed and turned off the light."

Joe looked to her open blouse and exposed breasts.

Lexan waited until he looked up. "I needed you to hold me." Her voice cracked and she took his hand.

"I, we, shouldn't have done that."

"We didn't do anything wrong."

"I kissed you." He looked past her head.

"That's an awful thing?"

"No, I don't mean that." He forced out a breath.

"I was scared last night, Joe." Her eyes caught the light from the street. "You needed me, too."

"No." He stood up quickly and held his arms out to the sides. "What are we going to do?"

"Stay, Joe. A little while anyway." She stood. "Unless--" Her eyes narrowed. "Wait. You think I lured you here, don't you. I got drunk so you'd have to take me home." She slapped at him.

He caught her hand. "What? No. Of course not." She sighed and he released it.

"Maybe I was flirting with you a little bit. OK." She jabbed at a tear on her cheek. "But I really am scared."

Joe turned away and pulled his clothes together.

She stood among the slashed pictures, arms drooping, shoulders slumped. "I can't stay with those awful pictures--"

He jammed his shirt into his pants. "I can help you with that."

Joe raked the snapshots into a pile and carried them out of her bedroom. He returned with a black trash bag. As Lexan slid the large portrait into it, their hands brushed. He wanted to hold her hand, but kept his focus on the painting. She followed him slowly into the kitchen.

"--copies. We can replace these, make copies from the negatives or the j-pegs--" His voice trailed off as he gestured vaguely at the trash bag.

"I know, but--" Her lip trembled.

Joe shook his head. "I can't stay."

She followed him out the kitchen and across the living room. He opened the door and turned to her. "I want to stay, Cathy, I do--"

"I'm Lexan," she said.

"Wait I--"

She shut the door between them.

CHAPTER SEVEN

K arl dipped the *Community News* page of the newspaper to get a better look as Pedro struggled through the maze of tables in the front of the diner. The younger man tried several aisles blocked by crossed legs, re-arranged chairs and diners who insisted on standing as they drank coffee, before arriving at Karl's booth in the rear corner.

"Thought you'd never get here," Karl smirked behind the once again raised *Stradford Star.*

"I couldn't see through the cigarette smoke," Pedro said, sliding onto the opposite bench. "I thought that was against the law."

Karl finished the paragraph, then carefully folded the paper along the crease and placed it on the table next to his plate. "It is in some places."

"It's a state pollution law," Pedro said as he tore a piece off his bagel. "Aren't we in Ohio?"

Karl wrinkled his nose in disgust. "Onion bagels are against the law, I know that for a fact. Smoking in The Donut Shoppe? No, that's been going on forever."

"A suburban tradition?" Pedro leveled the layer of cream cheese with his teaspoon. "That's an oxymoron."

Karl liked the man's vocabulary. "This place has been here since the cows outnumbered the people."

"Now it looks like a senior citizens center."

Karl looked around the room, nodding several times as eyes caught his. The gray cloud of smoke did match the dominant hair color, where there was hair at all. "A fair comment. The clientele may have aged a bit."

"If these guys are the movers and shakers, it's only because of the Parkinson's."

Karl nodded. "Guy over there talking to Alfie, is Lee Holmgren. Lee senior."

"Pamela's sugar daddy needs a walker?"

Karl shook his head. "Her father-in-law. Alfie used to own about a quarter of Stradford, where the Interstate is now."

"Made a few bucks when he sold it." Pedro nodded as he chewed.

"At the next table, Semproch, the banker and Fenster, from Fenster Construction. The two of them built almost everything around here, including the Cookie complex and PamLeeCo."

"Money, land, construction and politics," Pedro said. Karl could see Pedro's mind working beneath the comb-over. "So the women we work for are the next wave."

"Very astute," Karl said. "The politically correct next wave."

"Then their first order of business should be to shut this place down, huh?"

Karl laughed. "Kimberly and the Holmgren woman and the others will run things, but they have the good sense not to try that."

"That's why they call you the Professor." Pedro scanned the room again. "Where do we fit in this grand scheme?"

"You know how it is." Karl's voice lowered and his lips straightened into a hard line. "Nobody wants to do the dirty work."

"I never worked for women before." The space between Pedro's eyes narrowed.

"You'll have to learn how to feign," Karl said.

"A fancy word for lie?"

"I'm sure you can handle it, *compadre*." Karl kept his eyes on him.

Pedro sat quietly for a moment. "Don't they want the same things?"

"They do." Karl sipped his coffee. "But with women you can't come out and talk about it like guys do. You have to pretend to be interested in a bunch of their crap first."

"Can't just whack people."

"We can, but first they expect us to reason with them."

"Dr. Phil with a lead-filled sap." Karl couldn't tell if Pedro thought he was making a joke or not.

"So why are we bothering with all the campaign signs? It's a done deal."

"This is an election, so there have to be election signs. That's the other thing about Stradford you got to know. It's all about appearances," Karl said.

Pedro nodded. "Got it."

"I'm not sure you do." Karl carefully folded the paper and laid it down.

The man called Pedro looked up at him. "What do you mean?"

"This isn't the barrio, this isn't the coast, this isn't even Cleveland."

"This isn't a fucking geography class. Spit it out."

Karl's eyebrows lifted and his eyes narrowed. He waited till the smaller man pulled his eyes away. " We know the things you've done other places--"

"I fulfilled my contract. I never did anybody that I wasn't paid for." Pedro's voice harsh and raspy.

Karl held up a palm. "That may be." After a moment he continued. "I'm not saying you haven't done your job. We wouldn't have hired you otherwise."

"Then what the--"

"Your tone, *amigo,* your tone. This is Stradford." Karl looked left and right, lowered his voice.

"You want me to leave?"

"No, I want two things. I want you to do your job, and I want you to do it our way. Quietly."

"With the proper tone," Pedro sneered. "Where'd all this come from? That fat shit Oskar?"

"Tend your own garden. No, that wasn't your finest hour, but I'm in the midst of he-said and he-said. You both fucked up. The girl died and I'm not happy. You had better conform to the local mores."

"What?"

Karl sighed. "Establish the proper behavioral tone."

"And if I don't wanna play that game?"

"Prepare to be on the other end of the stick."

In the first weeks of school, the classroom had been Joe's refuge. With his students, he had forgotten his grief, or at least put it aside. He wouldn't ever forget her, but engaging his kids revived him. He didn't feel dead inside when he was in his element, not when he was teaching.

Speaking with them was good, but 'Grammarland' was even better; there he had more control. Leading his students through the forest of structures and rules gave him a clear sense of worth. He could see that his vocation, at least that, was still intact.

But it hadn't happened today. Now he was poised like a prison guard in front of the five straight rows of students, glaring at any who dared to lift a head. "Couple more minutes," he said to them in German. He glanced around to the ridiculous samples of their homework on the whiteboards and shook his head. "Then we'll try this again."

He realized he hadn't logged the attendance, and entered the names into his laptop. Fridays were usually speaking days. The kids had wanted to circle up the desks and ramble on about their plans for the weekend. They had grumbled when they saw the lined-up rows, but had gone to the board with their homework sentences, assuming that they would get to the fun part after they did their grammar.

Joe stood up and went to the board. "Let's get back to sentence number one."

Ketul Submarinian looked up, anxiety evident in his brown eyes. His fingers scurried across the desk, grabbing notes, pen and homework sheet.

Joe softened his voice. "Just read the sentence, Ketul."

The class rustled a bit, then settled as the boy read from the board, "*Grossvater hat einen neuen Hut. Er ist grau.*"

"So you used the pronoun *er*. That is correct. Can you explain why it's correct?" Joe turned away as he heard the door open.

"*Spaet!*" Chuck said. "*Sie sind spaet!*"

"He should get credit for that, Herr," Jodi Fenster said, "that was German."

Joe stepped away from the board and picked up his checklist. "A plus for Chuck and a minus for Jodi."

"That is so unfair--" she began. Joe lifted his eyebrows and she stopped.

"Band was late, Herr," one of the latecomers said.

"Put your late slips on my gradebook and get out your homework," Joe said.

"Mr. Boswell didn't give us passes."

"He kept the whole clarinet section, Mr. Lehrer."

"I'll have to check with him later, won't I, ladies?" Joe said and waited for them to find their seats. Thirty seconds after the room quieted, he took a cleansing breath and said, "OK, Ketul, *noch einmal*. Tell us why you selected *er*?"

The boy hunched his shoulders and ran his hand across his chin like a much older person would. The class around him was glad it was not their turn to explain.

"Isn't *er* the right answer?"

"Yes. The German isn't the problem," Joe said. "Read it in English."

"Grampa has a new hat. He is gray."

"Who is gray?"

"*Er* is masculine because Grampa is masculine. Right?"

"If Gramps weren't masculine, he'd be Gramma." Joe checked the class hoping for more than a smattering of laughter, then said to the boy, "But does the translation make sense to you?"

"*Er* means he, doesn't it? *Er ist grau*, he is gray."

"Class, any questions?" They stared at him blankly. Joe turned back to Ketul. "Are you talking about Grampa or the--?"

The loudspeaker scratched and Joe flinched. "Pardon the interruption."

"No problem." Joe tossed the marker at the tray. "We're just trying to learn."

"Please excuse any band members late to class," the disembodied voice continued. "They are to be admitted without passes. Thank you."

"See, Mr. Lehrer? We don't need passes."

"No, Debbie, you don't. That's what Mr. Weigel just said. Excuse me for asking."

The girl started to say something else, but saw his face and didn't.

"Now, can we get back to class? Ketul's answer is correct in German, but he translated it 'He is gray'." Lehrer looked at the faces in his classroom. "He is gray. Does that make sense?" The expressions ranged from confusion to catatonia.

He tossed his textbook onto the desk. When it landed with a thunk, the class looked up. "Do you even remember what a personal pronoun is?" Several nodded, but most looked down at their desks. "Uh-huh, a replacement for a noun. For a person or--?" He opened his palms and paused.

"OK, maybe it's all the distractions. Translate the sentences you did last night into English. Real English words that make sense. And do pages 62 to 64 in your workbooks in both German and English."

He kept his eyes on them as he sat down. "I don't want to hear a sound."

❂

Amy Michalik fished out the old coffee filter with her thumb and forefinger, and hurried to the wastebasket. The wet blob fell onto the lip of the can and wavered before dropping in with a sullen thud. Holding her dark blue skirt away from her legs, she twisted left and right. Exhaling loudly she found a clean filter in the cupboard.

Kimmy is in one of her moods, Amy thought. Looks like something the cat dragged in. She dumped a measure of coffee into the filter. Make-up all splotchy. Trying to cover up those bags under her eyes. Two measures is four cups. She's not as young as she used to be. She tapped the plastic spoon clean and dropped it onto the Formica.

"Be ready in a minute," she called.

Didn't get much sleep last night, that's why she looks like that. She watched the water rise in the carafe. The little red ball floated to a stop at four. Amy dumped the excess into the sink, closed the lid and punched the button. The light glowed orange and she set two cups on the counter beside the machine.

"Excuse me?"

Amy jumped at the small and unexpected voice. "You scared me," she said and stepped toward the girl at the door.

"These are, um." The girl looked at the card affixed to the cookie basket in her hand. "Oh, yeah, these are for Mrs. Horvath."

"You must be new here." Amy took the basket from the girl and looked at her. Slouching, skirt too tight, bored. "First of all, stand up straight and spit out the gum."

"What? Oh, yeah, sorry, I forgot." She put the gum in her hand and looked around the office.

"Use this." Amy handed her a Kleenex. "And fasten one or two of those buttons on your blouse. You look slutty." She watched the girl leave and exchanged the cookies for the clipboard on her desk.

Studying the schedule in her hand, she entered Kimberly Horvath's office. "Looks like a normal day," she announced. "Full, but same old, same old." She noticed the empty chair behind the desk, and found her boss at the window. "Oh, sorry."

"A lovely day," Kimberly said looking at the trees fronting the cookie factory below. "Too lovely to be called ordinary, Amy. But then it's also too lovely to have to work." She turned around and reached for the clipboard in the secretary's hand.

"Mostly campaign stuff." She stifled a yawn. "Alfie at ten and the girls for lunch. And that good looking police chief at two." She grinned at the mention of Amy's husband, and yawned again. "I suppose I can manage that."

"The coffee will be ready in a minute," Amy said. She ushered the candidate to a wing-backed chair by the window, turning it first into the light. "We'll get you all fixed up." As Kimberly sat down, her secretary opened the door of the bookcase and removed a tray of PamLeeCo cosmetics. She set them on the table and handed her a small mirror.

"Who is this hag?" Kimberly said. "I look 85 years old."

"It's not that bad. You're working too hard, you need to get more sleep." Amy wiped a cotton ball beneath her eyes. You need to sleep alone, she thought.

"It's not like you, Lexan. Those were my exact words," Nancy said. Joe watched her frown at the stack of papers that had slid off onto the desk. "You said you'd have the chapter four worksheets ready on the day of the chapter three test. Today." She counted five copies, tapped them together, and turned them face down on top of the others. "The other Spanish II teachers need them, not just you."

"I didn't get to it last night," the younger woman said, her voice squeezed tight.

"And I said it was OK." Nancy picked up the stack of worksheets. "I did them myself. In my prep period."

Lexan clutched her own papers to her chest. "I'm sorry, I--"

"--can talk about this later, Lexan." Nancy strode quickly from the office. Lexan dropped down onto her chair.

Joe looked at the blue half circles under her eyes. "Did you get any sleep?"

"After you ran out?" she snapped.

"After you threw me out." Joe tried to keep his voice steady.

"I look that bad?"

Joe reached his hand to her shoulder. She jumped as if shocked. "You don't, you look fine."

"You wouldn't have asked." She snatched her bag from the lower desk drawer and pawed inside for her mirror. "Like hell."

"Look, Lexan, I'm sorry, I--"

She dropped the mirror, "You're sorry I drank too much? You're sorry you slept with me?" She bracketed 'slept' with her fingers. "You're sorry you called me another woman's name? Which is it?"

"I'm just trying to make things right, Lexan, and I don't have a goddam clue how." He stood and reached toward her shoulder again, but stopped. "Maybe we can talk later."

When she didn't look up, he left the office.

From the top step of the doorway outside the language office, the color of the stream of kids leaving the building was denim blue with splotches of black, khaki and gray. "If they had to wear uniforms, they'd throw a fit," he mumbled.

Bright colors, like the high-pitched adolescent voices, were accents only, as were the occasional punk, Goth or farmer. Most were wearing the Full Stradford: jeans, cargo pants or shorts with a collared shirt or T for the boys, jeans or skirt with a J. Crew top for the girls. Even in the cooling temperatures, jackets were rare. Many of them spoke on cell phones as they walked. Those that carried books, carried lots of them, or struggled beneath large backpacks in the same tones as their clothes. Most strolled out of school empty handed, burdened neither by a book nor an apparent care.

Yellow buses stood along the curve on his left to the new football stadium past the school on his right. Most of the kids avoided them. The stream split in front of Joe, the younger ones walking through the buses to where their mothers double-parked the family SUV. The older ones walked between the front of the bus line and the auditorium, where the path to the student parking lot ran over the creek and up a low rise. It was too high for him to see into from this angle, but he knew it held more expensive cars than the faculty lot, and it would be the scene of at least one fender-bender this afternoon.

"There you are, Sunshine," Bob said. Joe flinched at the sound. The second time today. "Girls in the war zone said you might be out here."

"Like I need more stress." Joe kept looking at the fleeing students.

The door clanged shut and Bob sat down on the top step next to him. "With the sun out, it's not too bad out here. Looks like you need to lighten up."

"Not in the mood." Between two of the buses Joe watched a car screech to a stop.

"Almost got one that time," Bob grinned. "OK, no jokes, but you have to help me out here. Zimmerman wants to know what happened last night after you and Lexan left the bar."

Joe closed his eyes; black slashes on Lexan's face, blood on Cathy's face, Lexan's face next to his. "Why the hell is my personal life everybody's business?" he spat. "Tired of talking about Cathy's death?"

"It's just a stupid bet. Like we al--"

"No, it isn't." Joe stood up quickly and glared down at him. "If you two are talking about it in the Lounge, then everybody's talking about it. God damn, I hate this place. A fucking fishbowl!"

Bob pulled back at his friend's angry words. "Sorry, it's just a joke."

"My life's not a joke." Joe looked away as he lied. "It's screwed up, but it's not funny. Not even a little bit."

"I'm sorry, Joe, I didn't come out here to make you mad, I--"

"Why did you come out here? I was trying to get away from the crap inside."

"Why did I come out here." Bob narrowed his eyes and exhaled slowly. "For one, I think Lexan might be right."

"She talk to you?" Joe slumped back down onto the concrete. "Fuck."

"She told me about the break in," Bob said quickly. "Thinks it has something to do with Amber Larkin's death." He tried to see Joe's face.

"She's got a theory. Won't report it to the police, but she has a theory." Joe picked a pebble off the stoop and snapped it into the scrubby grass.

"For what it's worth, that's what I told her, too." Bob squinted in the light. "I'm sorry, man."

"It's OK," Joe said finally. "It's not like the rest of this day has been any better."

⟩⟨

"I don't need your help. I'm not some damsel in distress hoping a big strong man will ride in and rescue me." Lexan raised her chin at him, then took one hand from her hip and pushed a springy curl off her forehead. "I can take care of this myself."

"Your apartment was broken into," Joe said calmly. "You should file a report."

"They aren't going to do anything."

"So your point is you don't need help, or the police won't help you?"

Her eyes widened and filled. She turned away from him and snatched her purse from the desk, wiping a hand across her eyes as she did so. She strode past him and held the office door open. "If we're going, come on."

He caught himself before he said he was sorry. Instead he walked past her down the steps to the car. If he could just get her talking to the police, he could be done with it, and done with her. She followed him, the door slamming shut behind them.

The Stradford Police Department had been built onto the new City Hall. Across Center Street from the old Hall, now the offices of Cookie's Cookies, it sat on Towne Square behind the gazebo and beneath the blue water tower. A cartoon Ziggy Stardust looked down from it as they entered the low, cinder block structure.

"I still don't know what we're going to accomplish here."

"I witnessed a crime," Joe said. "I'm going to report it."

"It was in my house."

"That's right. You should be the one filing the report, but if you're not, I will."

She glared at him, and walked around him to the heavy glass window. "I'd like to report a break-in," she said into the microphone.

"Are you reporting a robbery?" The heavy-set clerk shuffled papers as she spoke.

"I don't know. Nothing was stolen."

"What is the nature of the crime?" The clerk raised tired eyes to Lexan.

"I don't know exactly, I--"

"Is Buddy Kramer available?" Joe said over Lexan's shoulder. He could see her confusion in the reflection. "We'd like to speak to him."

"Who are you?"

"Joe Lehrer."

"What is the nature of your involvement?"

Joe put his hand on Lexan's shoulder and leaned closer. "I'm a witness."

"One moment. I'll see if Detective Kramer is in."

"We don't need a detective." Lexan turned out of his grasp.

"I know Elmer Senior. He used to teach with us." The metal door buzzed and they followed the clerk through narrow hallways to a small office.

Kramer stood as he saw Joe and extended his hand. " Good to see you, Mr. Lehrer." A short man with closely-cropped hair, he focused cunning blue eyes at them from beneath thick brows.

Joe introduced Lexan as they sat down on gray metal chairs in front of Kramer's gray metal desk. The officer sat behind it. The three of them filled the room.

"So tell me what happened." Kramer's eyes darted from face to face as Lexan told the story, his hand taking notes independently as she spoke.

"Do you have anything to add?" he asked when she finished. Joe shook his head. Kramer looked down at his notes, paused and retracted the point of his pen. He laid it carefully next to the pad and looked up at Lexan.

"Are you sure there was nothing taken, Ms. Warner?"

She shook her head, no.

"And nothing was vandalized."

"My pictures," Lexan said quietly.

"The pictures," the detective repeated and glanced at his notes.

Joe watched his lips bunch into a line. "The intent was to terrorize her, Buddy."

"That may be, but it wasn't a burglary if nothing was taken."

"They broke into my apartment."

"Where she lives, Buddy. They destroyed her property, her--" Joe's voice faded off. Lexan reached for his hand.

"You're right, it's a B&E, but not like anything we're used to seeing. I'll send a team out, but 18 or 20 hours." He pursed his lips again. "You should have called us right away."

"There's nothing else you can do, is there?" she said. Joe watched her shoulders tighten around her neck. He squeezed her hand.

"What bothers me the most is why anyone would do this to you." Kramer's eyes seemed to pull together as he concentrated. "Do you have any known enemies?"

"She's a teacher," Joe blurted.

Kramer held up a hand. "Ms. Warner?"

"No, I, of course not. Nobody hates me enough to do that."

"Well, we'll put it all into the computer and see what we can find out." He jotted a note and continued to look at her across the desk. "I'll have a unit watch the area."

Lexan stood up. "Sorry to have taken your time." The men stood up as well.

"It's always a good idea to contact the police, Ms. Warner."

Joe tugged her elbow and said, "Give my best to your dad."

Kramer turned toward him. "I'll tell Elmer you were in."

"We'll be in touch, Ms. Warner," the detective said as they left.

Joe caught the door as she exited the police department. She stopped in front of the gazebo and whirled around. "That was just what I expected." The wind hooded her hair around her face but her hands remained on her hips.

"It was necessary," he said. "A step we had to take."

"A total waste of time. I can handle this myself."

Home-bound traffic filled two sides of the Square, a chain extending from the north and east. Joe thought how trapped the drivers must feel in the slow-moving traffic. "What do you want to do?"

"Me, what do I want? Nice of you to ask."

"Damn it, Lexan, I'm trying to help you."

"For the two hundredth time, I don't need help. I'm not the one who needs it."

"Wait, I thought it was your apartment that was broken into. I guess I got that wrong. My mistake."

Lexan saw him look away again at the commuters. "It was nice of you to help, Joe. Really." When he turned back to her, she said, "But the Larkins need help, not me."

"That again," he said.

"It's all right, Joe. You don't have to do anything about this." He felt her metallic gray eyes on his. "Or about anything at all."

"Sure I can't make you a cup?" Father Hastings stood at the counter with his back to Joe and measured cream into his coffee. After he sat down across from him, he carefully uncapped his fountain pen and skimmed through the notebook to find the proper page. It seemed to Joe that he was taking an inordinately long time to do it. He was probably mad.

"I haven't been by, because I thought I was better," Joe said. "Like you said."

At that Hastings looked up. "You canceled two sessions and I haven't seen you in church."

"Things have been better," Joe said quickly. "I'm not as crabby as I had been in class. I hate that, I hate yelling at the kids. They're the only ones keeping me sane. Except maybe you, but you're different. Anyway, the classroom's getting better, a small slip up, but most of the time anyway. You know how that goes."

"How were the parent conferences?" Again the concerned and reassuring voice, but Joe could hear within it that he wasn't happy.

"Parent conferences? I was worried about those, I really was. You know." Joe spoke quickly to demonstrate his progress. "I didn't want to lose it in front of the parents. I don't want to be Mr. Raging Emotions anymore. They went OK, went really well. I think some of them came to stare at me, to find out if I was crazy. Everybody likes a visit to monkey island, or a car wreck, and there I was." He laughed shortly. "There was some of that, but it didn't bother me. It was fine.

"I mostly got the helicopter parents. What can I do to help? I don't speak German. How can I help his grade? You're too hard. Where's the tutor? Can he drop? Bladdabladda. But I must be getting better, because I didn't get mad. I had my documentation. One thing about being alone, there's no reason not to have my grading up to date. Anyway, I didn't let them get to me. I got through it. It was fine, actually."

Hastings looked up after writing in his notebook. "I'm glad you did."

"Oh, yeah, wait, there was something else. This is the best part. You would have been proud. I pretty much, OK, I almost got completely through a confrontation with Mel. Would have killed me in the past. That's worth something, isn't it? Asshole cornered me in the office, no one around to hear anything. I hate that man, I really do."

Joe wished he hadn't said that, but Hastings only nodded for him to continue.

"So, yeah, I got through it. Took a couple low level shots at him to keep my sanity, but I didn't engage. Like you told me. I walked away from him. Literally."

"That is progress, Joe." The priest noticed Joe's lack of eye contact.

"Yeah, so parents, classroom and Mel. I got it going pretty well. Sense of humor even shows up sometimes. When it doesn't, I can cover it up. I couldn't do that before."

Hastings set the coffee cup down. "You haven't mentioned Cathy today."

"That still hurts like hell," he said. "The pain's not gone, no. Every night. I can't do it alone, it's, you know how it is, I've told you. But, I was getting through it, keeping my head together, not raging. It was fine. Then this."

"So there was something that brought you back to my door." The lines above Hasting's eyes arched up onto his deep forehead. "What happened?"

"What are the odds." Joe spoke quickly as he recounted the attack on Lexan's apartment. "Her face and Cathy's face. The same injuries. The same side of the face, the same cut, on the left cheek. Her left. I mean how the hell can that happen?

"Twice in one life? How can this happen to two random people in a year, let alone in the same year and to two women I know? Me, I know both women, with the same injuries. The mouths, the color even. God, it's not right."

"You should have come in sooner, Joe."

"No, I hear you. I got it under control. I am better. Really. I'm getting through it, I'm gonna get past it. I am not letting myself fall back in there. Not there. No, I'm not."

"You don't have to handle this by yourself. We can--"

Joe lifted his hand to his forehead. "Somebody is messing with me. Or they're messing with this girl. I don't care so much about me. I'm getting through this. I'm getting better. But." His open palm closed into a fist. "There is no way they, or somebody, or whoever the hell it is, nobody is gonna put a person I know through the shit I went through. That is not gonna happen. Not if I can draw one freaking breath, it's not. You know what I mean? It's not."

Hastings wrote 'rigidly adhering to his code' in the notebook and closed it. "What do you intend to do?"

"I don't know exactly."

"That's why you're here? So I can tell you how to act out your anger? Which damsel to rescue, which windmill to joust?"

Joe dropped his fist. "It sounds stupid when you say it."

"You know I'm not going to tell you that." Hastings' short laugh startled Joe, and he looked to the priest's face. "Besides, it sounds like you already have a damsel."

Joe looked past him out the window. "Got that part covered."

Hastings re-opened his notebook. "It's easier to help her than help yourself," he said.

"Maybe helping her, is helping myself." Joe noticed a cluster of statues in the grassy area outside the rectory office.

CHAPTER EIGHT

"My daddy will kill me if I let you look at the car again." Laurel Ann Brummelberger was a female version of her father, from the squinty eyes in her fat face to the dirty coveralls. "He's still mad at me from the first time." Her eyes darted furtively, a gesture that contrasted with her large frame.

"It's the first time for me to look at it," Joe said.

"But you're not the title holder." She tipped her heavy face in the direction of Sea Larkin. "She's not either, but at least she's in the family."

"Please, I have to get some books out of the car. For school."

"Same thing you told me before." Laurel Ann looked to the dark places in the ramshackle barn as if expecting something to leap out at her. Joe stepped closer to the door mounted on sawhorses that served as a desk.

"It's going to salvage on Friday," she said in a tiny voice. "Shoulda gone last week." She glanced from the computer screen to the door to his face.

"So what can it hurt?" Lexan said.

"Car won't hurt me. My daddy might."

Joe opened his wallet. "We shouldn't have to do that," Lexan said.

"Let's just go." Sea shook her head.

Joe handed a folded bill over the screen. "Oskar isn't here."

"Shoulda been home by now." Her eyes lightening bugs in the gloom, the money disappeared into her coveralls. "Car hasn't moved." She tilted her head toward the door.

Sea led them single file around the barn. Weedy grass grew through the wrecked cars and trucks, stunted life among the ruined vehicles. A cold wind eddied through the piles of junk.

"It's quiet back here," Lexan said. "Can't hear the traffic at all."

"The parking lot of the damned," Joe muttered.

They stopped suddenly, Sea holding a pale hand over her mouth. She nodded dumbly. It looked to Joe that she wanted to approach the car, but something held her back. Lexan put an arm across the girl's shoulders.

The front end of the car had been forced into the passenger compartment. The instrument panel was a V, the steering column a hand's width from the seat back. The roof was flattened and the windshield gone, glass sparkling instead on the floor and dash. The deflated airbag hung uselessly over a reddish-brown stain where Amber had died. Joe closed his eyes and forced the air from his lungs. When he opened them he saw the mangled door lying in the dirt beneath a space that was too small for a human being.

"Joe, you don't have to do this," Lexan said from behind him.

"I'm fine, it's just like C.S.I. Stay with Sea."

He blew air from his lips again, and crouched behind the left rear tire. The trim around the wheel-well and the tire itself were untouched, but both taillights were broken. He dropped to his knees and peered under the car. Finding no red plastic, he leaned back and inspected the bumper. A concave crease ran its entire length, marking where it had been forced into the car's body below the trunk lid. He got to his feet and backed away, stopping when he sensed a presence.

"Seen one wreck, seen 'em all," a slow voice said.

Joe turned around. "Oskar."

"You gonna pay me to look at this one?"

"Shouldn't have to pay anybody." Joe crouched again and ran his finger over the crease. He looked up at Lexan.

"It's blue," she nodded.

"I got lots of blue ones," Brummelberger said.

"The car is white, why is there blue paint on the bumper?"

"Car bounces around during a DUI. This one bounced around a lot."

Joe stood up between Brummelberger and Sea. "Her sister died in this car."

"Shouldn'ta been drinkin'."

Joe stepped closer to the fat man. "Shut up, Oskar."

Lexan pulled Sea behind Joe.

"You can't talk to me like that. This is my place."

"You don't know anything about the accident or the girl that died," Joe said.

"You don't know what I know." He jabbed a bratwurst-like finger at the car. "Sure as hell somebody was drinking. Them cans still inside."

"Yeah? Show me."

He waddled around to the passenger side and jerked open the door. "See for yourself."

As Joe followed him, Lexan crouched behind the car. She used a nail file to scrape some of the blue paint into an envelope, then snapped a picture of the bumper with her phone.

"You can't do that, it's not your property," Oskar said over her shoulder.

"And you're a lawyer? Come on, ladies, let's get out of here."

"You could at least pay me. You paid the girl."

"Send me a bill," Joe said.

Lexan spun the coffee around and clanked the spoon sharply on the rim of the mug. "The paint's blue, Joe, just like Oskar's tow truck."

"But what does that mean?" he said.

"It means somebody's blue car pushed Amber off the road, Herr."

"Or somebody's blue car bumped Amber's car sometime. We don't know when that happened, Sea."

"But if it happened that night, it changes everything," Lexan said.

"Sure, but it could mean nothing at all. Maybe she just backed into someone in the school lot. There's lots of blue cars and trucks."

Lexan and Sea stared across the coffee table at him. The window behind them was filled with SouthWest Mall. To his right he could feel Barnes & Noble's books, magazines and CD's gaping through the arched coffee shop wall. "But it is something."

"Tell him the rest of it, Chelsea."

The girl sat on the edge of the sofa, elbows tight to her body, forearms on her thighs. Her hands and her knees bracketed the mug. Behind the jagged curtain of jet black hair, she whispered into the coffee, "They killed her."

Joe felt his mouth tighten. It was different when the girl said it. "Why would they do that?"

"They wanted her, they wanted her to--" The words caught in her throat.

Joe looked a question at Lexan. She shook her head no.

"To, to do things. Things she didn't want to do." She spoke softly, into the cup.

"Sea, if this is too hard for you."

Her hair shook around her head, her face still aimed down. The tips of her white fingers appeared to float against the black cup. "No. I want to do this. I have to."

"Take your time." Faint music wafted in from the book store. Sea's black nails extended from her fingerless gloves and clicked against the ceramic.

She looked up at Joe and said, "They wanted her to fuck people. Strangers. People she didn't know. For money. Lots of money." Her face was visible to them for an instant, then disappeared behind fingers and hair. Lexan patted her shoulder.

Sea sighed, brushed the hair from her face, looked at him again, and said clearly, "They wanted her to be a whore. She wouldn't do it, so they killed her."

Joe looked from Sea to Lexan then back. "I don't know what to say."

"Just listen to her."

Sea let out another long breath. "Amber had this part time job, you know, selling cookies. After school, weekends. Drove around in one of those little electric CookieMobiles. Delivered to houses and shops, office buildings. Got to wear the uniform. You know."

They nodded and she continued. "She was so proud of herself. She went through this long interview. They told her what a big deal it was to be selected. They only took four girls out of the 83 that applied. Or more. I don't know. She loved the job."

"When was this, Sea?"

"Her Junior year, sometime last winter she applied. She worked all during the spring and through the summer. She didn't even want to go on vacation. We always go to the cabin in Michigan. Mom made her go and she was so mad. They had a big fight."

"Was she making a lot of money?" Joe tried to relax the tension in his shoulders.

"Money? Yeah, but it was more than that. For a kid's job it was good, I forget, 9 or 10 dollars? But it was like being a waitress. She made a lot more on tips." Her voice was stronger now, her words more connected.

"She and whoever she was paired up with would deliver those stupid cookies on a stick, flowers or teddy bears or whatever, and sing a little song, and they'd give them money. She could keep the tips and not tell."

"She liked working there," Joe said.

"It was fun. All the girls she worked with were her friends. The same kids she was in Show Choir with and on the dance line. It wasn't like work, it was like hanging out."

"Is that why she dropped Spanish?" Lexan said.

"Yeah, she wanted to work all the time. She never had a job before, and this was so much fun." Sea nodded. "After she got into the fight with Mom about vacation, she went to Mrs. Raymond and they fixed her schedule. She told Mom there was a schedule conflict."

"You didn't tell."

"I'm not a narc, Herr." The girl met his gaze.

"What happened then?"

"The job kept taking up more of her time. She even had to work some school nights. She told Mom she was at a friend's when she was really working."

"They deliver cookies at night?" Lexan asked.

"I thought that was funny, too. I guess they have business meetings and conventions and stuff like that. I don't know."

Joe looked at the empty mug on the table and the mall traffic on Center. He could hear the soft music again.

"Then it got funny," Sea said. "Strange."

Joe waited a second before looking at her. "What do you mean?"

"Late one night Amber came in, after work. She woke me up. She hardly ever did that. She asked me what I would do." Joe could only see the top of her head again.

"If somebody offered me a lot of money, what I would do." The girl's eyes looked at the cup, the spoon, the sugar packets, but not the two adults.

"What did you tell her?" Lexan said.

"I said no, it was gross, stupid. Strange men grabbing you, touching you. For money? I told her no, don't do it. That would make her a skank." She looked up at Joe. "I told her it was wrong."

Lexan rubbed the girl's back. "It's OK, Sea."

"She hugged me, Ms. Warner. She put her arms around me and cried. She told me she was quitting. She wouldn't do it. She never cries. Cried."

At that Sea curled herself under Lexan's arm and cried for her sister. Lexan patted her back, and when her eyes met Joe's over the girl's head, they were full.

"You told her the right thing," Joe said when he could get the words out.

"I did?" Her voice now brittle, her eyes red-rimmed. "Then why is she dead?"

Joe looked past her at the mall traffic and said nothing.

"It sounds like she had already made up her mind, Sea, and you were just confirming it," Lexan said. The girl shivered against her.

"When did she tell you this?" Joe shook his head.

"I don't remember exactly. A month ago?"

"Did they fire her?"

"No, but they cut her hours way down. That wasn't the worst part."

He looked to Lexan and raised his eyebrows.

"Her friends were so bitchy about it. They kept working." She spat the words. "Doing it. For money."

Lexan looked helplessly at Joe. "Her friends were whores."

"I don't know. I never saw them do anything." Sea shivered again. "I think so. But I told her I wouldn't tell anybody."

"Don't tell us names. That's OK."

"They stopped calling her, like, they cut her off. They were afraid she'd tell or something."

Several seconds passed. Lexan said, "Amber was killed to keep her quiet."

Sea opened her mouth but nothing came out. She nodded and swiped a hand across her face.

"I believe you, Sea," Joe said. "I'm sorry." His eyes drifted away to the Mall outside.

⋙╌╌⋘

I gotta make him pay.

Pedro was parked across Cleveland from Oskar's salvage yard, considering how to punish a man who has nada. The sway-backed barn? Hell, if I burned it, it would be a benefit to the community. The property might actually increase in value.

He looked past the barn to the rows of demolished cars, knowing there were acres more behind them. Steal his inventory? That made him laugh. A harsh rasp, not much more than a throat-clearing. You can't take something from a guy with nothing.

I was planning on riding this horse for a good long time, he thought. The perfect climate. Lotsa money and lotsa fools. He slammed the heel of his hand on the steering wheel. And that fat fuck squeals on me.

He took a cleansing breath and tried to relax. I could kill him. Big enough target. Couldn't miss him from across the street. But Karl would find out..

Thing of it is, the system here is perfect. They own everybody, the politicians, the police, and that fuckhead Karl may be right about it. Everybody keeps their mouths shut.

Except Oskar. Mouth as big as his double-wide ass.

He runs his mouth, and I could be out. He's nothing. A nobody going nowhere.

Me, I got skills, I fit here. They don't even know who I am.

Me, in plain sight in a school. He barked another laugh. Me, a principal.

And Brummelbag-ass is gonna ruin it for me.

Can't take his inventory, can't take his land, can't kill him.

He slumped lower in the car seat and peered through the traffic at Brummelberger's barn. The door opened and Laurel Ann emerged. The girl carefully locked it, then made her way across the yard toward the house.

Peter Weigel grunted a smile. But he does have a daughter.

"If you didn't let her dress like a tramp, Di--" Daniel Larkin let the rest of the sentence hang in the air between them as he frequently did. His wife knew what he meant. Not that she would do anything about it. "What else did she say?"

Diane Larkin was carrying an armful of dirty dishes and discarded clothing out of the living room and had to raise her voice. "Not much. She just said she was bringing her teachers." Her voice faded away and Daniel kicked his jeans into the closet and bent over to find his shoes. "So I have to get dressed up? I shouldn't have to do that in my own house."

"That's better," Diane said entering the bedroom. "You look nice."

"Is she flunking?" He set his beer can on the dresser to brush cigarette ash from his pants leg. "Didn't you meet her teachers at open house?"

His wife looked at him in the mirror, her hands brushing her hair. "Her grades were fine. I have no idea."

"It's all that black she wears." He crushed the empty and tossed it at the basket next to her dresser. "Not like Amber."

"It's just a style."

"Combat boots on a girl is not a style."

"She's different than Amber," she said.

"A young lady, not a punk or a Goth. Whatever the hell that is."

She laid the brush down and turned to him. "Leave her alone, Dan, she's under a lot of stress. We all are."

"That's your answer to everything," he said as the door bell rang.

In the living room several minutes later Daniel looked from Chelsea on the floor to Lexan and Joe on the sofa. "You're saying my daughter was killed?" Beside him Diane nodded dumbly, her eyes wide, her hand covering her mouth. "That's stupid."

"We don't know for sure, Mr. Larkin. Sea told us some things we felt we ought to discuss with you."

"We don't need to discuss our family with you. You're not the police and you're not social workers. You're just teachers."

"Excuse my husband, Mr. Lehrer, Ms. Warner. He's--we all are--under a lot of stress." He flinched when she touched his shoulder. "We told the police everything we know. They said it was an accident." Larkin stared at a spot on the carpet.

"Of course you did, Mrs. Larkin," Lexan said, "but Sea told us some things that maybe Amber hadn't told you."

"She told you her sister was a whore?" He jerked his arm away from his wife and glared down at his daughter.

"No, sir," Joe said. "Sea told us Amber was killed because she wasn't a whore."

"You're saying there's what, organized prostitution here in Stradford? With high school girls?" Daniel pushed his wife's hand away again. "That's ridiculous."

"Chelsea, how could you say that about your own sister?"

"Momma, I didn't say that. I said that other girls were doing it, not Amber. She wouldn't do that."

"I don't want to hear anymore." Daniel stood up, focusing his glare on Joe. "It's time for you to go."

"Is there is anything else you remember about this?" Lexan said quickly.

"We told the police everything we knew," Diane said and stood up next to her husband. Sea remained on the floor, arms wrapped around knees, her head down.

"My daughter is dead, leave us alone!" He took a step toward Joe; Diane clutched his hand.

"Sorry, but we thought--" Lexan began.

"The kid had been drinking. It's not some big conspiracy." Larkin yanked his hands free and waved them palms up. "A teenage girl just made a mistake. They all do. That's all it was."

Chelsea rubbed her sleeve across her eyes. "Amber didn't drink, Daddy, she didn't."

Daniel looked down at her. "You don't know anything." His daughter dropped her head.

Diane reached her hand out to Lexan. "Thank you for coming."

"We didn't mean to upset you."

"You meant well, I'm sure," Diane said. "Thank you again."

From the doorway Joe could see Daniel standing stiffly over the coffee table, Sea still crumpled beneath him on the floor. "We're sorry to have disturbed you," he said.

"Some detectives you are." Bob looked at them slumped on the sofa in Joe's living room. "What were you thinking?"

"The way they treat her is wrong." Joe looked away and set his glass down. "Sea was so upset, we had to do something."

"It's like they had one good daughter and one bad daughter, and the good one died," Lexan said, nodding to Joe for confirmation. "I hate them for that."

Bob reached for the bag beside his feet and said, "Maybe this stuff can help."

"More crap from the Attendance Committee," Joe snapped. He kept his eyes away from his friend's.

"Good stuff." Bob shot him a glance and laid several folders on the low table between them. "Computer records, back a couple years, plus some things I did myself."

Lexan pulled a thick stack from one of the folders. "You have tons of stuff. This took a lot of work."

"Yeah, maybe you'll respect me in the morning." He smiled when the young woman laughed. Joe beside her, glowered.

"What I did was sort of boil it down a little, and since I'm a guy with an ax to grind, maybe some of this is a little skewed to my particular bent." Bob stopped and waited for his reaction.

"OK, you like to say 'particular bent'," Joe said after several moments. "Get on with it."

Bob scooted closer and rubbed his hands together, satisfied that at least Joe was now looking at him. "I do love an audience. OK. Lex is holding a list of the kids with the most absences, and this is list of our college drop-outs.

"The Guidance Department has been tracking what happens to kids after they graduate. Do they go to a four-year college or a junior college, the military, other kinds of training? Do they get a job? Whatever.

"Then we find out how many kids stayed in college, and how long it took them to get a degree. It isn't pretty."

"What do they do after they drop out?" Lexan said.

"We don't know about all of them," Bob said, "but most end up back in the 'Ford saying things like 'you want fries with that?'."

"Where are you going with this?" From his seat on the sofa Joe could see through the hallway into his bedroom. The light caught the gilded edge of the photo on his nightstand. The picture of Cathy and him cutting the wedding cake.

"Hold on." Bob put a studious look on his face. "Here's where I've added my own malicious bent. I may like 'malicious bent' better than 'particular bent'."

"Quit wasting our time!" Joe said. "Just because you have an audience doesn't mean you can leave us hanging."

"When you think about it, Joey, that's precisely what it means."

The skin above Joe's eyes bunched together and Bob knew he had his attention. "OK, OK," he said quickly. "What I did was cross reference these lists with kids who had taken music classes, and it comes down to this." He looked triumphantly from one to the other. "As a group they missed more school time, but had better grades, got into college easier, but dropped out more, and more often than not came back to Stradford to work."

"So music kids are scum bags like you and Zimmerman thought all along," Joe said. "That's nothing new."

"Never understood in his own home, or your home, whatever," Bob muttered. "Look at the names. Stradford's best and brightest. Homecoming queens, cheerleaders, athletes, student council reps, show choir girls, look at them." He spread the papers across the coffee table. "Look at the highlighted names. The yellow ones."

"Why are they highlighted?" Joe·pulled the sheet toward him.

"One's pink," Lexan pointed to a sheet in the middle. "Oh, it's Amber."

Bob looked up. "The yellow highlighted kids worked for Cookies' Cookies."

"I don't get it." Joe shook his head. "So all these kids missed a lot of school."

"Excused or otherwise," Bob said.

"Right, and they were in the music programs, dropped out and got low-paying jobs in town." Joe's hands dropped to his knees.

"Keep going."

"They're all girls," Lexan cried.

"Not all of them, but most of them. Good."

"Slow down," Joe said. "What are you telling us?"

"One thing of course is the Music Man thing. They run around and tootle their flutes and sing and dance, and end up flipping burgers and selling cookies."

"OK, for the seventeenth time you've proven your life's thesis. Music is a scam. What's that got to do with Amber?"

"I'm getting to that. We have to do some more work," Bob said. "First, I believe that most of those girls, the high-lighted ones, were hotties. This is also a list of Stradford's cute girls."

"You're sick," Lexan said.

"So the cute girls sing and dance, get out of more school than most of the kids, and get crappy jobs in town. So what?" Joe's voice rose and sped up.

"Think a minute," Bob said patiently. "Why would these kids, Stradford's best and brightest, sharp kids with good personalities and good grades, why would they drop out of college and take these low-paying jobs? Or not even go to college?"

"I have no idea," Joe said.

Bob returned his disgusted look, and turned to Lexan. "Cool Hand Lex, what do you think?"

"There's only one thing that makes sense," she said as she put down the paper. "They don't need college, because these are not low-paying jobs."

"Bingo," Bob said and looked from her to Joe. "This is proof that Amber was telling the truth. Selling cookies may not pay well, but selling yourself does."

"Where do you keep the coffee?" Lexan's voice drifted down the hall into the living room.

Joe looked up from the papers on the coffee table. "I'll be there in a minute."

"It's so neat in here," she said as he entered the kitchen. "Everything's put away."

"I was going to say it's easy to be neat when you live alone," he said opening the cupboard next to the sink.

"But you won't because you've seen mine, right?"

"A gentleman never tells." He kept his head inside the cupboard. Yeah, I've seen yours, he thought. "Milk and sugar?"

"Skim and fake," she said, "if you got it. I mostly need the caffeine."

He closed the water lid on the Keurig, tapped the blue-rimmed button and set two mugs on the counter.

"Wait a minute," she said peering at the containers inside the cupboard, "these are in alphabetical order."

"Not all of them," he said crossing to her.

"Sure they are, 'cilantro, cloves, coriander and cream of tartar'." She turned to him. " I don't know if that's really clever or really creepy."

"It's the damn dill weed," he said, "is it a 'dill' or a 'weed'? There must be six of them in there." Her cinnamon scent flashed him back to her bedroom.

"You eat a lot of fish, huh?" On her toes to see, she leaned slightly against him.

"Brain food. I need every cell I can find." He brushed her shoulder as he turned and set three of the little canisters between them. "Oops."

"That's only three. You said there were six."

"I don't know, there may be a hundred."

She walked to the opposite end of the kitchen and returned with a step stool. "We'll just see about this." When she mounted the stool and leaned into the cupboard, her hips were eye level to Joe. He turned his head away.

"Hah-ha! Two more!" She twisted toward him, a dill weed container in each hand, and stumbled. He reached around her without thinking and she dropped onto him. He set her onto the floor and stepped out of her embrace. The cinnamon was stronger and he could feel where her breasts had brushed his face.

"I am such a klutz." Her face reddened, and he saw her next to him on the floor.

"I need a doctor," he said and crossed to the coffee machine.

"Did I hurt you?" Her eyes widened as she followed him.

"I think the coffee's ready." His hand shook a little as he pulled a cup from the machine and replaced it with another. "You Spanish might say *la blimpa munda*."

"That's not Spanish." She slapped him on the arm. " I mean really. Are you OK?"

He saw the serious look on her face, her dark eyebrows crinkled above gray eyes, and the soft line of her cheek leading to a heart-shaped chin. Incongruous yellow curls springing every which way from her head. He pushed a mug into her hand. "I'm fine."

She took it and stepped back. He sipped from his own, and the coffee scent replaced her cinnamon.

"You don't think I'm fat." She leaned against the counter next to him.

"Felt pretty good to me, but I'm no expert." He thought of cataloging her cinnamon with the other spices and crossed his arms.

She made a little sighing sound and leaned against him. "What do we do now?"

"About Amber?" he said quickly.

Coffee caught in her throat and she had to think to swallow it. She drew her hand across her mouth.

"Bob's an idiot, but there may be something to it. It does sort of make sense." Joe raised his hand to his chin.

"It does, and it fits with what Sea told us." Coffee sloshed out as she set the mug down on the counter.

"But even if it's all true, what can we do about it?"

"Do about it?" She stepped away from the counter and faced him. "We stop them! They're making prostitutes out of those children! Children we know!"

"I hear you, Lex, but--"

The speed and pitch of her voice increased. "Don't hear me, do something about it! How many other kids are involved? We have to do something!"

Her face was red again, this time angry. "I'm on your side," he said. "This whole thing is wrong. We have to do something. I just don't know what. We can't prove it."

"Chelsea knows, she'll talk to the police." She slapped a curl off her face.

"She can't even convince her own parents. Besides, what she knows is what she's heard. She hasn't really seen anything."

"Bob has records, they're--"

"--circumstantial. They don't prove anything."

She put her hands on her hips and glared at him. "So how do we get proof?"

He didn't know why she was angrier than he was. He wanted to both take her into his arms and tell her to leave. "I've got an idea, but you may not like it."

"Because I don't think he'll talk at all if you're in the room," he said. "Mindrivan's kind of a curmudgeon, hard to talk to. He works alone at night, for Pete's sake."

Lexan tugged her coat closer around her and pushed her shoulders back against the car seat. Joe looked through the windshield at the century home that was now Brian Mindrivan's insurance office

"Not too crazy to talk to, just too crazy for me to talk to. Is that it?"

"Yeah, I'm playing the men's club card on you, Lexan."

Gravestones in the city cemetery across Cleveland gleamed like teeth in a mandible as lights from a passing car lit them. "Look, if he doesn't have anything to tell us, I don't know what else we can do. I don't have a plan B."

She stared through the windshield. "You'll think of something."

"He was the HR guy for the schools; he hired me. Since he retired, he's gotten a little weird. I've hardly seen him." He spoke faster than he wanted to, as if he were defending himself.

"You go and talk to him," she said. "I'll wait here and cook dinner or something."

"Medium rare, please." He nudged her with his elbow. "Warm, pink center."

He shut the car door and walked across the darkened lot. The insurance company was housed in one of Stradford's first permanent structures. Tradition held that the Pennfield House had once been a stop on the Underground Railway. Joe doubted that, but knew the house had an enormous cistern in the attic to be used in case of fire. A single light now burned beneath it on the second floor. As Joe climbed the porch steps, he looked back at the car, but the reflection on the windshield blocked his view of Lexan.

The front door was unlocked and the old wooden stairs groaned despite the thick carpet as he climbed up to Mindrivan's office. Exit signs above the wainscoting and moonlight through the windows were the only illumination beyond a trickle of light escaping under the door.

Nothing was square in Brian Mindrivan's office. The ceiling slanted to the floor at both ends leaving the walls oblique. The dormers were rounded, tube-like extrusions, and the floor, planned to be rectangular with squared corners, sloped so badly that any sense of true horizontal was lost. The door fell open at Joe's touch and thudded against the wall. The floor creaked in protest as he stepped inside.

His eyes, adjusted to the gloom in the staircase, blinked several times in the slightly less gloomy light inside. Several computers hummed softly, but the room was deserted as if a careless person had left suddenly. Stacks of paper covered the desktops and spilled onto chairs and the floor. A wastebasket and its contents lay next to his foot.

"A visitor, at this hour?" The voice came from an alcove behind him on his right and Joe flinched.

"Little jumpy, too, I see. Out past your bedtime?"

An elbow at his stomach forced Joe back as the little man rolled past, his bald pate a blur in the darkness. Over his shoulder he called, "Least you could do is help."

"Mr. Mindrivan, it's me--"

"I know who you are," Mindrivan said, bursting past him again.

Joe followed the rotund figure through the doorway and around a sharp corner to where a copy machine stubbornly spat pages into a collating rack. Mindrivan turned quickly and thrust a stack of paper into his hands. They retraced their path to the main room, where Joe piled his stack onto an already full table.

"That'll do her," Mindrivan said and squinted up into his face. "You're Joe Lehrer. I never forget a face."

"It's me alright," Joe said, and looked at the clutter around him. "Can't you get a secretary or somebody to do this for you?"

"Like to get my own hands dirty," he said as he dropped into a desk chair. "Nothing wrong with a little honest work."

"Sure, but 9:00 at night?"

Mindrivan leaned forward and dropped his voice. "Whose name is on the door?"

"Yours," Joe laughed. "You got a point."

"Sure I do." He spun around in the chair and reached down to a desk drawer. "Can I buy you a drink?"

Joe looked at the chubby fingers clutching a bottle and a glass, the knuckles and veins bas-relief on the pale flesh. "One can't hurt, I guess."

"Now what can I do for you?"

Mindrivan's voice now had a hard edge Joe didn't recall. "How do you know this isn't a social call?"

"You must want something." Mindrivan tipped the bottle into his mouth without returning the smile. "Since I retired nobody comes here just to visit."

Joe sipped the Wild Turkey and looked at him. Mindrivan had been an energetic educational leader, a man who loved kids. He had been deemed so valuable at personnel matters that he was never given a shot at being a principal, yet he was also deemed not valuable enough to become the superintendent. Several years ago he had taken his retirement and opened the insurance agency. "Never could slip anything past you," Joe said.

"Like trying to slip the sun past a rooster, young fella." Mindrivan slapped Joe's knee and took another drink.

"Or a fast ball past Hank Aaron."

"Bad Henry, now that man could play," Mindrivan nodded as he screwed the cap onto the bottle. "OK, now, let's get down to business. What is it you want?"

Mindrivan's face like his body was round, his fair complexion blotched with red, his nose especially so. The lines around his eyes were deeper than the last time Joe had seen him and the laugh lines around his mouth droopier.

"Information, Mr. Mindrivan. You're the guy who knows where the bodies are buried."

Mindrivan's serious eyes studied his face. "How old are you now?"

"What? 33."

"Old enough to call me Brian."

Joe felt his throat tighten. "Sure."

"But why do you need to know? When I hired you, you had all the answers."

Joe thought a moment. "Now I'm not even sure of the questions."

"There you go. I knew you'd come around." Mindrivan laughed and retrieved the bottle. "OK, now, fire away."

Joe spoke for several minutes, summarizing their theory. The older man murmured several times as he listened, his eyes focused on Joe's, his hands on the bottle in his lap.

"Duh," he said.

Joe was surprised by the venom the man put into one syllable.

"Cookies is the largest employer in this town except for the schools."

"That makes sense," Joe said, "but the other part. What do you think?"

"You want to know what I think? Nobody wanted to know what I thought when I worked there." Mindrivan's hands shook as he dabbed his mouth. "You're right, Joe, they're whores. They're all whores. Everybody in the schools, in this whole town, is a whore. They'll do anything for money."

This clearly wasn't the man Joe remembered. "I know that, sir, Brian, what I mean--" Mindrivan waved him quiet.

"They don't care about learning, they don't care about people." He leaned closer to Joe and waved an arm at the window. "I had to get away from them. I loved the kids, but I couldn't stay there any longer." His head wobbled back and forth with each word. "But all they care about is the money. Only the money."

"But the actual prostitution--"

"The whoring. Of course. They're all whores. Like I said. Everybody has a reason for doing something, and in this town the reason is money." He tipped the barrel of the bottle at him, then drank from it. "What's your reason? Why are you here?"

"It's not money, that's for sure." Joe recoiled from his breath.

"St. Joseph, yeah, that's right, I remember. Everybody but you."

"I'm sorry to have bothered you, Brian." Joe backed his chair away.

"Joe Lehrer, the last of the teacher saints. You just want to help the kids." Mindrivan drained the bottle and tossed it into the basket under his desk. "Everybody in this town is a whore except Joe."

"I am doing this for the kids. You know that, it's the reason you hired me."

Mindrivan's shoulders slumped. "I used to be somebody in this town."

"You still are."

"Sure I am." He waved a tired hand at him. "Sure I am."

A floorboard squeaked and Joe looked over the old man's head to the door.

"This is quite a place," Lexan said as she wove through the clutter towards them. "I got tired of sitting there, and you took the key."

Mindrivan sprang to his feet. "Hah, there. See? You do have a reason. You're doing this for her. I knew it."

"No, I'm not."

"Like hell." He grabbed her hand. " She's lovely. Good choice."

"Nice to meet you," she said and edged closer to Joe.

"Bring her over here, son, and we'll talk about this." Mindrivan found a third chair and waved for them to sit.

"Now that I know your reason," he nodded at Joe, "I'll tell you everything I can."

"Reason?" Lexan looked at Joe.

"Mr. Mindrivan, Brian, was going to tell me about the prostitution when you came in. He's been in Stradford a long time."

"Many years. No one asks me, but I know stuff." He pointed at Joe. "Your boyfriend here has it pretty much figured out. Been going on for years. Everybody's a whore."

"I'm not her boy--"

"Even the school kids?" Lexan shot Joe a worried look.

"That's since I've been gone, but the housewives, they've been doing it forever. They're bored, their husbands are never home. It costs so damn much to live here. They need the money. Now the kids are doing it, too? Makes sense."

"We were right." Lexan shook her head. "Great."

Mindrivan nodded. "Cookie's Cookies is a front. It's how they launder the money. They run the sin cash through the legitimate business. Kimberly herself has been hooking for years. That I know for a fact."

"The school board president? Shit."

"Future mayor," he said. "Her reason's not the money, she's past that. It's power she wants. Kimmy needs to be in charge. She worked for her brother for years, now she's stepping up."

Mindrivan watched them exchange worried glances. "You two sure are the smart ones," he said. "Now the big question: what are you going to do about it?"

"We'll bring them down," Lexan said. "Somehow."

Joe nodded. "What they're doing is wrong."

Mindrivan laughed, a thin rasp that became a hacking cough. They waited as he wiped his eyes, wheezed again, and searched for another bottle. Finally he said, "You'll just tell them to stop and they will, huh? That's your plan?"

"We'll go to the police."

Mindrivan snorted. "They own the police, young lady. Her brother's the mayor and she's next."

"But you'll help us, Brian, won't you? You must have proof."

"Not me, I can't prove it." He shook his head and waved at the computers. "I set it all up for them, and turned it over to my wife. Only Eleanor can get into the system."

"You could testify," Joe said.

"Who would believe me? I'm just an old man, a drunk."

"No, no you're--"

Mindrivan held up a hand. "I'm a drunk and I'm a whore, too. I sold out years ago."

"No," Joe said. "I took this job because you did things the right way. I wanted to work for you." Joe felt Lexan's hand on his arm. "Damn it, I'm a teacher because of you."

"Thanks, son," Mindrivan's eyes blinked from his round face. "But it's too late for me. I made some bad choices, a lifetime full. I have to live with them."

"No. You're not one of them."

He shook his head. "I am. I got lots of money in the bank. Chose that. No real work to do. Chose that, too. Get out of here before you and the girl catch what I got."

"Wait, Brian, no--" Joe looked from him to Lexan. She took his hand and got up.

Mindrivan dismissed him with a wave, his eyes on the empty bottle in the wastebasket, his silhouette black against the computer screen. Joe stood at the door, watching, until Lexan managed to pull him out of the dark room.

CHAPTER NINE

From the landing Karl could see the top of the man's head leaving the hotel through the door below. Most people would say he meandered into the parking lot of the hotel, but to Karl it was more of a drift. Meander implied purpose if not exactly direction. This guy was lost. "It's on your left, next to the Hummer, asshole," Karl said out loud as he turned away from the window and started up the half flight of stairs to the eighth floor. He pushed through the security door into the hallway and pondered the correlation between blow jobs and orienteering.

"*Buenos tardes*, Maria," he said to the maid and held the elevator open for her as she maneuvered the cart past him. "*De nada*," he said as she thanked him. He stopped at 842 and rapped the door twice.

"Just a minute," a muffled voice called from the other side.

"Schedule," he called and looked at his watch.

The door opened and he pushed inside. April, or May he couldn't remember which, turned her back to him, reaching for her skirt with one hand and trying to cover her chest with the other.

"It's payday, honey, let's get a move on," he said. "He give you any trouble?"

"No, he's a sweetie," she said. "The old ones always are."

"Good. Turn around."

"Huh?" She turned toward him, her top clutched in front of her.

"Why are you getting squirrelly, girly? Show me." He nodded at her firm, round breasts and flat stomach. "You a gymnast?"

"Dancer." She moved from the first ballet position to the second, her hand in a fist on her hip. "Can I get dressed now?"

"Sure." Karl ran a hand through his white hair and appraised her as she did so. "You could lose a couple pounds in the caboose," he said after she finished.

"You could use Hair Club For Men," she said.

"A little attitudinal, but that's not all bad."

In the car, Karl watched her organize her money into two piles on her lap. When they arrived at the office, he said finally, "OK, I give up, are you April or May? I can't keep you girls straight."

"June," she said and hopped out of the car.

He reconsidered her ass as he followed her up the three steps and into the one- story building. They waved to the receptionist and entered the payroll office, a half-walled cubicle where Amy Michalik sat in front of a computer. June sat down next to her.

"Deliveries in this pile, specials in that one," Amy said without looking up. June put the bills in the appropriate stacks.

Karl got coffee from the pot, entered Pedro's office, and closed the door behind him. " What do you know, *mi amigo?*"

Pedro sighed and looked up at the taller man. "I'm kind of busy actually."

"No time for your *compadre?*" Karl put his feet on the desk.

"That will leave a mark."

"That time of month, huh?" Karl said and dropped his feet to the floor. "You're working too hard. You need to stop and smell the roses."

"I'm working double shifts." He arranged the thin strands of hair on his head.

"You undercover guys. Hey, Kimberly has this thing in the bag."

Pedro laid his pen down and sat back. "It's bad luck to say it."

"One Day at a Time, that's my philosophy," Karl said.

Pedro smiled weakly. "I'm working like a dog and you have too much free time."

"It's tough at the top." Karl wiped the desk top where his cup and feet had been.

Pedro looked past him through the glass partition. "How's she doing?"

"Typical smart ass kid. Chunky, but firm. Unlined. She'll be fine."

"She was a friend of that Amber kid. You never know."

"Got my eye on her." Karl stood up at the knock on the door.

"Oops, sorry," June said and jammed some money into his hand. "This is for you, Karl. Thanks."

"My pleasure." He shut the door behind her and said, "See, the young ones really are less trouble than the others." He nodded through the window as Vikki and Toni entered the office. "The old ones think they know everything."

Pedro shrugged. "Why do we keep so many of them around?"

"We need them. You see how business is." Karl rapped twice on the desk with his knuckles. "After the first of the year we'll prune the bush."

Pedro looked puzzled. "Yeah, right, we'll let some of them go."

Karl wondered again if the man had a sense of humor. "So to speak," he said.

At the coffee machine on the other side of the glass, Vikki shook the Splenda packet and tore the top off. "--watches out for them, settles their bills, drives them around," she was saying. "They're kids, they're not that good."

"You are, honey, so don't worry about it." Toni blew across her cup.

Vikki leaned closer, whispered, "But I don't look like them. I'm 36."

"You don't look it, that's what I'm saying. They don't know how old you are." She winced at the coffee. "Besides, you know stuff, girl, you do."

"I better get a good assignment at the Inaugural, that's all. If I lose another one to a kid half my age--"

"You'll do what, file a grievance?" Karl said behind her.

"Quit spying on me!" Vikki hissed.

"Plenty of work for everybody, my friend."

"It's not fair," Toni said. "We keep losing jobs to the high school girls."

"When Kimberly wins the election, ladies, our worries are over." Karl smiled down at them. "I can't stop the ravages of Father Time, but we will not lack for work. I can guarantee you that."

"I hope so, this sucks."

"That's your end of the business, Vikki, not mine," he said over his shoulder.

Toni furrowed her brow. "What did he say?"

Bob gestured with the bottle of Dortmunder Gold as he looked around Lexan's apartment. "You know, if you hadn't told me about the break in, I couldn't tell anything was wrong. You got it fixed up great."

"Nothing was trashed, was it, Joe? It never looked that bad." She was curled on the sofa next to him. Her hands landed on his several times as they darted around the room explaining how her furniture had been re-arranged.

"I know you changed the locks, but I think you're pretty strong to keep living here," Bob said as she finished. "I would have moved out."

"But you are a known wuss," Joe said.

"I am that." Bob lifted the bottle and drank. "Which brings us back again to good old Stradford. What the hell are we going to do now?"

Joe straightened up and twisted away from the girl, the smile gone from his face. "We know what's going on. They're running a massive prostitution ring, supported by the leaders of the community, the next mayor, the school board, and they're using girls from the high school."

"But we got no proof," Bob said.

"Your friend Mr. Mindrivan knows; he'll help us."

"You saw him, Lex. He's a drunk, a train wreck."

"That bad, huh?" Bob said.

"I feel like I let him down," Joe said. "I've only seen him two or three times since they canned him."

"Me, too." It was one of the things Bob liked best about his friend. "But he always drank a lot, you just never noticed it."

"It's not your fault." Lexan's hand touched Joe's.

"Maybe he can do something." Bob watched Joe pull his hand free.

"The thing of it is, the only ones who know anything for sure are the girls themselves," Joe said.

"What about the election?" Bob waited for them to look at him. "We're so depressed about the Cookie thing, we forgot all about it."

"I didn't forget," Joe said glumly. "Mindrivan told us Kimberly is running so she can control the police department, which fits. Then there will be absolutely no chance anything gets out."

"Come on, Citizen Kane may pull it out at the last minute."

"And Noah thought it was just a shower."

Lexan giggled and patted Joe's leg again. "That's funny."

"There's no way she loses," Bob said. "I was thinking about the school levy. If it fails, we'll really be screwed."

"They'll cut jobs and cram 35 kids in a room. And you call me Mr. Sunshine."

"I'm the one they start with, right?" Lexan said. "I'm the newbie."

"Nothing we can do about that either." Joe pulled his arms across his chest.

"We won't have to," Bob said, "that's the point. They can't let the levy lose."

"I don't understand," Lexan said.

"Look, their whole thing is keeping everything quiet, especially after the strike."

"There are no problems in Stradford," Joe muttered.

"Right," Bob said. "The sacred *status quo*. Keep the lawns mowed and the garage doors closed. That's why they caved last June after one day. The levy will pass to keep things the way they are. Lexy keeps her job."

"I don't know if I want to keep my job in a place like this." She had moved closer to Joe on the sofa, her shoulder against his.

"Come on, you two look like doom and gloom sitting there." Bob jumped to his feet. "I got one that'll cheer you up."

"It better be good."

"It is, and then I'll get going." He opened his hands and spread his arms. "The real question is what we call all this stuff we've uncovered in the 'Ford."

"It's prostitution, Bob, what else can you call it?"

"See, that's just negative, Joey. Come on now. They're prostitutes who work for a cookie baker, right? So do we call them Cookers or Hookies? Huh? What do you think?"

Lexan snorted, clapped her hands together. Joe tried to keep from laughing. "Hookies? At a time like this?" he sputtered.

"Hookies? You like that one better?" Bob looked as if he won the lottery. "I sorta liked Cookers, you know, they're so hot they cook?"

Joe laughed again. "You are one piece of work. This is serious!"

"Serious, yes, somber, no." Bob adjusted the collar of his shirt like Rodney Dangerfield. "Come on, we're teachers. We shut the classroom door, and teach the kids."

"Maybe Mr. Mindrivan will come through," Lexan said hopefully.

"We have to step out of our classrooms and fix this," Joe said. "It's not right."

"At least we're not doing it alone," Bob smiled. "But Linda's gonna kill me. I gotta get home."

"It's time for me, too," Joe said.

"You're not both leaving are you?" Lexan looked at Joe.

"It's late," he said zipping his jacket.

"9:30 is late for a man your age," Bob said.

"Don't start that," Joe said and stepped past him into the hall.

Bob gave Lexan a quizzical look and followed him down the walk. At the car he said, "You pretty much ran out of there."

"I got stuff to do, you know." Joe turned to wave at Lexan's silhouette in the doorway.

"Joe, we've been friends a long time--"

"Don't start that either," Joe said and slammed the car door. Bob watched him drive away, then waved goodbye to Lexan.

⟞⟊⟊⟝

The volume of noise surprised Amy as she opened the door from Kimberly's office into the conference room. It had been audible from inside, but it struck her now like a wave, and she felt her body move as she secured the door behind her. "I've got the numbers," she yelled into the noise, and waved a sheaf of papers over her head.

She repeated her message several times as she worked her way through the throng of campaign workers. Stacks of campaign literature stood next to computers on the long tables, and the candidate beamed energetically at the chaos from posters on the walls. By the time Amy reached the dais at the opposite end, the noise had ebbed and many of the volunteers had turned their faces to her.

"These are the final polling numbers," she said, and the crowd cheered. "Wait, you haven't heard them yet."

"We know what they say," someone called out. "Kim's the next mayor!" The women cheered again.

"You're right, of course," Amy said, "but don't you want to hear the numbers?"

They laughed and quieted as Amy cleared her throat. "All this yelling has hurt my voice," she said. "It's worth it!

"Our numbers, and these are the only numbers available because Mr. Kane apparently has no money to do any polling."

"He knows he can't win!"

"You're right!" she said after the laugh. "As these fig-ures indicate, Kimberly will receive 64% of the votes and Mr. Kane barely 30%."

The campaign workers cheered and several tossed confetti into the air. Amy grinned down at the bouncing, hugging women. "The school levy should pass, too," she shouted. It took her several minutes to work her way back through the crowd.

"That certainly fired up the troops," Ursula Hellauer said inside the office.

"Congratulations, Kimberly," Amy smiled to the ladies arranged in chairs in front of the oversized desk. "Or should I say Madame Mayor."

Kimberly tried to stop the smile from tugging at the cor-ners of her mouth. "It's still premature, but thank you. I couldn't have done this without you."

"You deserve it," Pamela Holmgren said, her elegant voice matching her elegant complexion.

"But you guys did all the work, really, I am so grateful for it."

"Now then, with the election next week, we need to look ahead," Ursula said. "We have to organize the Inaugural Ball."

"You're sure it's not bad luck?" Kimberly gave Ursula a thin smile and wondered why her sister-in-law looked at Eleanor Mindrivan instead of returning it.

"With numbers like those we can start planning now," Ursula said, finally smiling at the candidate.

"The Ball will be our first official moment," Pamela said. "It should set the tone."

"I've got the notes from when we talked about it last summer," Eleanor said. "We have the date reserved at the hotel, and we have the preliminary invitation list."

Kimberly nodded. "Work with Pamela on this, El. We'll sit down next week after it's official. Now then, what else?"

"There is one thing," Ursula said. "It could hurt us."

Kimberly saw how the older woman was trying to catch Eleanor's attention again. "Amy, make sure the polling numbers are posted outside, would you please?" She handed her a manila folder and waited for the door to close before she said, "This must be serious."

Ursula slowly shifted her gaze to the candidate. "Potentially."

"You told me we had no loose ends. Here we are planning the victory party." Kimberly dropped all traces of her smile, and looked coldly at her advisers.

Ursula said, "It's a personal matter."

"No, it's a business matter," Pamela said.

Kimberly looked from one to the other, following their eyes to Eleanor.

"It's my fault." Her round face was pinker than usual, and she looked down at her hands as she spoke. "I should have taken better care of it."

"He's a grown man, for God's sake," Pamela snapped.

"This is a precaution, nothing has actually happened," Ursula said.

"It appears that everyone knows about this except me." Kimberly glared at them. "It would be nice to know what the problem is." No one responded, and she cursed them silently. She calmed herself by stepping to the credenza and pouring tea into a Mary Engelbreit cup. "I gather this is about Brian." She remained standing and sipped.

"He's been a potential liability for years," Pamela said.

"Brian never said anything to anybody. He would never hurt us." Eleanor's voice was defiant but thin, her eyes searching the room for a safe face.

"We thought he wouldn't do anything after he was neutralized," Ursula said.

"And he hasn't, not once. Not one time."

Kimberly held her hand up to Eleanor. "Has he done something now?"

"He talked with Lehrer and that little Barbie, Spanish teacher." Pamela shook her head. "The one I told them not to hire."

Kimberly looked at the little girl with the broad-brimmed hat on the side of the teacup. "What did he tell them?"

"We don't know that he said anything," Eleanor said quickly.

"He could have," Ursula said. "He knows things."

Kimberly let out a long breath. "You promised to keep him quiet, Eleanor. That was the agreement we had."

"I did, I have, I.--"

"I have my reputation to think about," Pamela said. "In a sense you all do."

Kimberly raised her eyebrows at the interruption. "You know what this means," she said.

"No, you can't, we--" Ursula looked away as Eleanor said this. Pamela twirled her wedding ring. Kimberly set the cup on its saucer and pursed her lips.

"--no, don't, please, he's my husband." Eleanor covered her mouth with her hands.

"He could put us all in jail," Pamela said with contempt.

"He certainly could," Ursula said. "Get over it."

Kimberly waited for the realtor and school board member to catch her breath, and the others to stop talking. When the three looked to her she said, "There is nothing more to discuss today. Pamela, Ursula, thank you for your input." She stood up and walked to the door, the others following behind.

She turned and put her hand on Mindrivan's arm. "We're not going to do anything right now, El. Find out what you can, and get back to me. If there really is a problem, we'll deal with it at that time."

Eleanor glared at Ursula, as she grasped the candidate's hand. "You're not going to hurt him, are you?"

"Of course not, dear." Kimberly dropped her hand and hugged her. Over the woman's head, she locked eyes with Ursula. "Pamela will take you home."

Kimberly closed the door firmly behind them and looked to Ursula. Her sister-in-law said, "I'll tell Karl."

"Take it easy, son, it's just another trash fire. Nothing important is burning."

Grabowski slowed the big rig as it jounced across Brummelberger's rutted drive. "Right Cap, but you never know." The rotating lights made bloody smears across the barn walls.

The Captain smiled at the fireman, but his eyes searched for smoke from the barn or the house. "We may be lucky. Only flames I see are in the salvage yard."

They joined the crew outside the pumper, flattening themselves against the side as the ladder unit squeezed past. Behind them the electric-green EMS bus bounced to a halt. Their lights added to the gruesome scene on the barn.

"Better take a look inside anyway, Ski, then the house."

"Yessir," the young man said and trotted off.

The Captain followed the un-spooling hoses toward the junk yard. "Two lines gonna do it, Charlie?"

The squat man shaded his eyes from the bright, head-high flames. "I think so, Cap, it only looks like these two cars and a truck." The wrecks were stacked the way some-one would place twigs to start a fire.

"Make sure there's enough space around them." The Captain took a step back. "It's sure hot enough."

Charlie grinned. "Right. We don't want it to spread. Might lose something valuable."

The Captain nodded, but laid a hand on his shoulder. "You know what I mean."

"Yessir," Charlie said and joined a group of firefighters pulling debris away from the burning wrecks with long-han-dled rakes.

The Captain turned at the sound of footsteps behind him. He reached out his hand to Detective Kramer.

Kramer shook it. "These lowlifes got nothing better to do than set fire to their own stuff. Like shitting in your own bed."

"Wouldn't be the first time kids have started a fire here. Whoever it was used an accelerant."

"Probably an insurance scam then." Kramer shook his head in disgust. "Whatever. All it means is I gotta be here and I gotta file a load of paperwork bullshit." The two of them stepped back quickly as the pile of burning vehicles shifted and collapsed. Sparks shot up higher than the barn roof.

"Thing of it is, if it was kids, the yard is so big, they could be watching us. They know we'd never find them."

"It's not kids, it's that fat slob Brummelberger."

"Cap, there's somebody inside!"

The two looked from Charlie to the fire. What had appeared to be a headrest in the SUV was a head. Blackened, twisted over, silhouetted against the flames.

"Get more water on that car!" the Captain yelled. Charlie and the other hose-man moved in and attacked the flames. Kramer's phone buzzed and he stepped away.

The water turned to steam, the steam rose, and the smoked corpse emerged into view. The Captain sighed and ran a cloth over his face. "Whoever it was, I hope they were dead before--"

Kramer returned. "Want the good news or the bad?"

The Captain looked at him blankly.

"Two more dead tonight."

"What could possibly be the good news?"

"The neighborhood, Cap. A better class of corpse."

The fireman opened his mouth to speak, but Kramer was striding across the ruts to his cruiser.

"Gene ever tell you that story about the basketball game he played here?"

"No, Bob, he never did." Joe sat on the other side of Lexan, as sullen as she.

Bob scanned the cube-shaped gymnasium from the bleachers where the three sat. "The baskets are still up there, at one end anyway." He pointed to his right.

"Mr. Phillips played basketball? He's too short."

Bob nodded. "In the old days, Lex, you didn't have to be a giant."

"He's kind of heavy too, isn't he?" Her nose scrunched up as she said it.

"I've seen pictures of him in old yearbooks. I guess he was quite the athlete." Bob looked from the brooding Joe to the milling people below, the tables of paperwork and the screens linked to computers on carts. "Looks like we have time for a story," he said.

"You'd think with all the electronics and communications, we could get the election returns easier than this," Lexan said.

"This is the way they've always done elections, my dear. This is the real Stradford."

"Not very efficient," she said. Slumped next to her Joe said nothing.

"Anyway, Gene's story," Bob said. "He's playing freshman basketball in here, this was the original high school gymnasium."

"They really played basketball in here? It's so small."

"So was he, but hey, is there any chance of you saying something that approximates positive?" Bob turned to her. "What happened to Little Miss Perky?"

Lexan looked at Joe, then put her feet on the bench and sunk her head to her knees. Bob looked over her lowered head at Joe. " He's playing for Westlake, I don't know how long ago."

"His dad taught there," Joe said.

"Taught, coached, was the AD. Anyway, Stradford has the ball on a break from this end." B ob pointed to the stage on his left. " Gene's the only one back, and he knocks the ball away. The guy reaches for it and Gene opens the door."

"Those doors we came in?" Joe nodded to his right.

"Yeah, under the basket, two feet from the baseline. The guy can't stop and goes right out the door. It's winter, he's outside in the snow. Gene lets the door fall shut behind him, picks up the ball and passes it back up court."

Joe snorted. "How does the guy get back in?"

"Banged on the door till the ref finally opened it." Bob saw the slight smile on Joe's face. "My all-time favorite Gene story."

Lexan punched Joe's knee. "Some returns are in. Look."

There was a white SmartBoard for each precinct in Stradford. The computers displayed the names of the candidates for the mayoralty and city council, the municipal issues and the school levy, and the votes cast.

"Why do they do this by precinct?" Lexan said. "Where's the total?"

"Rhetorical question?" Bob was focused on the numbers on his yellow pad.

"OK, you said seven times, that's how they've always done it."

"I got it. Levy looks good. At least that."

"How much of the vote is in?" Joe said.

"About a third. That's enough usually to tell." Bob closed his pad.

"Two thirds left and you're done?" Lexan demanded.

"I've seen enough. Cookie lady has almost 80% of the votes."

"We're screwed," Joe said. "You were right, Lexan."

"I didn't want to be right about this. She controls the whole city. What are we going to do?"

"The Stradford Squat," Bob said. "Keep our heads down and wait it out."

"And let them get away with it?" Lexan's voice was a harsh whisper.

"I can try Mindrivan again. I don't know what else we can do." Joe's feet dropped from the bench, his shoulders slumped over them.

"We need Hawk," Bob said. "Or Bubba."

"Not Win either." Joe shook his head. "We're teachers, not detectives."

"That's why we need them." Bob smacked a fist into his palm. "I hear you. It's not a book and we can't go to the police. Maybe we should contact the Feds."

"They'll need proof, too," Joe said. "We don't have anything for them either."

"The FBI will get the proof," Bob said. "That's what they do."

"So while we're waiting for them to find it, how many more girls die, Bob? How many more are abused?"

"I know what we can do." The two looked at Lexan. "We get somebody on the inside who can find out what's really going on."

"Might be the only way we could prove anything." Joe nodded, then spun toward her. "Who would do that? Not you."

"I can't, they know me."

"Then who?" Joe said. "We got nobody to do that." His voice was flat and lifeless. He sounded to Bob like he had at Cathy's wake.

"Chelsea Larkin," Lexan said. "She'll do it."

Joe shook his head and didn't look at her "No way, Lexan, no way at all."

"She'd never do it," Bob said quickly. "Why would she?"

"To get the assholes who killed her sister. No better reason than that."

"Lexan, come on, she's a kid--"

"That's the point, Bob. They're children. They're preying on children!"

"They killed her sister," Joe said, "and they'll kill her too."

"They don't want to kill the girls, they want to abuse them," she snapped. "That's the whole problem!"

"Maybe they'll make a mistake. We know what to look for now." Bob smiled thinly and arched his eyebrows. They both glared at him.

"So we sit and wait for them to make a mistake. Great," Lexan said.

"It's the best we got," Joe said.

Karl shook his head and cracked the window open. "You been at a barbeque?"

"New after shave." Pedro jabbed at his phone.

"What's it called, Smoke Gets in Your Eyes?"

"No idea what that means."

Karl sighed. "I pride myself on my patience, *compadre*, but I swear to God, you check the time again, I'll put the bullet in *your* head."

Pedro had a belly-full of the Spanish crap he had to take from his boss, but instead of killing him, relaxed his expression. "Sorry, Karl, I get jumpy before a job. You know."

"I know you're not taking care of yourself. You don't eat right, you don't get enough sleep. You smell like smoke. I'd bet your electrolytes are all out of whack."

"Fuck my electrolytes. Aren't those people ever going to bed?" Lights burned in the ground floor windows of the house.

"One day at a time, my friend. Or in your idiom, re-fucking-lax. See, they're heading upstairs now." Karl pointed to the house. "Just a few more minutes."

Pedro watched several lights blink off downstairs and on upstairs. "So now I get to hear another one of your stories," he said. He could kill Karl whenever he wanted to.

"Merely an observation."

"I am so fortunate."

"You are." Karl liked the sarcasm in his partner's voice. It meant he was irritated enough to argue with him. "Women are cats and men are dogs."

"What the hell is that supposed to mean?" Pedro said.

"You know how cats play around with mice, instead of just killing them? They bat them around, ignore 'em, then pounce? Play with them, you know?"

"It's the fucking Animal Channel."

"Cats could just kill the thing, like a dog would, just rip its head off and eat it, but cats'd rather watch it die slowly."

"Locked in a car with Steve Irwin."

Karl didn't know who that was. "Whatever."

"Like I care. Hey, the last light went out, it's all dark."

Karl leaned past him to look. "We have to wait till they're asleep."

"I really don't care, but what caused this epiphany?" Pedro flicked the dome light switch off. "Finally doing this job?"

"No, this was a logical build. It has to be done because the isolation didn't work." Karl released the cylinder of the .38, pushed it through with his thumb, nodded, and snapped it closed. "The Lehrer job last summer. We shoulda killed him then. After you guys botched it--"

Pedro ground his jaw, then muttered, "That was Oskar."

"In either case, the ladies hoped scaring him would shut him up. It's not working with the Warner broad either. She keeps right on yapping."

Karl glanced at the house and continued. "That's my point. With her it was just the first shot, a base line. With Lehrer they were beyond that. All last spring he kept stirring things up. Him they wanted to hurt."

Pedro nodded in the darkness of the car. "Cats."

"There you go. Kill his wife, break him down, watch him bleed."

"I almost feel sorry for the poor bastard."

"If this works, maybe we don't need to kill him, too. And remember the tone." He waited till Pedro looked at him. "None of your kinky shit."

Joe heard the giggling as the book hit the floor and used his teacher glare to restore order. As he swung his eyes over the test-takers like a searchlight, their heads fell forward and their eyes found their own papers.

"Herr Lehrer?"

He ratcheted down the glare and motioned Jodi Fetzer to his desk. "*Ja?*"

"Is it OK if we make a list of the pronouns to use on the test?"

Joe looked at the class behind her and several heads ducked back down. "Like a cheat sheet?"

The girl's face blanched as she held out a blank sheet of paper. "No, there's nothing on this. I just want to write them down so I don't forget them. For the test."

"That's OK, but it won't do you much good when you speak."

"I know, I just get so flustered on tests."

"You're allowed to. Sure. You'll be fine."

He watched her return to her seat. The room was quiet and his mind wandered behind the glare until someone knocked on the door. He kept his body facing the class and opened it.

"Sorry to bother you," Roberta said softly. "Test day?"

"Either that or I'm playing Whack-A-Mole. What's up?"

She handed him a slip of paper. "Special faculty meeting after school."

"Election report, no big deal."

"It's more than that," she whispered. "They won't say what it is."

The department chair disappeared into the hall and he glanced to the clock. "Fifteen more minutes for the test."

An hour and a quarter later, Stevens did not hesitate in bringing the meeting to order. "We need to get going, people, this is an emergency meeting." The staff settled quickly and the late-arrivers quietly found their seats.

"I have some bad news, but all is not completely dire. In fact there is also good news," the Principal said. "As I'm sure you know by now, most of you anyway, the school issue passed last night." Several teachers applauded and he looked surprised. "Passed quite easily as a matter of fact. Most of the funding issues in the state failed, and we got, let's see, almost 55% of the votes."

He peered up from his notes. "More good news. Mrs. Horvath moved from the school board to city hall in a landslide. That and the new tax revenue mean we are in reasonably good condition for the next year or so. That's good.

"The evening did bring tragic news however." He cleared his throat and placed his hands carefully on the podium. "We just received word, and that's why I called this meeting. The police just now called us, to say that there has been a death, two deaths actually, here in, um, Stradford. One of our own, Brian Mindrivan, and his wife Eleanor were found dead in their home this afternoon."

Several in the room gasped and Joe felt Lexan's hand clutch his forearm.

"We, and the police, have no further information at this time. They don't know what happened." Stevens' voice faded out and Peter Weigel stepped forward. With his hand on the principal's shoulder, he spoke into the microphone. "As you can see this is quite an emotional time for all of us, especially those in the administrative family." The room stilled. "All we can tell you at this time is that the police are investigating and they will let us know what they find."

He patted his boss and stepped in front of the podium. "We didn't want to upset you folks. We just wanted to let you know before you heard it on TV or read about it in the papers tomorrow." He pushed a stray hair across his broad forehead and dismissed the faculty.

Bob checked the hallway before closing his office door. "Everyone's gone," he said to Joe and Lexan, and dropped down into his chair.

"They killed them both." The skin on her face was taut and colorless.

"We don't know that," Bob said.

"Yes we do. He talked to us and he's dead."

"Lexan, this is hard enough." Joe kneaded his eyes.

"Hard for you?" she said sharply. "The Mindrivans are dead!"

"What the hell do you want us to do about it?" Bob's voice echoed off the concrete block of the tiny office.

"I want you to stop saying we don't know for sure," she shouted back. "They were killed because of us!"

"In the paper tomorrow it will be a murder-suicide," Joe said. He brushed the scar on his forehead and tried to keep his voice under control.

"That's how they'll cover it up," she snapped.

Bob's chair bumped against the wall. "The shitty thing is, he talked to us but it didn't make any difference."

"The shitty thing is, he's dead. He was a good guy." Joe bunched his eyes together to clear his head.

"He died for nothing is what I mean," Bob said. "We still can't prove anything." Joe watched him dig the nail of his index finger into the cuticle of his thumb, his eyes unfocused, roaming.

Lexan opened her mouth, but hesitated. She took a breath and said carefully, "All the more reason we have to do something." Joe could see it was hard for her to speak. "His death, both their deaths, have meaning only if we act on what he told us," she said.

"We talked about this before," Bob said.

"But things have changed," she shot back. "They killed two people."

"Lex is right. We have to do something," Joe said clearly, his eyes locked on hers. "But I can't put Chelsea or you or anyone into danger."

"Give me another choice then." Her voice matched his.

"They shot two people in their beds, Lexan."

She waved a hand at Bob, her eyes not leaving Joe's. "It's our only chance."

"You may be right, but I can't do it. If she gets caught, she'll die too." Joe shook his head. "No."

"Then I'll do it without you." Papers fell off her lap as she stood up. "I don't need your help."

"Come on, Lexy," Bob said.

"Yours either," she barked. "And if they killed the Mindrivans for talking to us, that means they're coming after us, too!"

Joe reached for her. "Wait--" She slammed the door behind her.

"Pretty quiet in here without her, isn't it?" When his friend didn't respond, Bob let out a breath and said, "We can't let her do this alone."

"I hadn't thought of it. We probably are in danger." He picked her papers up.

"Better if we stick together."

Joe shook his head. "No more death."

"You can't pretend you aren't involved."

"I don't have to go chasing it."

"You can't walk away from this, or from her."

"Her?"

"Are you blind? I know you're not stupid. The girl's in love with you."

"You don't know what you're talking about." Joe raised his voice in warning.

"Can't you see it? She spends every minute she can with you."

"You have no idea." Joe held up his hand.

"Maybe this is exactly what you need."

In the picture behind Bob's head, a knickered Payne Stewart pumped his fist as his putt dropped.

"Cathy's gone, Joe. I know how that must have hurt. No, wait," he said at Joe's expression. "I can't know that, it's beyond anything I know."

Joe dropped his eyes from the print.

"No, really, Joe, she's gone, but you're not, you're--"

"So I'm supposed to forget all about her? Is that it? Just start screwing around with anybody out there? Forget the seven years I was married?"

"Don't forget her, I didn't mean--"

"Then what did you mean?" Joe's voice sped up. "Take off the wedding ring? Did that. Get rid of all her clothes?

Check. Learn to cook? Visit her grave? See her every time I freaking turn around?"

"Shit, man, I'm sorry."

"I can't forget her, I just can't do it. I am physically. Unable. To forget her."

Bob paused, then lowered his voice. "But it might be time. Lexan adores you."

"Yeah, well I waited. I waited almost four whole months before spending the night with her." He rubbed the back of his hand across his forehead. "The night of the break in."

The color drained from Bob's face. "You slept with her?"

"I wanted her in the worst way."

"You didn't--?"

"In my mind I did. Shit. I didn't think I was like that."

"No, of course not. You're Saint Joe."

"She wanted me to stay, I had to run out of there."

Bob nodded. "Like the other night."

"I mean, I mean I really wanted to, want to--"

"--so you're blaming yourself for a sin you didn't commit? Come on, even for you that's a stretch."

Joe waved a hand to stop his friend. "Blaming no one but myself. I can't forget Cathy and I cheated on her. I know it's not cheating, I know. Fuck."

"No, you didn't," Bob said and laughed. "Joe, you are the hardest hard-head in the world. It can not be cheating if you didn't sleep sleep with her."

"I have no idea what you just said." He opened his hands and faced Bob. "It feels like I'm not being faithful."

"You were faithful." When Joe nodded absently, Bob continued. "You're a goddam code hero, Hemingway." He opened a can of Altoids and slid it across the desk. "Here. Being a saint must be really hard on the throat."

"Asshole." Joe put a mint in his mouth. "I couldn't love another woman like I loved her. I don't want to."

"No doubt about it." Bob shook his head. "No, I'm just saying."

"She died in June, Bob. I'm not ready for this."

Bob's arms rested on the desk, his fingers spread apart. "Joe, you won't ever forget Cathy. But you got to consider the possibility."

"I know. I don't know. No."

CHAPTER TEN

"I must really be good at this," Fr. Hastings said as he filled the coffee machine on the protruding shelf of the bookcase. "A couple of months ago you were blaming God, then you cursed God, and now you want to be God," he said. "I think I have a gift."

"It's more than that, Father," Joe said.

"Megalomania always is. De-caf?"

"No, thanks." Joe stuck his hands under his arms to keep from kneading them, and focused on the statue in the courtyard outside. "I have to do something, but I can't put her in danger. Either of them."

"Yourself either." The leather-covered recliner whooshed as Hastings sat down, but he managed not to spill the coffee this time. "The real progress you've made, Joe, is we're talking about acting. You're back in the present."

"How is that better? The abuse has to stop. They have to stop hurting kids." He slapped his knees in frustration. "But I don't know how to do it."

Hastings closed his eyes. "That's an awful story, horrific. I can't imagine--" The priest's face was unnaturally pale.

"But grist for another mill." Hastings looked closely at Joe. "For our purposes here--" He swallowed, then began again. "You've got acting confused with controlling. You're responsible for your actions, not anybody else's. You know that."

"She's just a kid."

"You're just a man. A man who hasn't had a good night's rest in months." He smiled weakly. "At least you're trying to be an active, concerned God."

"Does that make me a Deist or a Theist?"

"You remember the weirdest parts of religion. You really do." Hastings swirled the coffee around his cup, knitting his brows before speaking. "You're working for justice, that's a good thing. The problem is you can't go to the police."

"It would be easier to shoot the bastards."

Hastings nodded. "That would be more convenient, but--"

"I know Jerry, it would make us no better than them."

"Do you mean that, or are you just saying the words?" He set his cup on the end table, and focused directly on Joe. "Look at the cross. He had every reason to take revenge. Think about what it is that makes us Christians."

"I know, I know," Joe said. "I saw the movie."

"Maybe I'm not that great a counselor," he said. "You're still a smart ass. Always have the deflector shields up."

"You're not going to change that part of me."

"Lord knows I've tried." He tapped the cup on the table. "OK then, so your plan is not about revenge. It's about justice. Fine. But who are you to hand out justice?"

Joe splayed his hands out in front of him. "Where else is she, or any of the girls, going to get justice?"

"You're her teacher, you're not a cop, nor her parents nor her priest."

"So you're telling me to keep out of this? That's not right either."

"All you can do is explain the risks to Chelsea as much as you can, and you absolutely have to talk to her parents. Pray they make a good choice. I will too."

Joe nodded. "Not that I'm an expert on good choices."

"No, you're not, but let's stay on point here. This is not about you. This is Chelsea and her parents' choice, not yours."

"What if they chose to do it?"

"Free will. You know, maybe that's what this is all about." Hastings glanced around the room as the thought coalesced. "That's the hidden sin of prostitution. Those girls get locked into that kind of life, and lose their ability to choose. Breaking that system would give them back their free will. Give them a chance anyway." Hastings spoke slowly, hoping Joe would speak. "I hadn't seen it like that before. Never realized what it was." He paused. "Joe?"

He waited another minute. "There's something else, isn't there."

Joe kept his gaze away from the priest. "Isn't this enough?"

"Only you know that," Hastings said. He gave him another several moments before nodding, "Well, my friend, you know where to find me."

≈✦≈

"Why would Stevens hire somebody like Weigel?" Roberta aimed her furrowed brow and pursed lips at Joe and Bob.

"Don't you remember what Stevens said about the interview? 'He answered my questions so well, I thought I was interviewing myself'." Bob chuckled. "Shit."

"So he hired his assistant to be just like him," Joe said.

"But Weigel has the leadership skills of a jellyfish," the French teacher said.

"Try to keep up, Bert, that's what I said."

"Come on, he's an administrator," Joe said, "he's got to be a mammal."

"A vertebrate at least," Bob said. "So he could stand up."

"The last thing they want around here is somebody who would stand up."

"Just like the old days, boys," Bob nodded to his two friends crammed inside his office. "Door locked, subversive conversation. You'd think Mel were still around."

"I'd say this with the door wide open," Roberta said. "Weigel's a nebbish."

"Nebbishes got spines?"

"What I don't understand," Joe said, "is why everybody is scared of him. The girls in my office jump every time he appears."

"That's easy. He's a lurker," she said. "You never know where he'll pop up."

"I've heard some women are afraid of him because he's male." Bob saw their blank expressions. "What? I'm a counselor, people tell me stuff."

"He does drive a gynormous truck," Joe said.

"What's that all about?" Bob's lip curled up at one side. "It's too big for him."

"Come on, he's in a position of authority." Roberta counted on her fingers. "He has his hands on all kinds of details, and he's never in his office like Bob said. You have to pay attention to him."

"And he's six-four with a voice like Darth Verizon? Come on, he's a little runty guy with a comb-over." Bob slapped the edge of his desk.

"However he does it, he has some fatal effect on the staff," Joe said.

"This is too complicated for me," Bob said. "All I want to know is where did Weigel come from?"

"Some place out east, right?"

Bob nodded. "I heard that, but where exactly?"

"Somebody said he was an old buddy of Radburn's. Same college." The bell rang and she stood up. "Probably some school with an insect as a mascot, maybe a gnat."

Joe stood up too. "See you later, Bert." The noise from the class change dropped as she closed the guidance office door. "You coming over tonight?"

"With you and Sexy Lexy?" Bob leered. "Should I come late or leave early?"

"Not funny. We got to talk about the Larkins. Only way I'm doing this is to get them involved."

"I'll be over after I eat. What if they say no?"

Joe waved through the window at a passing kid. "She's their daughter."

Bob's grin was gone. "They weren't very receptive the last time."

"Their only daughter," Joe said.

"So are we ever going to talk about this or are you going to keep avoiding it?" Lexan's words came out in a rush and Joe had to concentrate to hear them. He turned off the water faucet.

She stood next to him at the sink where they were cleaning up after dinner. Her hands placed the casserole dish onto the drying rack then buried themselves beneath her folded arms. "Well, are we?" Her face was turned up toward him, flushed from the hot water or the words she'd said. A hand pulled a curl off her forehead and darted back to its place. "Because I don't want you to think I'm that kind of person. Especially after losing Cathy."

He turned toward her and leaned against the counter. Islands of pink speckled her fair skin, and red rimmed her eyes. "No, Lex, that's not it."

"After the stunt I pulled in the car, you must think so."

"The car?" Joe thought quickly. "Oh, God no, I never thought that."

"I hate the whole 'it's OK I was drunk'. I'm not like that. But I really don't know what happened. I was fooling with you in the car, a little bit, but you said no, and you meant it, I was sure you did, and then in the apartment I was mad at you for not believing me. The last thing I wanted. Then I saw the pictures."

Her eyes were fuller now, rounder, the gray in them bluer. "Don't blame yourself, Lex."

"Blame myself for what?" She turned to face him squarely. "You think I should feel guilty? Do you?"

"No, that's not what I mean, I--"

She jabbed a finger at him. "No, wait, I remember. You're the hero and I'm the helpless damsel who needed to be rescued."

"Wait a minute here. You were the one screaming, right?"

"My apartment had been ransacked, whatever. What was I supposed to do?" She poked him again with her finger. "Besides, what did you do about it?"

"How could I do anything about it?" he said. "You think you can do everything yourself."

She pulled her hands back under her arms. "Admit it Joe, you're the guy with all the answers and you didn't have one. Still don't. You've been avoiding me ever since."

"What I'm trying to say is, we barely know each other. I--"

The front door slammed open and Bob's voice called out, "Anybody home?"

Lexan looked at him, then ran toward the bathroom. "I have to fix my face."

"Wait!"

"Now here's a domestic scene, washing dishes together at the sink," Bob said entering the kitchen. "You know, you could get the dishwasher fixed."

Joe turned off the water and wiped his hands on a towel. "You have no idea."

"So where is the little tyrant? Wait, ty-runt. That's a good one."

"You two talking about me? Dirty old men." She marched between them through the kitchen and paused in the doorway to the hall. "Let's go, we have a lot to discuss."

"She probably doesn't mean 'discuss,' does she," Bob said.

"Probably not."

They found her in the family room perched on Joe's recliner, and sat down on the sofa, Bob between them. "I assume you've already started," he said, "fill me in."

She shot him a look. "As a matter of fact I have. Did you notice anything different about Chelsea, today?"

"Sea?" Joe shook his head. "No, I don't think so."

"Not Sea, Chelsea, that's the first thing."

"That is her given name," Bob said, "but she never uses it."

"It is, and now she's going to use it. We decided," Lex said. "We talked about it earlier this week. If she's going undercover--"

Joe raised his voice. "Hold it, we haven't decided that."

"I said 'if'," she shot back. "We still have to talk to her parents, and we can't do that looking like she does. So we gave her a make-over. She had on a real pretty green top and a skirt today."

"No more black nails? No studded dog collar? I gotta see this."

"I'll send her down to your office tomorrow, Bob. We changed her jewelry, covered up some of the tattoos."

"She has more than the butterfly on her ankle?"

"It's a cute little snake with wings. That one will be hard to disguise."

Joe cupped his chin with his hand and watched them talk.

"The hardest thing was her hair, getting all that black out of it. We had to strip it. The color's not right yet. I don't really know what color it is, but we got it a lot lighter."

Bob turned to him. "It's amazing that Joe didn't notice all this in class."

"He's not real observant." She kept her eyes on Bob.

Joe kneaded his temples.

"Kinda grumpy, too."

"Damn it, Bob, this is serious."

"We are serious," Lexan said.

"I'm talking about her life, you're fixing her makeup. We haven't even decided to do this." Joe stared from her to Bob. "We're not doing anything without her parents' consent."

"We already have decided, with you or without you." Lexan glared back at Joe. He noticed she had dropped the 'if.'

"I feel like John McEnroe's little brother," Bob said with a dopey smile. "Looking left, then right, then left--"

"Shut up," Joe and Lexan said at the same time.

"At least I got you two to agree on something."

"Asshole," they said.

"No really, you both need to lighten up. OK?" He poked each of them in the shoulder. "What I don't get, Lexy, is why you did this before we spoke to the Larkins."

"So we *could* speak to the Larkins. They think they lost their good daughter and Chelsea is nothing but a waste. They don't listen to her. You saw that."

"I guess it wasn't a bad idea," Bob said.

"It's sick," Joe said. "Girl has to disguise herself to talk to her own parents."

"It is sick and it's wrong," Lexan said. "But I think it will work."

Joe knew they both wanted him to agree. "I don't know what else we can do," he said. "It's up to her parents."

"It seems funny without her here, you know, odd like." Amy whispered. "I don't mean laughy funny." She squinted to emphasize the distinction.

"I know what you mean," Ursula said. "But why are you whispering?"

"Eleanor is dead," Amy said as if bringing the news from Marathon.

"I was at the funeral. We both were. On the credenza is fine."

The secretary reverently set down the tray with the brightly colored cups and saucers next to the carafe. "She was like, you know, always here."

"A terrible thing."

"They still don't know what actually happened," Amy whispered.

"Her husband shot her then killed himself. You forgot the cream and sugar."

"Darn it," Amy said, then "oops, sorry," as she spun to avoid Kimberly and Pamela who were entering the office.

Kimberly took a quick look. "What did we miss here?" She didn't like it when people were in her office without her.

Ursula closed the door behind the secretary. "Nothing, really, but I think the story is holding. Amy has no idea."

"She's not the sharpest tool in the shed," Pamela said as she and Ursula sat down in front of Kimberly's desk.

"Looks like the coffee's ready. Help yourselves," she said brightly to what she mockingly referred to as her inner sanctum. Pamela's best quality of course was her family's money. Ursula was pretty sharp actually, but would soon be leaving town with Alfie. Amy did have some bookkeeping skills, but they had to keep her out of the loop. She was only involved because she was the way to control her husband and the police department. "Do you think we still need that chair, ladies?" she said.

"Isn't Eleanor--" Ursula began, and then put a horrified hand to her mouth.

Kimberly paused a beat. "You were saying, Uschi?"

"It was expensive. Not, not the chair," her sister-in-law said haltingly. "Something we had to take care of. But money well spent. It, he, a loose end." Pamela beside her nodded in agreement.

Kimberly waited for the babbling and head nodding to stop. "Moving on to a cheerier topic, how are we coming on the Inaugural Ball?" She slowly shifted her eyes from Ursula's reddened cheeks to the artificially unlined visage of Pamela Holmgren.

"My committee has been decimated as you know," she said dryly, "but I have risen to the challenge and made some progress."

Kimberly let a small smile tease the corners of her mouth. The woman thought she was the Queen of Sheba. "Do you need some help?"

"I can get some girls from PamLeeCo if I need them, of course, but I presume you have input to make." Kimberly noticed how the upward cadence of her voice allowed assistance without admitting need. The woman was good at this.

"I have some suggestions about the guest list," Ursula said.

Kimberly realized Pamela was enjoying the attention too much. "We're not going to waste time with this now. Give your personal ideas to Pamela in writing, and she will go over them before we meet again."

"Before we move on, I do have a couple of professional issues." Kimberly shot her a look, but Pamela continued. "Pedro and Karl, in or out?"

The door opened and Amy re-appeared, creamer and sugar bowl in hand. "Do you wonder about them?" she said. "I always do. Especially Karl, he has those, you know, delicate features?"

"This has no place in our meeting," Pamela huffed.

"He dresses well, better than me actually, and his nails are to die for," Amy said.

"Thank you, Amy, you may join us." Kimberly waited for her to sit down.

"It's not like you two never wondered," Ursula said. "I know I did."

Kimberly clenched her hands in her lap. "In answer to your question, the original question, Pedro yes, Karl no."

"That's settled," Pamela said.

"Why one and not the other?"

"Ursula, think about it," Pamela dismissed her. "And the police department?"

"Detectives and higher, no uniforms." Kimberly gave Amy a quick nod.

"One last question--"

The new Mayor held up her hand. "No, Pamela, this is exactly what I wanted to avoid. We're not spending any more time on this. Take care of it." She held her eyes until the woman looked away. "Now then Amy, where are we on the number?"

"A lot of people are eager to donate. I told Juan at the Marriott 375 maybe 400. Girls may be a problem." Amy scanned her notepad. "I hope we have enough."

"Counting the people who worked on the campaign and our regulars?"

"400 guests are a lot to service, especially with all the celebrities," Amy said.

"Hire some temps if you need to," Kimberly said to stop them. "OK then, hospitality?"

"Oh, that's me too. Eleanor was going to handle this." Amy opened the Vera Bradley tote at her feet. "Goody bags. Pamela has graciously donated cosmetics. Like she always does."

Kimberly watched Pamela tip her head to her secretary.

"We have a donation of bottled water, Evian. Tina at the Flower Gallery is providing dried flowers, really cute, I saw them and oh, wait, this is the best." Amy looked up from her notes and gave first Kimberly then the others a goofy smile. "Chocolate. The new shop in the mall, I talked to, who was it, Samantha, and she is providing these little baskets of chocolate, wrapped in pretty foil. You'll love it."

"Chocolate works for me," Pamela said.

"Sounds like you have it under control." Kimberly said. "Ursula?"

"Getting there," Amy said quickly. "I'm sure I'll get some more stuff, too. Cookies, of course."

"Fine," Kimberly said curtly. "Publicity. Ursula."

"It'll be all in the papers," her sister-in-law said. "Mr. Stevens found me a girl in the high school tech class, and she's doing a website for the Ball, and--" she looked down at her notes, "--and she's contacting social media outlets."

"Very good, Ursula, that's a great touch," Kimberly said and gave them a satisfied smile. She was glad she wouldn't need to deal with them much longer. "I think we're in good--"

"Just one more thing," Pamela said and waited for Kimberly's irritated expression to fade. "Uschi mentioning social media, gave me an idea. A concern actually."

"This better be important," the Mayor-elect said icily.

It's a pronoun substitution, Joe thought sitting on the pink and gray sofa in Larkins' living room. It's the same sofa and the same room, the same pink drapes and the same gray carpet, but they're substituting Chelsea for Amber. I'm watching a living grammar drill.

"Sure I can't talk you into a cold frosty, Lehrer?" Daniel Larkin said with a beery grin and a brown bottle of Amstel Light.

"No thanks, but please, call me Joe." The man slapped him on the shoulder and the pink and gray sofa billowed as he plopped down onto it.

"I thought German teachers liked German beer, Joe."

"I do, and thanks. Amstel is Dutch actually. From Amsterdam."

"Dutch, Deutsch, I'll drink it," Bob said and the three men laughed.

"It's nice he doesn't want to drink all the time," Diane Larkin said, her hands smoothing her skirt as she spoke, her eyes guiding them.

"Whatever. I'm just a man in a good mood," her husband said. "I got a daughter back and I have you people to thank for it."

"We are so very grateful to you, Ms. Warner. She looks so nice."

Chelsea was wearing a skirt and collared blouse, pink like the room. She sat on a chair opposite the sofa, her ankles crossed above gray Steve Madden flats.

Camouflage, Joe thought. Blending into her environment.

The girl directed a smile to the adults around her, nodding to Joe as if agreeing with him.

"It wasn't me," Lexan said, "it was Chelsea. I just helped her."

"She's getting a job and finally growing up." Larkin said and tapped his bottle on Bob's. "That and my new job, I'm a happy camper."

"You're OK with it?" Joe asked. "Chelsea working at Cookie's Cookies like Amber did?"

"Why wouldn't I? A job's a job. My job, your job, hers."

Bob looked away as Larkin aimed the bottle at his wife. "The thing is, she's given up that individuality shit and joined the real world."

Joe looked at the girl in pink and gray. Sea's eyes burned from Chelsea's face.

"No more black or that stupid dog collar. The piercings, metal dangling all over. How'd you fill in all those holes, Chels? A little spackling?"

Joe forced a smile as Larkin's hand slapped his knee. He opened his mouth, but Lexan's look told him to close it.

"Daniel, please," Diane said still examining her skirt. "We have guests."

"And I'm damn glad we do," he said. He set his drink down and looked at the teachers. "You know, I was wrong about you. Last time you was here, I about had to throw you out. But I'm a fair man, I'll admit it. You turned the girl around."

He sat back on the sofa and encompassed the room with his arms. "There Diane, is that polite enough for our guests?" When no one responded he lowered his voice and said to Lexan, "She always tells me I get too loud."

Chelsea's face revealed nothing.

"You're fine, Mr. Larkin, thank you," Lexan said and stood up. "We should get going. I'm sure you have things to do."

"Thanks for everything," Bob said.

Diane rose and gripped his arm. "No, we should thank you."

Joe said to Larkin. "You got a new job, too?"

"Just came through. Over to PamLeeCo. Got the Holmgren's to hire me."

"It's only part time, Daddy."

"It's a foot in the door."

Bob turned to him as they walked from the room. "What they got you doing?"

"Security for starters, they're working me in. If it goes good, I'll be full time and I can dump the trucking company."

"Good deal for you," Joe said. "Hope it works out."

"It will. We're so proud of him." Diane stepped between her husband and her daughter and put an arm around each. "I'm proud of both my new workers."

They said their good byes and crossed the lawn to where Bob had parked. Joe looked at the neighboring houses as he held the door for Lexan. Like his own street, the lawns were neatly trimmed, the leaves carefully bagged at the curb. Thin trees staked upright, wrapped at their base against deer, and plots of manicured shrubs on strategically placed mounds. The effect was one of sterility and forced, artificial beauty. The area too clean, too new, neither lived in nor appreciated. As he turned to get in the car, he caught sight of the Larkins. Posed on the front porch as a happy family, Sea's eyes the only things out of place.

Bob tooted his horn as he passed Lexan's apartment. Joe watched the Cobalt until it disappeared into the darkness. He turned away and followed her up the stairs inside. She walked like an athlete, the weight on the balls of her feet.

"Thirsty? I'll get us something to drink," she said in the hallway.

"I don't know if I'm staying, it's late."

"You're staying." She spun through the dining alcove into the kitchen.

He shook his head.

She handed him diet soda, plopped down onto the sofa and kicked her shoes to the floor. He saw his car in the street behind her head as he sat down next to her.

"I bet you were surprised."

He made his face a blank.

"You were so sure there'd be a big fight about it, but no, I was right."

"Oh, yeah, the Larkins."

"Hello, where were we?"

Joe took a drink from the soda. "I never thought we'd get them to agree, even though it was only about her taking the job. But I admit, you were right."

"Now she goes undercover and we can get some proof; that will be the dangerous part." Lexan pulled a curl off her face, her eyes animated, sparkling. Toenails painted dark pink peered from beneath her jeans. He continued to look at her as she talked.

"I mean it's good and it's bad both, you know?" Her hands moved nearly as quickly as she spoke.

"I know."

"It's sweet you worry about Chelsea, but she'll just be selling cookies, not doing those horrible things."

"You did a nice job on her make-over, she'll fit right in."

"That was fun, and it will keep her safe, won't it? Now you got me worried." Concern appeared on her face.

"She'll blend right in. She's a pretty girl." He moved the soda can from one hand to the other. "As long as everything is pink and gray."

She laughed. "Do you think that was a bit much?"

"It was hard to see her in her natural habitat." She placed her hand on his.

"She's a woman. We have to adapt to our environment."

"A learned behavior of the weaker sex."

Lexan leaned back into the sofa, took his hand in both of hers and pulled it to her. "Joe, you started to say something the other day about planning."

"When we were interrupted by Mr. Bad Timing?" Her hand felt good in his. "I've been thinking about it Lex, thinking a lot about it. You're right, I'm a control freak. Always have been. That's how I am. But, come on, you are too."

She squeezed his hand. "Guilty. No, I didn't mean that," she laughed. "Go on."

"OK, and as you said yourself, I'm not like that either. I wasn't expecting anything to happen between us. It's not been that long since Cathy died." He paused, "I'm so sorry I called--"

"--I was such bitch. After all you've been through. I should have stepped back. I'm sorry, too." She pulled his hand to her cheek.

"We've both been stressed."

"My turn," she said and released his hand. "I need mine to talk. We are alike. I'm used to being in charge, and that doesn't seem to work on you." Her hand paused to push a curl off her face. "I don't know what happened either, but something did, Joe, we can't ignore that."

Before he could respond, she was on his lap, her arms around his neck. Her lips soft, her mouth half open, and he kissed her. She sighed as his hands ran up her back. Her tongue a butterfly, darting to meet his, fleeing, returning.

He pulled her away. "Lexy."

"Wait, I'll be right back," she said and was gone.

He gulped from the soda can and it wobbled as he set it back on the table. "What the hell am I doing," he muttered and stood up.

"You're leaving?" Lexan stood in the bedroom hallway and beckoned him. She stepped toward him as he crossed the room and clutched his hand. "You should stay."

Her lips were shiny from fresh lipstick and he could smell her cinnamon. He pulled his hand away.

"Please stay. I want you to," she said and followed him to the door of the apartment.

He opened it. "I can't."

"You can't keep walking away from me."

"I have to. I don't know."

"Joe, I'm not Cathy. I can't be Cathy."

"You don't have to, but I don't know who I am, who we are."

She opened her mouth to speak again, but her chin quivered. She covered it and turned away. He pressed his chin into the base of her neck and wrapped his arms around her. Her shoulders heaved.

"The last thing I want is to hurt you, Lex. The second last thing is to use you."

She struggled to turn and face him. "It's not like that."

He kissed her quickly.

"Then stay with me now. Tonight." Her eyes glistened.

"We're not ready. I'm not."

"Then go." She stepped back and pushed the door closed between them. Without thinking he reached for the knob. "Lexy, open it."

The door made a hollow, empty sound as he struck it, the echoes reverberating in the stairwell. He pounded the metal door again then exhaled loudly through his mouth. Shoulders slumped, he turned and walked down the steps to the street. The rhythmic clicking of his heels striking the concrete, a contrast to the uncertainty he felt.

CHAPTER ELEVEN

"What is the matter with you, boy?" Bob moderated the volume of his voice but not the tone.

"Leave it alone, I'm trying to hear." Joe warded him with a hand and kept his face turned to the spindly figure of Principal Gale Stevens at the lectern.

Bob tried again. "You don't want to listen to him."

"I don't, but at least he's not yelling at me."

"Shit," Bob muttered as he tried to get comfortable. The choir room was quiet and most of the staff appeared to be listening to the Principal address another special faculty meeting. The hard plastic chair seemed to be tipped too far forward.

"--one special note before I introduce our special guest." Stevens smiled at his quip and looked hopefully at the staff. "We have been invited to participate in the Mayor's Inaugural Ball." He nodded and smiled when several teachers clapped. "Yes, the Cookie Lady wants us to come to her big party!"

"There has to be a catch," Joe said.

"Lighten up, Cinderfella."

"You and Tricky Dicky up there deserve each other."

Stevens had raised his arms in a V trying to regain control while enjoying the enthusiasm. "I told you she wouldn't forget her friends at the high school." He flashed a mouthful of white teeth.

"Now we weren't technically invited to the Ball itself." The noise subsided but not his grin. "As you know Mrs. Horvath has donated thousands of dollars over the years to many local charities through her foundation, 'Cookies for Kiddies.' This is so Kimberly," he said as if speaking to himself. "She would like her Inaugural to be a revenue stream for her charity, and so has asked us to help." He shook his head and giggled. "It might have been at my suggestion."

He refocused his gaze and continued. "Instead of paying a large amount of money for the help she will need in putting on the Ball, she asked us and I accepted. I hope you don't mind." He flashed another smile at the teachers. "She asked us to donate our time, and she will funnel the money saved to her foundation and help the children." He extended his arms toward them, horizontally this time. "And we get to mingle with all the famous people."

Bob elbowed him. "Cheap labor."

Joe didn't move. "NAFTA."

"It will be a great night for people watching." Stevens reached into the podium and retrieved a paper. "This is just the tentative guest list. Dick Goddard, the chief meteorologist on Channel 8. Kyrie Irving of the Cavaliers."

He pronounced it like the church word, then dropped his voice to a whisper. "And maybe that famous hoopster from Akron." He returned to his normal voice with a conspiratorial smile. "The new Coach of the Browns, and even Drew Carey from Parma." He nodded. "I knew you'd be impressed. Michael Brantley and Corey Kluber from the Indians. Former Congressman Dennis Kucinich, you can't keep him away from a party, just a whole raft of people. Oh, and the Governor, too, Governor Stanic, can't forget him."

"You may be in a funk, Joseph, but not our colleagues. Listen to them."

"This might work out for us," Joe said. "We can be our normal unimportant selves and still get in to the Ball."

"I think we can all agree," Stevens continued, "that we have seen enough of those celebrity scandals on TV, the internet, well, everywhere you look it seems. Now, with all these famous people coming to our fair city, Kimberly, Mrs. Horvath, I guess I should call her Ms. Mayor now, asked me if we could help her with this sensitive issue. Since these famous people are coming here to help us, to help Stradford, she felt it would be in our best interest, and the right thing to do, her words, if we help them protect their dignity." He looked up. "She and the city have decided that smart phones, phones with cameras and internet capabilities, will not be allowed at the Ball. That way the dignitaries can enjoy themselves without worrying, and there won't be any pictures making Stradford look bad. If anybody at the Ball, you guys, too, want to take a few pictures, they will lend you disposable cameras and they'll have these kiosks, where you can upload them. Right there in the hotel, and the best ones will appear on the website. He looked up and shook his head at Zimmerman's raised hand.

"You don't even have to ask about the Fourth Amendment, Mr. Zimmerman. The phones will be held by hotel security, not the police. The guests will be advised beforehand of course."

The math teacher adjusted his glasses and sat back down. His face red, he muttered something to Wosniak beside him.

"I hope I didn't overstep when I volunteered us to help her out, but I thought you would like the opportunity to participate," Stevens continued. "There'll be sign-up sheets on line when you submit your lesson plans this week. I'm excited about this; I think it's a win-win for all of us." The Principal put his hands on the podium and released a breath.

"I am excited as well to present our next speaker, our business manager, Mr. Mel Radburn."

The larger man shook Stevens' hand and whispered something in his ear before stepping to the microphone. The Principal shook his head no, his smile gone.

"While we are pleased that the levy passed," Radburn intoned, a deliberate hint of West Virginia in the vowels, "we must remain vigilant. The 7.5 mills will indeed begin to trickle into the district's coffers after the first of the year. Money that we desperately need, and the voters have graciously given us, to use on behalf of their children.

"It is not money for ourselves. As the number of children increases on a daily basis," he shot Joe a stare as he said this, "these monies will be stretched ever thinner, by the demands of quality education, that Stradford is known to provide. We have, however, avoided the dagger of personnel cuts, that has hung over us for so long. For the time being."

"Man can suck the air out of the room," Bob said out of the side of his mouth.

Joe muttered, "Fuckin' A."

Radburn raised his huge head from his notes and peered at them over his Buddy Holly glasses. "While we are grateful that we have not been forced to cut any teaching positions, at this time, it is well for you to remember, that this is only temporary. The growth of the district is constant, and the will of the voters fickle.

"My Daddy used to tell me, education is like rust," Radburn continued. "It never sleeps. We are constantly asked to provide, the very best, for the children, of the voters of Stradford. This is not to say, we are unhappy with the outcome of the election, far from it, but to serve us as a reminder." He glared at the teachers in front of him. "We must convince these voters, that we are not wasting one, single, dollar. Their money is being well spent, and they can count on us, so we may count on them, the next time, we put an issue on the ballot. Thank you very much for your kindly attention."

The teachers returned his look in silence for a moment. Scattered applause joined into a polite, curt show of appreciation, and they stood to leave. Stevens stepped in front of Radburn, clapping, and thanked his mentor.

"I'm inspired," Bob said. "I can't wait to strew filthy lucre wantonly around the halls of academe."

Joe gave him a small grin, then turned his head toward the door where Nancy and Lexan were exiting.

Bob nudged him. "So what happened?"

"Like I said, I'm not ready." Joe looked at his hands as he stood up to leave. "I feel like shit, but I'm not staying just because she's offering."

"That would be reprehensible." Bob tried a pious tone. "Morally wrong."

"You know, being my friend and all, you really are an asshole."

"I am," Bob agreed, clearly glad to get any response. "But at least I'm consistent."

"Mel is consistent."

"You fit right in. You're consistently hyper-critical of yourself."

"I probably blew it," Joe said and kicked the leg of his chair. "She hasn't spoken to me in three days."

"She'll get over it." Bob took the silliness out of his voice. "You know, I probably would have done the same thing myself."

"But I wouldn't have given you an entire ration of shit about it."

Bob laughed and patted his back. "You probably wouldn't have. Hey, I got a thought. What about Larkin?"

"What about him?"

"That job he took with PamLeeCo. Think it could be a payoff?"

"Are the Holmgren's involved with Kimberly?"

"Thick as thieves." Bob clasped his hands. "Literally."

"You think they gave him the job to keep him quiet about Amber?"

"Why else hire a bitter man with a drinking problem for security?"

"God, I hope not," Joe said. "They killed his daughter."

Bob snorted a cleansing breath. "Wouldn't be the first time somebody in this burg thought money was more important than people."

"Or celebrity," Joe said. He knit his eyebrows. "How do you read this bit about no cell-phones?"

"It's about control," Bob said. "In Stradford if it's not money, it's control."

⊷⊶

"We want to express our deepest condolences, Chelsea." Amy Michalik cast her eyes downward. Behind her Karl nodded meaningfully. "Amber was a good worker for us."

Chelsea gritted her teeth and looked at them across the desk in the Personnel Office of Cookie's Cookies. "Thank you," she managed. "She loved working here."

"Quality worker." Karl nodded again.

"So what is it I'll get to do?" Chelsea swallowed the lump in her throat. "I mean my sister told me some stuff and all."

Behind the desk Karl looked at Amy. "First, you need to lose the gum."

"Oops, sorry. I forgot." The girl put the wad into a tissue and stuffed it into her purse. "Amber told me you didn't like gum."

"It is inappropriate in a business environment," Karl said.

Amy waited for Chelsea's eyes to meet hers. The girl was dressed well, the skirt not too short, the top conservative enough, the hair neat and dark blonde. "To begin with, you'll be making deliveries. Our product is fresh baked every day--"

"--every night," Karl said. "We are nocturnal bakers."

"Every morning we have a fresh batch of cookies to deliver," the police chief's wife said in a tight voice, her eyes holding Karl's before moving across the desk. The man could be an enormous ass. "We need to get them to our clients as fast as possible."

"Do I get to sing?"

Amy let a smile play across her face. "Your sister must have told you."

"That was her favorite part," Chelsea said. "I like to sing, too."

Amy shuffled the papers in the folder. Karl better be right about this. "You did very well on the singing portion of your interview."

"I'm not as good as Amber."

"You'll do fine, I'm sure. So then, what we'll do is start you out with a partner, someone's who's done this before, and she'll kind of break you in. Then if it works out, and we have no reason to believe it won't, we can send you out on your own."

"You're forgetting a piece, Mrs. Michalik," Karl said.

"I'm not forgetting anything, Karl." Amy held her eyes away from his. I've done this before, you blowhard. "Before we send you out into the field as a Cookie Girl, we will take you through our day-long training session."

"Cooking with Cookie," Karl said. "You'll get to meet Cookie herself, the new Mayor, and...they let you take samples."

Studiously ignoring him, Amy continued. "We'll show you the entire process of baking, from the raw materials, the ovens, how to insert the sticks, even the packaging."

"It's a hands-on program," Karl said. "You get to wear a toque."

"Maybe you should continue, Karl. I don't want to leave anything out."

"You're doing fine, Amy. It lasts all day, Ms. Larkin. They put you in a classroom and explain the temperature of the ovens and all the technical data, and you get to make some of the cookies, the actual cookies. My favorites are the Wal-Mart face smilies."

"It all sounds great. When can I start?" Chelsea beamed at him across the table.

"It is. The best part is the decorating. I come along with the new groups."

Sure you do, so you can scope out the new talent. Amy smiled and said, "Let me see, the next training day is, next Thursday, 9:00 am."

"Wait, I can't, that's a school day."

"Not a problem, Chelsea Larkin," Karl said before Amy could. "Just see your counselor for a pass. It's all approved."

"I don't have to go to school? That's even better!"

"Ms. Raymond in Guidance handles all this for us." Amy closed the folder. "I guess that's about it. Do you have any questions?"

"After the training and I get out on my own, if it all goes well and you like me, do you think, is it possible, that I could work at the Inaugural Ball for the Mayor?"

Amy nodded. "Karl, I'm sure you want to handle this."

"No Ma'am, it's not my department."

"Never stopped you before." Amy looked at the applicant. "If everything works out in the probationary period, and you're doing the great job we're sure you will, we'll get you something to do at the Ball."

"We'll need you, it's a big event." Karl nodded confidently.

"If you do well," Amy cautioned.

"I'll do my best, Mrs. Michalik, I want this job."

"I'm sure you do." Amy stood and extended a hand across the desk. Chelsea shook it and Karl's, and left the office.

"Is she worth the risk?" Amy said as the office door closed. "She's got the look."

"Dime a dozen," Karl said. "That's not the problem. We had to get rid of her pain- in-the-ass sister."

"Nothing leaked, did it?" Amy frowned in thought.

"No, but do you have any idea how much work it was?"

"You and your people did fine, Karl." She pursed her lips as she looked at him. "It will be easier to keep an eye on her when she's working for us."

"But I'll have to deal with it if something goes wrong."

Amy nodded sympathetically.

"Maybe Chelsea will like the money and get into it," Karl continued. "That could happen too."

"Maybe," Amy said. "It worked with her father."

A string of accordion-bellied witches hung from the arch separating the coffee house from the magazine racks at Barnes & Noble. As the air currents buffeted the orange and black crepe paper, Joe watched the hook-nosed ladies cling to their broomsticks, and wondered if they had a quidditch team.

"Chelsea, this is when you have to make the final decision. It's your call." Bob looked evenly across the small table at the girl, his hands in his lap.

"We can back out now, it's OK," Joe said.

"She doesn't want to back out," Lexan said quickly. "Do you."

Chelsea's eyes were calm as was her voice. "I want to do this."

Bob rubbed his hands together. "OK then, we're on. Lex, you have a camera?"

Lexan laid her iPhone on the table.

"It's small so she can hide it in her pocket," Joe said, "but it will still be hard to get in and out of the hotel."

"We're hoping they don't search the maids when they come in to work."

"I don't like it," Joe said.

"I'm sure they don't frisk the cleaning staff," Lexan said. "If they do, she can pick up one of those disposables Stevens talked about."

"Maybe," Bob said, "but I'm concerned about the picture quality. How's the lens on this? Does it have a flash? That could get her in trouble."

"It's the newest version," Lexan said sharply. She gave him a look and handed the phone to Bob. "It works in low light."

Bob took a couple of shots with the flash on and then off. "OK, now show me how it zooms."

Chelsea focused on the string of witches and showed them the image. "The one on the end looks kind of like Mrs. Turner."

The teachers laughed. "I guess you're feeling all right about this," Joe said.

"I am," the girl said. "You guys don't need to worry."

"We're going to worry and you can't stop us," Bob said. Joe nodded.

"I'm just going to snap pictures of people going in and out of rooms. We can time stamp the pictures so we'll have a record."

"Right, and if someone comes along?"

"I toss the camera into the cleaning cart."

"Keep your head down. No eye contact."

"I've taught her some simple Spanish," Lexan said. "They'll never notice her."

"I wish I could go back to my black hair, I'd look more Hispanic."

"Sorry, Kiddo," Joe said. "You got the job as a blonde, you gotta stay blonde."

"They have me wearing this real nice cap-thingy with the uniform, so it doesn't matter." Chelsea sipped some latte. "It's wearing a costume and pretending."

"Halloween's been over a long time," Bob hooked a thumb at the decorations. "Nancy and her posse didn't get the message."

"No, I mean it. It's like this stuff happens and everybody smiles and pretends it doesn't." Chelsea's eyes avoided their faces, but Joe felt her voice speak directly to him.

"They go into a room and come out again. What they do inside is like a play, an act. You know? They make all this money, and pretend it didn't happen. I hate it."

Her face locked onto Joe's as she spoke. "It's all a big game to them, and it's supposed to be about love." She snorted the word in disgust. "Love, it's not love, it's not even playing really, it's, I don't know, but I hate it.

"Those girls, they do it and don't mean it. It's all a waste. They make sure everybody sees their new clothes and all the money they have. Their cars. It's worse than pretending." She shook her head like she was trying to shake out the images. Joe laid a hand on hers.

"They tried to make Amber do it, too. She. . . she wouldn't."

"You don't have to talk about it," Joe said softly.

"Yes I do," she snapped. "Everybody knows about it, but nobody does anything. They killed her, Herr. She wouldn't do it. She wouldn't be like that. Now she's gone."

Chelsea wiped a hand across her face. "My parents don't have a clue. The police don't help anybody. The mayor, all these people are involved with it. They act like it's not even happening. They're having a party to celebrate it."

She looked to the three teachers. "You guys are the only ones who care."

"You're taking the risk," Bob said. "It's not worth you getting hurt."

"I have to do something, Mr. McCauley. What they're doing is wrong."

"It is," Joe said. "So you take a couple pictures from a safe distance, and get out. We'll keep an eye on you. You run away if there's a problem. Any problem."

"I will." She squeezed her fingers around the iPhone.

"We'll make the pictures public and maybe we can stop this." Lexan gave her hand a squeeze. "You're a brave girl."

"I don't feel brave inside."

"No prob," Bob said, "we can't see inside. You need a lift home?"

"I'll take her," Lexan said and stood up.

"Let Bob take her, Lex," Joe said. "I'll buy you another coffee. Sit down."

"No, it's on my way." Lexan dropped a dollar on the table.

Still seated, Joe caught Chelsea's eye. "You're pretty popular."

"It's a burden," the girl said with a grin.

"Come on Chelsea," Lexan said.

"I get dumped?" Bob opened his arms in supplication.

"Joe can buy you a coffee," Lexan said and turned away. "He's rich."

"Bye," Chelsea said to them and followed Lexan toward the door.

Bob dropped onto the bench next to him. "Things a little frostier than I thought."

"Arctic," Joe said.

CHAPTER TWELVE

Five Months Ago

Constantine tapped the window in the meeting room of the Board office with his knuckle and turned away. He could almost smell the brats grilling in the parking lot below, and the peaceful-looking scene reminded him of his time as a teacher. But the Assistant Superintendent also remembered how his previous comments had been received, and instead of saying what he thought, he merely nodded as Board President Kimberly Hellauer Horvath summarized the feelings of the others in the office. "How dare they?" she said. "Who do they think they are?"

Seated at the conference table, Eleanor Mindrivan echoed her. "I can't stand to even look at them. Come back to the table. They didn't do that kind of thing when my Brian worked here."

Constantine followed the tall woman and held a chair for her, thinking the 'Minivan' had mentioned her husband three, no four times already. This would be a long night.

The Board negotiating team, Supt. Metcalf, Rev. Patterson, Constantine and Radburn, was joined by their attorney, Eric Tuttle, Mindrivan and Horvath, and two district administrators, Beverly Hallik, the principal at Raub Elementary and the high school principal, Gale Stevens. Some of them had managed to skirt the picket lines and enter the offices through the middle school, while Patterson and Metcalf had given television interviews in front of the library, and boldly walked across the street and through the picketers. That had been several hours ago, and now it felt to Constantine as if they were being held hostage.

Tuttle spread his hands and said, "However it used to be, the fact is we are here, now, and we need to decide how we want to handle this situation."

"Fire 'em!" Patterson said. "We have hundreds of applications on file, don't we Mr. Radburn? There are many, many unemployed teachers that would love to work here."

Radburn nodded his head. "We could do it, and it would save us money. We could hire two young teachers for what we pay one of those tenured employees. A lot of money." He bunched up his lips and nodded his jowly face.

And lose all that experience, Constantine thought.

"They're holding the exam grades," Stevens said. "That puts us in a bad spot."

"Can't we just give the kids grades? Do we really need the exams?" Mindrivan said.

"The Building Principal has the statutory right to assign grades, the classroom teacher actually doesn't," Metcalf said. "But that would cause a good deal of trouble." Next to her, Stevens flushed red.

"More trouble than that rabble outside has caused already?" Patterson boomed. "Looks like a band of immigrants invaded us!"

"The TV coverage, the crowds, the traffic disruption, as if we were in Cleveland or on the Mexican border." Horvath said. "It's all over social media. We can't have that in Stradford. We simply can not."

"We could get rid of the disruption, by simply getting rid of the strikers, Kimberly, it's as simple as that." Constantine scanned the other faces to see if Patterson's words found any traction. Mindrivan and Radburn nodded, Metcalf and the other administrators did not.

"It would set off a firestorm, Humphrie," Kimberly said. "There would be even more TV, more meetings, more disruption . . . not less."

"It's the end of the school year. We give out the grades, high grades, everyone will be happy, and go home for the summer," Patterson said. "By the fall, all will be forgotten."

Mindrivan nodded enthusiastically. "Sure. We give the grades, ignore their demand to be recognized as a union, and we won't hear a peep out of them for years."

Constantine watched the Board President exhale and place her pen exactly in line with her notepad. If this discussion went the way it usually did, Horvath would prevail. She held an amazing amount of power over the Board and the school administrators. "No," she said. "I don't want to trade definite chaos now, for a possibly peaceful future. I say we end this today, and run Commencement as planned." She fixed the others around the table with her stare, then said, "Ms. Hallik, I have a job for you."

As they climbed the steps up into Georgia Campbell's enormous RV, Bob patted the sign next to the door advising him to leave if he found the vehicle rocking. "Makes me laugh every time."

"I hadn't noticed," Joe said and punched his shoulder.

Inside the RV, Georgia had set up a table large enough for the strike committee. Around it sat Prusnek, the OEA rep, Gene Phillips, the President, Terri Dieken, Zimmerman and several others. Gene was pointing to the screen on his laptop.

"Glad you got here, Joe, they're playing the video again."

The committee made a place for Joe to see. "The Channel Three interview?"

"You nailed it," Gene said. "Just what we needed."

"Wait, here's the best part," Zim said.

They watched as Joe turned from the reporter to the camera and said, "This isn't about money or power or 'Union' tactics, Hollie, it's about the caring and nurturing interactions that take place in our classrooms on a daily basis. We want to do the best we can for the children of Stradford, because, well, we love them."

"Damn, but it looks like you're shedding a tear there." Bob laughed.

"Come on, I meant it," Joe said.

They laughed again and someone slapped him on the back.

"You can't buy that kind of press," Prusnek said. "However you meant it, it was gold."

"OK," Gene said, "let's see where we stand now." He rotated the computer toward himself as the others sat down. "I've spoken with the bus drivers, and they will honor the picket lines tomorrow, if we need them to."

"That's big," Dieken said.

"It is." Gene nodded. "The press coverage so far is good, the buses are good, but I need to get a feel for the average parents. Are they with us or not?"

"If you can tell by attendance, they're with us. It was down today, maybe fifty per cent," Zimmerman said.

"The Board reported seventy-five," Georgia said. "That's what somebody told me."

"No way, not at the high school," Bob said. "The student parking lot was nearly empty. Not even close to half full."

"Moms drove the younger kids today," Dieken said, "but what will happen tomorrow?"

"Let's hope there is no tomorrow," Gene said, then laughed as he heard himself. "Maybe not so dramatic as that. The Board put out a feeler a few minutes ago." He looked to Prusnek, who checked the computer screen and said, "Maybe a half hour now."

"Anyway," Gene continued, "it was a back-channel type of thing, so they can easily deny it. They got Hallik, the principal at Raub to float it."

"She's not even on their team," Joe said. "What's she got to do with it?"

Gene opened his palms. "Maybe nothing, but she said that she felt the Board was ready to talk."

"After one day?" Bob said. "They want to give up after one day?"

"They listened to our reasoned position and came to their senses," Georgia said with a wide smile and open face.

"No, Joe made all the moms shed a tear, that's what it was," Dieken said, and they all laughed.

Gene was the chairman of the social studies department, and had taught history for many years. He loved political intrigue. "No, nothing as local as all that," he said. "I believe it has to do with the governor."

"Stanic?" Bob demanded. "Is that redneck even in town?"

"Wait a minute," Terri Dieken said. "He's giving the commencement address."

"He's using it to tout his new school funding initiative," Gene nodded. " I'm getting the feeling, and it's only a feeling at this point. They're afraid, they'll have to cancel the graduation ceremony on Sunday, and the governor won't be able to give his speech."

"So we win!" Zimmerman said. "They fold after a one-day strike, and we get recognized as a Union!"

"What do they want in return?" Bob said. "They must want something."

"They do," Prusnek said, "but we can live with it. What we hear from Hallik is they want assurances that we would support a levy in the fall."

Joe joined in the celebration, happy that their efforts appeared to be successful. He smiled and slapped palms with the others, but couldn't quite shake the feeling that they hadn't won because of their concern for the kids, or fair representation. They had won because the strike had embarrassed the Board.

CHAPTER THIRTEEN

"This is from LeBron James," Juan said as Amy opened the penthouse door for him. "So I brought it up myself. There are little 23's in between the flowers."

The hotel manager struggled beneath the enormous arrangement, bending his knees and turning sideways to get it through the opening. Despite his efforts a dark red bloom snapped off and fell to the floor. "I am so sorry," he said.

"We don't have much more room," the secretary said and picked it up. "Put it over there, I guess." She gestured to the wet bar in the corner. "Every place else is full."

"Where should we put these?" Juan said as two bellhops behind him pushed baggage carts into the suite, each one loaded with flowers. "There are more in the lobby."

"You brought more?" Amy snapped. "Put them in the banquet room. It's starting to smell like a funeral home in here."

"But with the tables set up for the auction and all the guests--" Juan began.

"Open the extra section if you have to, you can't put them here." Amy stood with one hand on her hip and pointed to the door with the other.

Juan, dark skinned, balding, and shorter, thought about standing up to her for a moment. Instead he made a quick bow and said, "As you wish." He ushered the others from the room with an elegant wave and closed the door softly behind him.

Amy tossed the broken flower into the waste basket, and spun around the sofa past the large windows overlooking the MetroPark. The penthouse floor of the Marriott extended around the corner of the room where Amy found the Horvaths, Tom closing the clasp of Kimberly's necklace. "Thank you, dear," the Mayor said and turned to her.

"I'm glad you decided against the suit," Amy said. "This is a party. You can be businesslike the rest of the week."

Kimberly adjusted her breasts inside the low cut bodice so the large green stone lay centered between them. "You don't think it's too much?" She glanced past Amy to the mirror and ran her hands down the tight-fitting, silver-sequined dress.

"I think you look great," Tom said. "Or is it hot, they say?"

Kimberly shook her head at her husband and looked to her assistant.

"He's right. You're definitely glowing."

"A drink, Amy?" Tom said on his way to the wet bar.

"No, I have to run and check on Steven. He can't do his necktie."

"No one can," Tom said, then put his hand on his wife's shoulder.

"Careful, don't muss me," she said and crossed her arms over her flat stomach.

"I'll be good," he said. "Look at that stream of traffic, Honey, down I-71 and both ways on Center. They're all coming to see you."

"Not all of them."

"Look at the line waiting to turn into the parking lot. They are." He took his hand from her shoulder and pointed it down to the right. "All those big cars."

"They are, aren't they?"

He saw the corner of her mouth lift up in a smile and nodded to her reflection in the glass. "They're driving in, my dear. That means you've already arrived."

"We look like Bob Hope and Bing Crosby in one of those 'Road' pictures," Bob said. "I'm the good looking funny one, and you're the wormy straight man." He fancied himself a film connoisseur almost as strongly as he appreciated his own sense of humor. "But at least we're not checking handbags for contraband phones. Poor Nancy."

"Neither of us can sing a note," Joe said. "Besides Tom Hanks was in 'Road to Perdition,' not Der Bingel."

"Bingel, schmingel, that car's yours," Bob said. "I got the Escalade behind it."

Joe opened the passenger door of the Dodge as Bob trotted away. "Good evening, Rev. Patterson. Welcome to the Ball." He gave his hand to the School Board member.

"Thank you, Mr. Lehrer. This is my wife, Bernice."

Joe nodded to the gray-haired lady hovering at the bumper. "Nice to meet you."

"Should I leave the keys in it?"

"That will be fine," Joe said.

"He teaches at the high school, dear," Patterson said and led her toward the doors.

Joe watched their backs through the windshield as he put the SUV into gear. He pulled under the archway and across the long side of the rectangular building, and parked it next to a white Mercedes.

"Must be administration night," Bob said. "I had Dr. and Mr. Superintendent."

"I don't care whose turn it is, I'm not parking Mel. I'll take Stevens, not him."

Bob spoke over his shoulder as they threaded through the cars. "Don't worry, they won't let him in here with that beater truck of his."

"This is a Clampet free zone?"

"No, they're afraid you'll run it into something."

"Cops coming?" The two stopped as Joe pointed to the flashing blue and red lights atop a line of silver Ford Explorers entering the lot through the exit.

"State troopers, five, no six of them," Bob said, checking the time on his phone. "It must be the Gov, but he's early."

"Show off. Helicopter must be in the shop."

The line of vehicles stopped as one under the covered arch. The doors of the first and last opened and uniformed men jumped out. Two went directly to the door of the hotel, the others spaced themselves around the cars. From the valet parking stand, the teachers could see the men carried weapons and wore body armor.

They watched the hotel manager and a tall, white-haired man approach the middle car. They both shook the Governor of Ohio's hand after holding the door and helping him step out. A small cheer wafted through the crisp air from the gallery behind the barriers. Thompson Stanic smiled, waved, and reached back for his wife's hand. Bracketed by officers, his entourage processed down the carpet into the hotel. The white-haired man, Karl, spoke into a lapel mic and followed.

People turned their heads and conversations stopped mid-sentence. The Governor's procession muted the Ballroom the way the ocean smooths the sand on a beach. Lexan noticed the sudden quiet and paused with a cornucopia in her hands halfway to the table she was setting. Several seconds passed, then the crowd clapped as the Governor and his party took their seats directly in front of the dais. The black-clad troopers melted into the dark edges of the large room.

Lexan placed the horn of plenty in the center of the table. "Why do you suppose the Governor isn't sitting at the head table?" she said to the server she had been assigned to work with. "Isn't he important enough?"

The older woman straightened up and wiped her hands on a towel. "I just do what they tell me," she said with an exasperated shake of her head. "They don't ask me about the seating chart." She lifted another centerpiece off the serving cart with both hands and carried it carefully toward the next table.

Lexan wheeled the rest of the cornucopiae to the other end of the banquet hall. On the way the cart rolled over pieces of straw and dried flowers that were part of the harvest theme. Large bundles of hay stood at the corners of the hall and in the center, with pumpkins and smaller gourds displayed at their feet. Arrangements of dried flowers in dark red, burnt orange and gold sat on the head table at the short end and on the auction tables along the sides. On the curtains behind the dais sparkling letters in the same colors proclaimed the Ball's theme, "Giving Thanks to Stradford."

"Watch where you're driving there, girl," Roberta called with a grin.

Lexan yanked her cart to a stop. "Sorry, I was asleep at the wheel."

"Almost dumped my load of cream and sugars. We need a traffic cop."

"Plenty of security. Did you see the state troopers?"

"The Ohio Patrol and Nancy," Roberta said. "She fits right in."

"Tell me about it," Lexan said. "She's probably getting fitted for a uniform."

"I heard she actually took LeBron's phone away from him. Can you imagine her telling him he has to use those disposables and upload them in the kiosks like everybody else?"

"She's the only one who could do it," she said to Roberta with a forced smile. She hoped that Chelsea had managed to get her iPhone past security.

⟞⟨┼┼⟩⟝

The key-card was attached to her wrist by what looked like an old-fashioned telephone cord. Maria Fuentes held it in front of Chelsea's face. "Tonight we're starting on four, but if we have to work on the top floor, we need this card. "No one can get onto the penthouse floor without it." The elevator doors thumped shut.

Squeezed into the service elevator with the maid and two cleaning carts, Chelsea said, "Not even Governor Stanic?"

"Not even the highway patrol. Everybody needs a card."

"I don't have one."

"You have the uniform like me, and you have the cart like me." The woman shook her head. "But they didn't give you a card."

"Do they use those cards on the stairs, too?"

Maria's eyes nearly disappeared behind her round cheeks as she squinted at the girl. "We can't bring the carts up the stairs."

"No, they're too heavy. I didn't mean that."

The elevator jerked to a stop with a bing. "Girl, you ask too many questions."

Chelsea started to ask another, but pulled her cart out of the way and held the door for the woman to pass. It slammed onto her own cart as she exited, and the girl stooped to pick up the bottles of shampoo that landed on the deep red carpet. Maria was waiting at the door of the first room with her hands on her hips when she caught up to her.

Chelsea stood there as the maid sized her up. "This job is hard work."

"Yes, Ma'am, I'll work hard."

"My cousin Juan is the manager. He told me I have to work with you, but you young girls don't know how to do hard work." Her eyes lost their friendly shine and bore into her.

"Thank you, Maria, I'll do my very best."

Maria huffed a short breath. "You'll have to." She shook her head as if not believing it. "The hotel is almost completely full tonight, so we'll have to work quickly. Leave your cart here." Maria took an armful of linen from the stack and marched into the room.

"Aren't I going to clean my own rooms?"

"You don't know how." Maria put the sheets onto the bed that was made up and ripped the covers from the other bed to the floor. "And you ask too many questions." She looked at Chelsea, expecting her to follow her example.

Chelsea nodded and pulled the bottom sheet off the corner of the mattress. As Maria remade the bed, the girl carried the soiled sheets to her cart in the hall. The cell in her pocket banged against the rim and she looked up, startled, but the maid had not heard it.

"What else?" she said as she re-entered the room.

"Look around," Maria said and raised her arms. "If it's dirty, you clean it. Check the bathroom, wipe off the water spots. Run the sweeper. They won't be in here very long, so we don't have to do the whole room. Bang-bang," she said.

Chelsea looked at her quizzically as she ran her dust cloth across the desk top. "Bang-bang," Maria said again, her voice hollow in the tiled bathroom.

"Did you see the cruise package?" Roberta tugged Lexan's arm. "On the silent auction table?"

"Aruba or Cozumel? I can't afford either."

The French teacher lowered her voice. "I put a bid in. For our anniversary."

"Are we allowed?" Lexan said.

"Why not, it's for charity. I'm going over to check it."

"Finished yet?" a tired voice said behind her. "No, you're not." The server's heavy shoulders shrugged and she hefted another cornucopia from the cart.

"Almost," Lexan said and followed her.

Roberta parked her cart between a pair of round ten-tops. The rectangular silent auction tables ran the length of the hall, the items themselves or pictures of them stood near clipboards on which the bids were entered. She picked up the Aruba cruise bid sheet and saw that she had been overbid. She drew a line through it and entered a higher amount and her own code number on the line below.

Excusing herself as she moved past a clump of bidders, she noticed several time-shares being offered. One was a condo in Aspen for a weekend getaway, one for a week on Captiva Island, another in Jamaica. Next to this was a glass sculpture of a dog, the current bid at $1100. Several frames held certificates for maid service. A wicker basket on the next table held assorted jellies, an autographed football and a pair of Browns-Steelers tickets. She was tempted by another maid service and a massage, but checked her bid on the Mexican cruise. She was still the highest; she slid the clipboard behind a frame holding two tickets to *Cabaret* in Playhouse Square and a night at a Cleveland hotel.

"You have to leave the clipboards in full view." The bare arm of a blonde in a skimpy green gown reached past her and retrieved the bid sheet. "It's not fair."

"Sorry," Roberta mumbled. "Do you work here?"

"Employees shouldn't be bidding," Vikki said.

Before Roberta could respond or comment on what was obviously a wig, Vikki reached for the hand of a man passing them and steered him farther down the table. "You might be interested in this one, sir," she purred and gestured to an item in a gilded frame.

Roberta placed two sets of cream and sugar on the next table and watched. The blonde looked like Vana White selling a vowel. Probably an I or a U. The man picked up the clipboard and checked his watch. The woman said something that made him laugh and walked away. The man wrote on the sheet and set it down, his eyes on the blonde woman's ass.

"The creams and sugars. Tonight, missy," the server said in Roberta's ear.

Roberta turned the cart around and sped toward the head table.

"Teachers," the woman said and shook her head.

"I don't understand why we can't spend the night in our own bed, Uschi." Alfred Hellauer yanked the bow-tie loose and began once again to tie it. "It's a waste is all it is, and so is this damn tie."

The outgoing mayor looked into the mirror to see his wife's face at his side. "Let me try it, dear."

"I never had to make a big show like this, and I was in office 14 years. Ow."

"Don't be such a baby."

"Inaugural Ball, my ass. The expense alone--"

"Alfred, stand still!" Ursula tugged the ends of the tie and stepped back. "Looks pretty good, despite all your complaining. Quit fooling with it."

He frowned and turned his back to the mirror. "I hate tuxedos."

"I know you do, dear. How do I look?" She checked his face as she twirled around. She liked the feel of the dark purple material and its Empire waist.

"As good as the day I married you," he said and stopped her by holding her elbows. "The best day of my life."

She smiled into his tan, weathered face, different than it looked forty-two years ago, but the same as well. Reassuring, especially the eyes, clear and kind. She pecked his cheek. "Mine too, and you're right about Kimberly."

She stepped to the side and smoothed her dress in the glass. "This is ostentatious, a public spectacle. Something you would never do."

He shook his head. "I didn't need to."

"Your sister does. It's her defining moment."

"I'm glad we're done," Alfred said holding open the door of their suite. "I've had a belly full of Stradford."

"So we dance the night away and leave it to her. Thank you, sir," she said and took his arm. The plush carpet in the hallway muffled their steps and the recessed lighting glowed warmly as they made their way to the Presidential Suite at the far end of the hall. Alfred muttered good evening to the security guard halfway down.

"Be good now," Ursula said and gripped his arm tighter.

The door swung open before they could knock. "Welcome to party central," Amy said loudly. She stood aside for them, one hand on the heavy door, the other holding a drink. A blue gown hugged her slim figure, her feet bare.

"Steven, you're looking well," Alfred said to Amy's husband behind her.

"I look like a penguin and so do you," the police chief replied. "I hate these things. Can I get you two a drink?"

"I think you might."

"Alfred, you look wonderful." Kimberly enveloped him in a hug, then stood back to admire him. "And Ursula, that color is fabulous."

"But you, Kimberly."

"Tom thinks it's too much." She dropped her brother's hands and spun around.

"I think it's not enough," Alfred said. "Tom, good to see you."

"My wife is something, isn't she?" Horvath was a bookish looking man, with close-cropped black hair and rimless glasses. His face was flushed, perspiration beaded his lip.

Steven Michalik returned and distributed drinks from a round tray. Pamela and her husband had glasses already in hand. "Drink those up, the Governor's party just arrived," he said.

"It's my party and I'll be late if I want to," Kimberly sang loudly and the others laughed.

Ursula spoke to Amy in a low voice. "Is she OK?"

"She's really excited about her speech."

Ursula clinked glasses as the new mayor circled the group. "You have the figures?"

"It's all in the report." Amy pointed to the iPad with the blue cover on the table by the door.

"Don't lose it."

"It's all set, Ursula. You just relax and have a good time tonight."

"OK, everyone!" Kimberly stood in the center, her arms above her head. "It's time to leave for the Ball!"

"Before we go downstairs, I have something to say," Pamela said.

"Here, here," her husband said. An arm around his wife's waist, Lee saluted the mayor with a tip of his glass.

"I would just like to say a few words, here in private, before we face the crowd below." Pamela's face was exquisite as always, her hair up in a simple, yet equally elegant twist, her gown ephemeral. She looked the part of the queen mother.

"This is a proud moment for Stradford. Kimberly, you have united us in a great cause. Under your leadership we have put our skills and hard work together, and look at what we have accomplished."

Amy let out a whoop and Pamela glared at her.

"No, that's OK, that's how I feel too," Kimberly said. "Yes! Whoo-hoo!" Her arms upraised, she danced around in the circle and the others joined in.

"So much for decorum," Pamela said. Alfred shook his head in agreement.

"I'm your 10 pm, darlin', says so right here. Ready to share some time?"

Lucy pushed the gum to the corner of her mouth and looked at the paper the man had forced into her hand.

Thirty-five or so she thought as he grinned at her chest and adjusted his cummerbund. "You can call me Jim Bob."

"I'm Luscious." She opened her arm toward the elevator to give him a side view.

"Yes, you are."

Lucy looked behind him to Karl on the far side of the lobby. The white-haired man tipped his head slightly. "Right this way, sir."

She leaned against him in the elevator as the doors slid together. "Push four." She watched his finger extend and jab the plastic disc. The car jerked upwards.

"Pretty good deal you people got around here," he said. "Time shares, that's funny." Lucy adjusted her butt on his hip as his hand reached down from her shoulder.

"Hmm," Lucy murmured. His breath was beery but he was better looking than most. Almost cute. She could feel only a small mound of fat around his middle with her back. No nose hair, either. The door binged open.

She turned toward him to take his hand and stepped out of the elevator into the path of a cleaning cart. "Shit," she said. "Get out of the way!"

"*Por favor,*" the maid said, turning herself and the cart away. "*Buenos noches.*"

"Oughta have us a green light," Jim Bob laughed. "You alright, darlin'?"

Lucy stood with her hands on her hips and glared at the maid on her knees hurriedly returning supplies to the overloaded cart. "Immigrant bitch should watch where she's going."

"Whoa, pardner. Not only a green light, we need us a green card around here too!"

"You're so funny," Lucy said and pulled his hand. "Come on, this way."

Chelsea watched them as she pretended to pick up the little bars of soap. Lucy and the man stopped several doors down the hall, 442 or 444. She tossed two bars into the box and reached for the cell. Around the corner down the hall, Maria's cart stood outside 465.

"Here we are," Lucy said and handed Jim Bob the card. She leaned her back against the door and looked up at him. "You can put it in." He grinned and inserted it.

"Lucy Patterson," Chelsea said softly as she zoomed in to their faces. "Dance Team captain, cheerleader, Amber's best friend at Raub." The camera clicked when the girl's back arched toward the man's kiss. "Ex-friend," she muttered.

That's a good one, Chelsea thought. The two figures laughed and their faces rotated toward her. Other pictures had been dark or blurry, and she hadn't known all the girls. She clicked once more as the man entered the dark room behind the ho. Thinking it would be safer, she slid the phone into the cart underneath the towels.

At the intersection of the halls, Maria looked to her right at the two entering the room, then to her left at Chelsea, crouched behind the cart with the phone in front of her face. She quickly stepped back out of sight.

"One, two, three, rock," Joe said.

"Nope, paper covers rock, I win!" Bob shuffled his feet in a clumsy dance.

"OK, I got Mel, but if he tips me, I'm not splitting it."

"If he tips you, it'll be the first time. I got the one behind."

Joe opened the door of the Buick. "Good evening, Frau Radburn."

"Thank you, son," a voice boomed at his back. "Try not to spoil the paint job."

"I'll try, sir, but there are a lot of maniacs on the road tonight."

Radburn's eyes were beads behind his thick glasses. "Nice to see you with a tie."

"You're looking rather spiffy yourself. I'm Joe Lehrer," he said to his wife.

"That's my Bonnie," Radburn said, "my bonnie lass. Don't guess you've ever met."

Mrs. Radburn was a small woman, but her gaze strong and her grip sure. Joe didn't think Mel could bully her. "Nice to meet you finally," she said.

"Lovely dress," Joe said climbing behind the wheel. "Have fun tonight." As they entered the hotel, he heard her say to her husband, "He doesn't seem so bad."

Bob met him after he parked Radburn's black sedan. "I got a theory."

"A professional paper-rock-scissors league?"

"That's an idea, this is a theory. Not a bad idea though."

They hurried back to the valet station. "What is it?"

"There's a fixed amount of beauty you can have in a relationship. Only a certain amount. That's why nerdy guys got hot wives."

"You must have parked Stevens," Joe said. "Tommi is way hot. Scalding."

"Admit it, I'm brilliant."

"And it explains you and Linda. Wait." Joe pointed to Peter Weigel walking through the dark parking lot into the lights at the entrance. "What about Petey?"

"He must have one seriously hot babe at home."

"I don't think he's even married."

Bob thought a second. "You know what, I don't know if he is or not. My turn."

Bob jogged over to the next car and nodded slightly to Weigel. Joe was turning to open a car door and didn't see the hostile look Karl gave the Assistant Principal as he passed.

"You only finished one?" Maria said several minutes later as Chelsea came out of the room with an armful of dirty sheets.

"Only one more to go."

"Let me see." Maria pushed past her into the room. "This is clean, OK," she said when Chelsea followed inside, "but you have to work faster."

The girl stretched her lower back and sighed. "Yes, Ma'am."

"I wish we could call Chelsea," Bob said when Joe returned from the lot.

"Too dangerous." Joe looked up at the hotel looming over them. "Can't we just go up there?"

"Staircases are locked and we need a key for the elevator." Bob looked at him.

Joe kicked a pebble across the asphalt. The rain had stopped and the rough surface reflected the lights from the hotel rooms. "We should have checked that."

"I'm sure she's all right."

"Sure." Joe kicked the pebble again. He wouldn't be able to handle it if she wasn't.

Karl followed Weigel into the hotel, stopping in the lobby as the thin man continued into the ballroom, then nodded to his man posted at the elevator bank. He turned the corner to the door of the stairwell, and ran a passkey through the slot. He found Oskar Brummelberger loitering on the second floor landing. Even dressed in a blue security blazer the man looked like a pile of dirty laundry.

"That shithead here?" Oskar said.

Karl nodded, keeping his eyes from the bulbous face.

"Gonna let me kill him? You gotta let me kill him."

Karl sighed. "We been over this several times."

"I been patient, Karl, you can't say I ain't been patient."

Karl nodded, his eyes scanning the stairs.

"He killed my girl!" Oskar's voice a hiss.

"We had to wait until the Ball was over."

Oskar's tiny eyes swelled. "Tonight."

"Tonight, my friend, tonight." Karl patted Oskar's arm and continued up the stairs.

Chelsea looked around the hallway and didn't see Maria. Glad to be finally alone, she pulled the slip of paper from her apron pocket. She checked once again and unlocked room 404.

The room was in much the same condition as the others had been. The bedspread lay in a heap at the foot and the pillows were shoved into a lopsided pile. The sheets looked like Katrina wreckage. That made them easier to change; the corners on the side facing the window had sprung back toward the center of the bed. She held her breath and rolled the sheets into a ball.

She emptied the ashtrays and put the dirty glasses onto the rack in her cart. She returned with the vacuum and her dust rag, and wiped the surfaces of the desk and the low coffee table. Disgusted, she tossed several empty bottles into the trash. She quickly ran the sweeper over the center of the room and checked the bathroom on her way to the corridor. Hey, you don't look nervous at all, she said to her calm expression in the mirror over the sink. She wiped the sink dry. But she was.

Chelsea took the ball of soiled linen to the cart to exchange it for a fresh set, leaving the bed for last as she always did. The elevator binged and another couple crossed the short space to the room opposite her. She pulled the cart in front of her room and dropped behind it. She reached into the stack of towels, then slid her hand under the stack of clean sheets. She frowned, stood and moved to the other side of the cart. Across the corridor the door thumped shut. Again she ran her hands deep into the cart, bending nearly double to do so. The iPhone was gone. Frantic, she pulled all the dirty sheets out onto the floor and moved the clean ones aside. Still nothing.

"Looking for something?" a voice behind her asked.

CHAPTER FOURTEEN

Kimberly framed herself beneath the shimmering letters on the curtains and behind the low, glass lectern she had insisted upon. The money I paid for this dress, she thought, they sure as hell will get a good look at it. She raised her arms over her head to still the wave of adulation.

"As I said this is not a political speech, and this is not a chance for me to gloat about our victory. Mr. Kane was a worthy opponent." She smiled benevolently at the scattered applause. "This is a speech of thanksgiving. A short speech." She smiled again, this time at the laugh.

"The person I wish to thank the most is my brother, the outgoing mayor of Stradford, the honorable Alfred Hellauer!" She stepped away from the podium and clapped her hands, urging a crescendo that filled the room. When it began to fade, she chanted "Alfie, Alfie!" and pumped her fist. The noise intensified, refilling the hall. At Ursula's urging, Alfred rose to his feet at his table, red-faced and beaming, and waved a long arm to the crowd. After a minute the siblings exchanged blown kisses, he sat down, and Kimberly returned to the center of the stage.

"Thank God, I never had to run against him," she said. "He would have crushed me!" The crowd laughed, and that launched another wave of applause.

"Good luck in your retirement, Alfie. You're the best big brother a girl could have." She wiped a pretend tear from her eye and flashed a quick smile at the collective 'aaww.'

At the rear of the hall, Roberta parked her cart full of dirty dishes next to Lexan's. "She raises her arms again in that silver dress, I'm yelling 'Evita! Evita'!"

"She makes me puke," Lexan said, "but she knows how to put on a show."

From the stage the new mayor of Stradford proclaimed, "Let the party begin!" The band struck up 'Fight On, Old Stradford,' balloons cascaded from nets above, streamers exploded into the air, and another wave of cheering competed with the organized chaos. The crowd rose from their seats, some flowing to the stage where Kimberly reached down to take their hands, others making their way to the dance floor.

Lexan looked at Roberta. "She puts on a show and we get to clean up the mess. Come on." They maneuvered their carts away from the celebration.

They will not make me cry. Chelsea pressed her nails into her palms and clamped her jaw until the muscles bulged under her cheeks. The pain helped, but she could feel her throat constrict and knew tears were close. She was sitting in a small room in the basement of the hotel across from Karl and Det. Kramer. A third man was in the room behind her.

"Why did you have your cell phone with you, when you knew they weren't allowed?" The policeman's voice was hard, his words direct but not unkind.

"Like I said before, sir, I'm a fan. I wanted to take pictures of the celebrities."

Over her left shoulder the other man muttered something, but stopped when Karl looked at him.

"A fan," Kramer said. "Not an employee, a fan."

"Yes sir." She swallowed and the words came faster. "Because LeBron and Chrissie Hynde and the Governor and all those--"

"Big crowd," Kramer said to Karl, then directed his eyes to hers. "A lot of famous people on the fourth floor?"

She squeezed harder. It hurt, but kept her hands from shaking. It was cold in the small, windowless room, and the light in her eyes made it hard to see. "I wanted to get down there, maybe on my break, and I hoped I'd see them when they left maybe. When I was done."

"Her break, sure, maids get breaks," Kramer said. Beside him Karl nodded for her to continue.

"That was my plan, sir." Chelsea pushed hair behind her ear and gave him a smile. "But I never did get to my break." She hated her voice and the way the words fell from her mouth. She sounded like a little kid.

"There's only pictures of girls," Karl said swiping through the images on her phone. "Nobody important."

"Why'd you take their pictures? They're not famous," Kramer said.

Chelsea shivered. "They're kids from school. I know them." I hate them. "They'll pay me," she said. "They either want the pictures or don't want them seen."

Karl nodded his head. "Either way they pay. Not a bad scam."

"A bunch of shit." The voice behind her said.

Karl shook his head, then said to her, "So you're not like your sister."

"No sir," she stared back at him trying to keep from spitting. "She was stupid, I'm not."

Kramer looked at her. "You need to delete the pictures. All of them. Then you'll have to give us the phone like everybody else."

"All the pictures?" Chelsea managed to say. Now we won't have any proof.

"Right, but we can't confiscate her personal property," Karl said.

Kramer shot him a look, then nodded. Karl came around the table and showed the phone to the man behind her, then handed it to her. "When you're done, I'll hold it till the end of your shift."

Chelsea turned to see who it was, but Karl poked her shoulder. She nodded dumbly, swiped a tear and began deleting the photos.

"I guess that's enough," Kramer said to Karl and got to his feet. "You're lucky you're not going to jail, young lady." Chelsea swallowed and kept deleting pictures. When he turned his face away, she released a breath and her fingers began to relax.

"You want me to take her home?" Chelsea turned again to the sound, but Karl blocked her view.

"That OK with you?" Kramer said to the white-haired man.

"No," Karl said. "We need her to finish her shift, Pedro. I'll take her back upstairs."

Kramer came around the desk and stood so close to her she had to tilt her head back. "If you step one foot out of line--"

"Yes, sir, thank you sir," she said. Karl took the phone with one hand and steered her out of the room with the other.

Weigel shut the door behind them and stepped into the light in front of Kramer. "I don't like it."

"You don't have to."

"She's a loose end and all you did was slap her hand."

"And kept us all under the radar. That's how Karl plays it."

"Shit." Weigel glared at the detective through his dark-framed glasses. "You're not even sure she's working alone."

"That's why we let her go." Kramer's voice was calm in the hard, cold room. "Karl can keep an eye on her here."

"You'll let me know if--" Weigel told him.

Kramer's upraised palm stopped him. "There's always time for that." He didn't like Weigel's tone or the man's priorities. Karl should keep him on a tighter leash.

At a table in the ballroom directly in front of the podium, the Governor's administrative assistant shaded his mouth with his hand. "You have an important phone call, sir."

A confused look passed across Stanic's face, followed quickly by a smile as he remembered. "I gather I should take it."

"You might want to, yes sir," the assistant said.

The governor was a tall outdoorsy looking man, whose delicate hands didn't seem to match his image as a former athlete and an NRA card holder. He pushed his chair away from the table and set those hands on his knees. "Ladies, I'm afraid I have to leave you for a moment or two."

"Something urgent, dear?" His wife posed the tea cup over her mouth. "A pressing governmental concern?"

The assistant's wife said, "It must be, to pull him away from the Ball."

"My time is not my own." The Governor shook his head sadly then brightened. "But I leave you in capable hands."

As he stood he straightened his wife's cup which now lay in the saucer on its side. He pressed his wife's shoulder with his other hand. "Be good," he whispered into her ear.

Chelsea tried to see her face in the reflection from the burnished metal trim on the elevator wall. She imagined she was still flushed and her eyes still puffy, but at least the elevator was unoccupied. If I see another girl with her 'date,' I swear I'll punch her.

But they'll have to wait until I'm finished with Maria. The maid had to have narced me out to Karl. They took the pictures. Now I have no way to prove anything.

Maria and her cart were halfway down the long hall, the maid's pear-shaped body turned away from her. Chelsea grabbed her arm and turned her around.

"Did you tell Karl?"

The woman looked at her numbly, a tissue in her hand darted to her eyes.

"Well did you?" she demanded. "He took the pictures off my phone!"

"They're so young," she said, "so young." She wiped her eyes and pulled out of Chelsea's grasp.

"Did you?" Chelsea, followed as the maid opened a door and entered 462. "I thought they were going to arrest me!"

Maria pushed past her and closed the door. "Stop it!" she said sternly, and Chelsea stepped back.

"I thought we were supposed to keep the doors open."

"You should keep your mouth shut," Maria said and held her hand out. "Here, use this."

When it finally dawned on Chelsea that the maid had given her another cell phone, she looked up in wonder to find tears streaming from the woman's face. "They're so young," she said and dropped onto the bed.

"Maria, thank you, but, I don't understand." Chelsea sat down next to her. "Why are you crying?"

"The girls, the little ones in my village, before I came here," she began, her voice low. "They had to do things like that, things with men, grown men, disgusting things. My cousins and I, we, we came here, we had to get away from that place. Little girls with men!" she cried, her face ashen.

Chelsea forgot her anger and put her arm around her.

"My cousin and I want to own our own hotel one day. But we found young girls in this hotel, these girls who have everything, they are doing the same things! They don't have to do it, they want to! For money! It's wrong." She put her face in her hands. "That's not how Juan and I will run our hotel."

Chelsea hugged her tighter and said, "That's why I was taking their pictures."

The maid dropped her hands. "I know that now. Juan told me. I thought you were one of them until Mr. Karl took you away."

"You didn't tell on me?"

"No, I was watching you. When they took you away, I called my cousin." She pointed at the cellphone. "We think you should use it. They won't listen to us. Maybe they'll listen to you."

"First we're car parkers, now we're security guards." Bob held the door open with his foot while Joe maneuvered the bicycle rack into the narrow entrance hall.

"At least we're in show biz," Joe said. "If the star gets sick, maybe they'll let us go on. It always worked for Crosby and Hope."

"From the sound of that band, it's too late." He helped Joe set the metal grating in line with the others. "It's amazing they're doing security checks on the way out, too."

"Think Chelsea will have trouble getting away with her phone?"

"They only confiscated phones at this door. She went in with the work staff."

"Like at the airports?" Joe said. "They screen the passengers but not the baggage handlers."

"Could you be more cynical? Hopefully she can get it out the way she got it in."

"Think she got her phone in?"

"Bing, you got to stop worrying." Bob wiped his hands on the seat of his pants.

"Me, I'm OK, I just hope Chelsea is. Hey, look who's coming."

"It's either Ceasar Romero or our white-haired boss, and a guy wearing Dudley Doright's jacket and Jarrell's hat." He followed his friend's gesture to the inner door where Karl and a state trooper were leaving the lobby.

"Gentlemen," Karl said. "Looks like everything is under control. Lt. Jordan?"

The officer gave them a look that graciously could be called a sneer. "Just these two handling the main entrance?"

"Of course not," Karl said. "They're valets. My hotel security boys will be here when it's closer to time."

The highway patrolman scanned the narrow pass-way that ran between the metal racks. "It'll do." His eyes were hard to see under the brim of the peaked hat, his chin blue-black with late day stubble. "The guests'll bitch about it, sure as hell, like they did on the way in."

"The Lieutenant and I have been discussing civilian responses to authority," Karl explained. "He sees it as whining."

Jordan grunted, his head swiveling across the lobby entrance in a constant arc, his eyes never seeming to blink.

"Is it normal to run them through metal detectors on the way out?" Bob asked.

"When there's a need." Jordan didn't look at him. "It'll make it easier to return their phones."

Joe nodded to Karl. "That would be whining."

Karl looked at Bob. "One of you needs to stay in this position, the other can take a break. Officer." Karl gestured to the door.

After the two men returned to the hotel Joe said, "I think he recognized your incompetence."

"Honed right in on it. You want to break first?"

"No, you go. My luck I'd run into Lexan."

"Yeah, she might want to make out or something." Bob jumped aside to avoid Joe's swipe.

"Nobody says 'make out,' you asshole." Through the glass door Joe saw Bob enter the lobby, then his own reflection. The black smudges in the pale white oval were his eyes.

⤝┼┼⤞

It was easier working as a team, Maria standing watch and Chelsea taking pictures. In their uniforms and speaking Spanglish the two of them were practically invisible. The phone was a Droid, not an iPhone like hers, but she managed to take pictures of several high school girls and their 'dates.'

They weren't invisible to Karl. He appeared suddenly from the stairwell and Chelsea stepped quickly to put Maria between them. "Hands up, ladies," he said. "Security check."

The large man frisked her efficiently. "You already took my phone, sir," Chelsea managed.

"That I did, girlie, and now I am checking you again." He reached into the pockets in her apron, then examined the cart, Maria's as well. Seemingly satisfied, he straightened up.

"That's done," he said. "*Buenos noches, Senioritas!*"

The two maids looked at each other and responded.

"You see, this is America, and our great country has always been about second chances. Maria's entire life is a second chance, coming here from Ol' Mexico--" Karl tried to pronounce the word correctly. "--and our young friend Chelsea, well now, she has had quite the evening so far, and is clearly interested in her own second chance.

"I then, am playing the role of Uncle Sam." He pointed to his white hair, struck a dignified pose, and continued. "Even illegal aliens should get a chance at citizenship, and paying their taxes." He whispered the last part. "Our little Chelsea here has indicated an interest in a career change, and as it appears there is nothing untoward happening, I am granting her a second chance as well." He produced a leather zippered bag and handed it to her.

Chelsea gave an embarrassed look to Maria and took the bag. It was heavier than it appeared.

"Take that downstairs and give it to the manager at the desk in the lobby. Juan is his name."

When Chelsea reached the elevator and was waiting for it to arrive he added, "I don't have to tell you not to talk to strangers along the way, do I."

His manner of speech and tone of voice were light and playful, but the look in his eyes was not. Chelsea shuddered and entered the elevator. Inside she patted the phone on her head underneath her cap.

⊷⊶

Amy Michalik returned from the Governor's table and took Lee Holmgren's empty place next to Pamela. "I talked to his aide," she said.

"It's all set?" A small measure of distaste tugged at the corner of the older woman's mouth. It had no effect on the rest of her perfectly smooth face.

"You're not OK with this, are you," Amy said studying her.

"I suppose it's the price one must pay." Pamela dabbed her lips with the heavy white napkin. "However offensive."

"See, that's the thing." Amy turned toward her and laid her fingers on the older woman's forearm. "She likes doing it. It's not offensive to her, and it works for us."

Pamela flinched at the touch. "It's offensive to me."

Amy watched the cosmetics queen pull her hands into her lap. Get over it, queen bee, she thought. "It's all set," she said.

"Did you bring the report with you?"

Amy's eyes widened as she searched the table and the floor beneath her chair. "Damn. It's on the iPad. I must have left it upstairs."

Pamela shook her head. "You'll have to go up and get it, Amy."

"Get what?"

They stood up quickly and Kimberly engulfed each in an enormous hug. Straightening her dress after disengaging, Pamela said, "Amy left the report upstairs."

"No problem, Kim," Amy reached for her small clutch on the table.

"No, I can get it," Kimberly said. "I'm going upstairs anyway."

"You shouldn't have to bother," Pamela said. "And leave your admirers."

"I'm the Mayor and I can do what I want." Kimberly turned with a flounce and began weaving through the tables to the lobby. The two watched her stop along the way and exchange hugs and handshakes with well-wishers.

"It'll take her all night."

"It's her night," Pamela said.

Several tables away, Mel Radburn got to his feet, then bent to help Bonnie. They watched as Superintendent Karen Metcalf stepped out of Kimberly's embrace and introduced her husband. Radburn kissed her quickly on the cheek when his turn came and said, "This here is my Bonnie. She voted for you, too. We all did," he added with a sloppy grin.

"Thank you, sir, and you too, Bonnie. We think very highly of your husband, as I'm sure you know."

"That's nice of you to say, Mrs. Horvath. Thank you."

"Kimberly, please." She gave her hand a squeeze and smiled. "You school people were so important to our campaign and a big help to us tonight; I can't thank you enough. I hope you have a good time. I'm sorry to have to run."

"Please, I know how it is," Metcalf said. "You must have a million things to do."

Kimberly lowered her voice and the others bent conspiratorially closer. "Actually, I am on a mission."

"We'll let you go then," the former Principal boomed and backed out of her way. "Good night."

"Congratulations," Metcalf's husband said as she left.

"Great lady." Mel reached for the arm of a passing server. "Miss, we need coffee here, all around." He released her and made a circle over the table. "She'll make a great mayor."

"Four coffees, right away sir," Lexan said and continued on.

"Carmello, wasn't that one of our teachers?" Bonnie said.

He slapped his hand on the table top with a loud laugh. "Hell, I'm not the principal anymore. How am I supposed to know?"

Bonnie looked doubtfully over her shoulder then to Karen. "It's a big district," the Superintendent said and waved to someone at the next table.

⚔

The music in the hall spilled over into the lobby, and it was hard for Juan to hear the girl. "Where did you get this?" he asked again.

"From Karl, the man with the white hair. He told me to have you put it in the safe." Chelsea slid the canvas zippered bag across the counter. "I don't know what it is."

"Oh, *si*, Mr. Karl, good, good." He covered the bag with both hands and pulled it closer. "From which floor, please?"

"The fourth, the 400 rooms." She faced the man directly and spoke slower.

He made a note on a sticky. "That is Maria's floor, my cousin."

"Oh, I work with her. She's very nice."

Juan smiled. "She working you pretty hard?"

"She is, I should get back," Chelsea said dropping her voice. "I wanted to thank you--"

Juan shushed her with a look and turned away to a customer. Chelsea crossed the lobby, and peeked into the ballroom. A middle-aged band was playing hip-hop and she laughed at the way people were trying to dance to it. The dresses on the women were fabulous and she was tempted to step inside and get a better look, but she remembered Karl and turned back to the bank of elevators.

"I wonder, could you do me a favor?"

She spun her head at the sound of the woman's voice. "Oh, the Mayor, Mrs. Mayor," she stammered, embarrassed by the warmth on her face. "Sure, I'd be glad to."

Kimberly smiled. "Mrs. Mayor, I like that."

"I'm sorry. Mrs. Horvath." The elevator doors opened and she cursed herself.

"I need you to run something back down here for me, something from my room."

Chelsea pushed the button for four before Kimberly inserted the penthouse floor key. "We're going up to the top if you don't mind." She wondered if this was the other Larkin girl.

"No, that's fine."

The car stopped at four and a man with an envelope in his hand lurched off with his date. Chelsea saw the two carts when the door opened, but neither Maria nor Karl. "That's where I'm working tonight."

"We'll get you back there in a minute. I appreciate you helping me out."

"No problem," Chelsea said. "I really like your dress."

"You do? I wasn't sure."

"You look great, Ma'am."

The girl examined the smile on the woman's face and dug her nails into the palms of her hands.

Bob stood aside and held the ballroom door for the elderly couple, then kept holding it for the several couples that followed. Their presumption that it was his duty to serve them pricked his ego as the women's perfumes irritated his mucus membranes. He was cursing their arrogance and his attire, when the last man in the group shoved several bills into his hand.

"Thank you," the man said.

"No, thank you," Bob replied automatically and stepped through the doorway into the ballroom. It was loud inside, amplified music blaring through man-sized speakers, and dancers swaying like a windblown field of live maize amidst the bundles of dead cornstalks. Bob stayed on the perimeter of the room and tried to find Lexan.

A hand touched his, he flinched. "Hey."

"I guess you didn't see me," Lexan said. "Sorry."

"I'll be OK when my heart gets back to normal."

"A little wound up. I am, too." Lexan stood with her arms clasped across her chest.

"I'm worried about Chelsea."

"I saw her a minute ago and she's fine. Looked fine anyway."

Bob pulled Lexan away from the last table and deeper into the shadows. "She was down here? What was she doing?"

"She just poked her head inside the door and was gone before I could get to her." Lexan frowned, her arms still tight around her body. "I'm sure she's fine."

"She's back upstairs with the whores and the johns and a dozen security people. What was I thinking?" Bob stepped in a half circle and slapped his arms against his legs.

"I didn't mean that."

"We have no idea how she's going to get the camera out."

"Great, now I'm hysterical, too. Is that what you wanted?" Lexan spun her face to his and glared. Her eyes were half-filled and it looked to him like she was clamping her chin shut to keep it from quivering.

"Hey, sorry, Lex, it just seemed that Joe and I were worried and you weren't." He put his hands lightly on her shoulders. "You've been so strong the whole time."

Lexan stepped back and wiped a quick hand across her eyes. "I'm worried, too."

He studied her expression. "But not just about Chelsea."

She looked away. "It's that obvious?"

He smiled hoping she would too, but she didn't. "I'm a trained professional."

"I'm an idiot, that's what I am," she said, her mouth a tight, flat line. "I keep throwing myself at him and he keeps running away."

"Give him some time."

"I would, I can see that. I get it. But he won't open up to me at all. I think, I guess I just imagine it, but I see flashes in his eyes or something he says. I don't know, then the door slams shut and he's gone. Like he's not there."

"He really loved his wife."

"I know. That is the worst thing imaginable. And she was pregnant." Lexan wiped away a tear that had already dried. "But what can I do about that?"

"You don't have to do anything. He needs time to get over the loss." Bob waited until she returned his look. "He's afraid, Lexan."

"I am too." Her eyes returned from his to the dancers in the ballroom. "I need to protect myself."

Bob cocked his head and furrowed his brow.

"I'm taking your advice, Mr. Counselor." She released her arms and blew out a long breath. "It's over. I tried, but he's not ready. So I'm done. We're done."

"That's not what I meant."

"Probably not," she said. "But you can't have it both ways."

The elevator pinged and the door opened to the eighth floor.

"It's right down the hall," Kimberly said, "both halls actually. It's a corner suite." Chelsea followed her sliver-clad figure down the carpeted hall to the right.

"We'll go in the back door," the Mayor said. "I left it open." She faced the girl and gestured to her dress. "No place to put the key!" They passed a bedroom and a bathroom on the left, and followed a short hall around a corner into a living room. A plasma TV stretched across one wall above a fireplace, a wet bar stood in a corner. A large leather sofa in a U faced them. Other groupings of chairs and tables covered with flowers were spread across the immense room. Through the wall of windows red and white lights on the highway below blinked in the darkness.

"You like the view?" Kimberly took a quick look around, then turned in mid room and stretched her arms as if she actually owned the place.

"Gorgeous," Chelsea said. "I think I can see downtown Cleveland from here."

Kimberly picked up the small blue-clad iPad and held it out. "Take this downstairs to Amy. Mrs. Michalik. You do know Mrs. Michalik, don't you?"

"Yes, Ma'am, she hired me." Kimberly gestured with her arm, and the girl took the computer down the hall and opened the rear door.

"Be sure that Amy gets that," Kimberly called from behind her.

Her hand poised to call the elevator, Chelsea waved at the mayor who was now leaning out of the other door to the suite. Kimberly returned her wave and Chelsea could see a tall man in a tuxedo inside the room behind her. She supposed he had been in one of the bedrooms.

Chelsea waved to the guard at the far end of the hall as he pushed open the door to the stairs and continued his rounds. She couldn't see him very well, but he reminded her of the fat man from the junkyard. When the door closed behind him, she hurried back across the hall to the mayor's suite.

She pulled the rear door shut behind her, muffling the sound with her body. She checked the cell was on and the flash off, laid the iPad on the small table, and followed the hallway toward the voices in the living room.

"Tommy Boy, so nice of you to drop by," Mrs. Horvath was saying. "Would you like a drink?"

"I would say it's always my pleasure, Cookie, but that's the point isn't it?" Governor Stanic stood in the center of the room and admired his reflection in the windows. "I bet you could get used to living like this."

"Beats the old days." She kicked off her shoes and handed him a glass.

"The no-tell motel." He grunted a laugh and set the single malt on the mantle.

"Not drinking tonight?" She turned her back to him and he unzipped her dress. From behind a table filled with flowers, Chelsea's eyes widened. She slid the camera from photo to video and punched the red circle.

"No, I want to keep a clear head," the Governor said. "Unlike the old days."

When Kimberly dropped the dress his eyes followed it to the floor, returning to her breasts as they always had. "You still look good," he said.

She took his hand and led him toward the bedroom, but he stopped after two steps. "No, the old way."

"I don't do that anymore." She watched him loosen his belt.

"Yes, you do." His mouth in the grin she hated, his pants dropped to the floor.

She faced him with her hands on her hips. "You know me too well."

"I know you'll do whatever it takes to be the next governor."

She refused to lower her eyes or move toward him.

"The cheroot's not enough this time."

"You're not the president."

"Not yet, but I got the job you want." The Governor took a step forward and put his hands on her shoulders. "It's all about give and take. You give and I take."

She tensed at his touch and he laughed.

"Just relax, Cookie." His hands kneaded the muscles of her neck and a sigh slipped through her teeth. "No one else calls you that, do they."

She hated the warm pressure radiating from his fingers. "I'm the next governor."

He remembered the huskiness of her voice from the other times. "That's the deal. I move to Washington, you move to Columbus."

Unable to pull her eyes from his, she felt the pressure of his hands increase. Her knees buckled and she settled onto the floor below him.

"Have I ever lied to you before? Cookie?" He reached for the scotch.

Chelsea kept them in frame, making sure the red square was on and it was recording. She took as much as she could, clicked it off, and cursed under her breath at the sound. Then she silently got to her feet and crept down the hall. Their awful grunting pursued her to the door. She cracked it open and peeked out.

Karl stood at the elevator, his arms folded and his eyes scanning. She pushed it shut and leaned her back against it, her breath a rapid gasp. She was trapped.

"I'll just pop into the bathroom a sec and then you can leave." Kimberly's voice grew louder as she approached. The girl darted into the small bedroom as the Mayor's bare feet padded down the hall.

She tried to calm her breathing. The wall thudded as the powder room door closed and the fan began to hum softly. She peered out of the bedroom into the dimly lit hall and saw the iPad where she had left it by the door. The toilet flushed.

If she sees it, I'm dead. If she sees me, I'm dead. Chelsea held her breath and crossed the hall. A rhomboid of yellow light flashed out of the bathroom onto the wall beside her. She snatched the iPad. Maybe she stopped to check herself in the mirror. The light snapped off and darkness refilled the hall. Panting, open-mouthed in the bedroom, she heard Kimberly's soft tread fade away.

The red numbers on the alarm clock by the bed told her she had been gone from the fourth floor for nearly half an hour. That explained Karl's presence outside.

The front door of the suite thumped closed. Did they both leave, or only one? She looked at the clock again. I can't call Ms. Warner or Herr, they had to turn in their phones.

She forced herself to breathe from her diaphragm and that helped. Her eyes slowly adjusted to the half darkness, and her breath slowed somewhat. She heard another thump and strained to hear the elevator bell. After five agonizing minutes she risked opening the door. No sign of anybody.

Chelsea opened the door a bit more, still no one. She looked down the hall the other way and stepped out. She crossed the hall and into the stairwell, clutching the blue covered tablet and carefully placing her feet on the metal stairs. Heavy footsteps clanged up toward her as she descended, and she hurried to open the door on four and escape into the corridor. She looked left and right for her cart, raced to it and shoved it around the corner. She would worry about the iPad later.

⚊⫶⊱

Roberta took the last tray of dessert plates and coffee cups off the cart and set them on the counter next to the washing station. She wiped a bead of sweat from her upper lip and said to Lexan, "Hey, I forgot to tell you something I heard before."

The younger woman rubbed her lower back and furrowed her brow. "What?"

"Too loud to talk in here. Come on." Lexan followed her out of the humid din to a short corridor that led around a corner to the loading dock.

"The smoking lounge, I guess." Lexan pushed a cigarette butt across the cement with her foot. "What did you want to say?" She held herself against the cold.

"Typical Stradford story. All the fancy people and one of our kids gets busted."

Lexan riveted her eyes on the French teacher. "Who was it?"

"One of those girls working upstairs got caught by the police. Probably stealing something," she said. "That's what gets me, kids around here don't need--"

"Who was it? Who was the kid?"

Roberta was puzzled by her interest. "Does it matter? One of Stradford's finest. The school gets another bad rap. I'm just glad the levy's passed."

"Do you know her name or not?" Lexan demanded.

"No, I don't, that's all I heard. Hey, where are you going?" Her mouth still open, she watched Lexan hurry back into the hotel.

⚊⚊

Chelsea found Maria's cart outside 442 and willed herself to slow down as she entered the room. She wanted to shout about the pictures she had taken, but took a deep breath, then another. Maria nearly dropped the towels in her hand when she saw the girl.

"There you are. I was so worried about you."

"I'm fine, really," she rushed, then paused seeing the concern in the older woman's eyes. Chelsea put a hand on her arm and explained what was on the phone. "Really, I'm OK, but since they turned off the wifi we need to find a way to get it out of the hotel."

"The children are bad," Marie said, "because they see their elders doing bad things."

"We can stop them if we can get the pictures out of here."

"But they're screening everyone in the lobby, that's what Juan told me," Maria said. "They have metal detectors and wands."

"We didn't have any problem getting the phone in."

"That's how they think around here. We're all thieves. We're not bringing stuff into the hotel, we're carrying it out." She squinted her eyes nearly shut and shook her head. "Getting anything out of here tonight won't be easy."

Chelsea tapped the phone case with her thumbnail. "Can we open a window? Herr Lehrer and Mr. McCauley are downstairs. I could drop it to them."

Maria sat down on the edge of the bed and patted the space next to her. The girl sat down. "Whatever happens," the maid said, "I'm proud of you. The windows won't open and are too thick for us to break. But you, you're one of the good ones--"

"Taking a break, are we ladies?"

The women stiffened as Det. Kramer strode into the room and looked down at them. "It doesn't look to me like this room is clean."

Chelsea opened her mouth but no words came out. Beside her Maria struggled to stand up and Chelsea thought too late about shoving the phone into one of the maid's pockets. She waited behind Maria as long as she could before standing and saying to the detective, "Why are you here?"

Kramer held her eyes as she reddened. "You shouldn't have to ask that."

"She is doing a good job," Maria said. "Very good."

"Is she?" Kramer flicked his eyes from one to the other, enjoying their fear. "I am here to give your assistant a ride home. I hope you can manage without her."

The cell phone with the pictures burned in Chelsea's mind. She tried to catch Maria's eye, but the maid was standing between her and the policeman looking down at the floor. "Wait, the iPad," she said quickly. "I have to return the iPad. To Mrs. Michalik." She turned to the left and the right trying to remember where she had left it.

"iPad?" Kramer's voice was hard, short.

"I was supposed to give it, it's blue, to Mrs. Michalik, you know--"

"I know who she is."

"--from Mrs. Horvath, the Mayor, Mayor Horvath wanted me to give it to her."

"The Mayor is in the penthouse. How did you get it?"

"Mrs. Horvath, saw me in the lobby, downstairs, and took me up there with her."

"You were in the lobby? And the penthouse?" The lines between his eyes and his hairline deepened. "You were told to remain on the fourth floor."

"Yes, I was, and now Mrs. Michalik needs it. I don't know what's on it, but--"

The detective lifted his hand to stop her. "I don't know anything about an iPad. I'm taking you home."

"Wait let me show you." Chelsea jostled Maria as she dashed around her into the hall, and jammed her hands under the towels in her cart. When she turned around with the iPad, Kramer was close behind her.

He snatched it from her and brought it back into the room. He opened the cover, then tossed it onto the bed. "Now turn around and face the wall."

Maria stood horrified as Kramer searched her, roughly. The girl looked ready to cry but held her mouth clamped tight.

The detective jabbed a finger at Maria. "Now your turn."

"No cameras, no phones," he said when done. "Let's go, Chelsea."

Maria gave her a quick hug, then watched her disappear into the elevator with Kramer.

⇥⇤

Lexan was waiting under the canopy as Joe jogged back for his next set of keys. The band had stopped playing and guests were leaving in a moderate stream, pausing to upload photos at the kiosks, and picking up their own cell phones from Nancy and hotel security. He only caught a glimpse of her in the shadows between the passing cars, but could tell she was upset.

"They caught her," she said as he stopped in front of him.

"Chelsea? Who caught her? You sure?"

"I don't know, I just heard. Roberta told me. Said they caught a girl upstairs. An hour ago. The police," she blurted before Joe could ask again.

Joe led her by the elbow away from the guests filing through the security check. "They caught her taking pictures?"

"Probably. Roberta heard it was for stealing, but that doesn't make sense." Lexan pulled her elbow free and took a step away.

"Do we know for sure it was her?"

"You gonna help me or not?"

Bob jogged up to them, panting. He tossed a set of keys to Joe. "Chelsea's in trouble," Lexan said. "If she took any pictures, they're gone now."

"The police? The police got her?" Bob said. "Shit. What are we gonna do?"

"What can we do?" Joe looked up at the lights on the fourth floor. "We can't get up there, and she can't get down until her shift is over."

"We have to do something." Lexan said.

"Are you sure it was Chelsea?"

"No, I didn't get a name. Who else could it be?" Her tone was angry and Bob's eyebrows arched as he heard it. Joe looked away.

"It could be anybody," Bob said. "A lot of kids were working up there."

"He's right," Joe said softly, looking at the wet pavement.

"So all we do is wait? We do nothing?" Lexan put her hands on her hips.

"What else can we do?" Bob's words hung unanswered in the air between them.

CHAPTER FIFTEEN

B ob set the empty can of Pabst Blue Ribbon onto the coffee table in Joe's family room with a soft tink. He thought about crushing the aluminum against his forehead like he usually did to get a laugh, but when he looked at the two of them, Joe was slouched back with his legs splayed out blindly facing the TV, and the tightly wrapped bundle of Lexan on the cushion next to him was an IED waiting to go off. He exhaled instead.

It had been an hour since the three of them had left the Marriott. The last of the volunteers, they had dragged their feet outside the hotel security perimeter hoping to see Chelsea, or at least get some definitive word on what had happened to her. They believed she hadn't left before them, but were not sure of anything.

Bob tapped the bottom ring of the can on the marble inlay hoping to spark a reaction from them. Even the anger that had erupted earlier.

"OK, we know you want to do your can thing," Joe said without looking at him.

"Get it over with," Lexan muttered.

"You'll have to beg," Bob said and looked from one to the other. When nothing happened, he tossed the can at Lexan and tapped the power button on the remote. Neither moved. He sighed again, and stood up. "You two are absolutely no fun."

In the kitchen he opened the refrigerator and pushed aside an oddly shaped package of mayonnaise. There was one more beer in the carton. He pulled it out and shrugged at the bottle of Rolling Rock. Not finding a bottle opener, Bob tried his fingers, cursed the pain, and used a drawer handle to pry it off. The cap dropped to the floor, and he decided against looking for it. He was worried, too.

Beer in hand, he turned the corner from the hall into the family room and saw lights flash in the driveway. "Somebody's here," he said, and his friends leaped from their stupor.

"Is it Chelsea?"

"Sea's here?"

Joe had ripped open the front door and now stood on the porch. Bob watched Lexan move to Joe and place her open hand on his back. Bob stepped past them and waved. "Chelsea, where you been, girl?"

The car, a plain gray sedan, flashed its lights as she reached the steps. Bob looked closely at it, then joined the others in hugging Chelsea. The family room was a brighter and louder place when they returned inside.

"I hope you weren't worried," the girl said. "I'm fine."

"We weren't worried, kid, we were flat out scared to death," Bob said.

"Not me," Joe said. "I was a rock. I knew you were too tough to be in trouble."

Lexan slugged him and laughed. "He was a basket case."

"They both were, OK, all three of us." Bob joined in their laughter.

"You look fine," Lexan said taking a step back. "Why are you so late?"

"We heard you were arrested," Joe said.

"Is that why Det. Kramer dropped you off?" Bob watched Lexan's eyes flash from the girl to Joe and back.

"I wasn't arrested. They yelled at me, twice, but I'm OK." She sat hunched forward on the sofa, her hands clasped around her knees.

"Did they take the camera? Did you get any pictures?"

"She's safe, Joe, that's the thing," Lexan said, the first time she had responded to him in anything other than anger.

"You're right, sorry."

Lexan gave him a soft smile. "Did they take it from you?" she asked Sea.

"They made me delete the pictures on my iPhone, and held it until they let me go. There were maybe twenty. Amber's friends, kids in my grade. They're gone."

Joe looked at Bob and shook his head. "Who's they, Chelsea, who took your phone?"

The girl continued looking at the floor and it was hard to hear her voice. "Det. Kramer, Karl, and some other guy."

"Did they hurt you?" Lexan asked, her hand drawn to her mouth.

Chelsea shook her head and looked up. "They scared me to death."

"So then they sent you home? That's why you're late?"

She sat up straighter and let out a long breath. "No, they needed the help so they sent me back to work. Back upstairs to change dirty linen." She spat out the last words, and a disgusted look crossed her face.

"Well, at least you're safe now."

"You're a brave girl, Chelsea Larkin," Bob said. The girl shook her head.

"I'm just so glad," Lexan said.

Bob watched Lexan smile at Joe, this time longer, and he smiled himself. "Guys, we dodged a bullet," he said. "And our plan worked, from a tactical standpoint anyway," he continued as they glared at him. "Come on, it did. We really had them."

"The point is," Joe said shaking his head, "Chelsea is safe."

Chelsea looked at their serious faces. "So you guys aren't mad at me for losing the pictures?"

"Mad at you? You're the hero," Joe said.

"Then I can tell you the rest of it." Chelsea grinned at them, her hands still clasped in front of her. "We may still have a chance. Maria gave me another phone and I got some good pictures."

"Who's Maria?"

"Pictures of what?"

"Where are they?"

Chelsea laughed at their spate of questions, explained, and finished with Kramer's appearance in the hotel room.

"So you stuck the phone in the towels when you pulled out the iPad. Pretty clever." Joe nodded.

"I hope Maria realizes it's there. Detective Kramer would have found it on me for sure. He even looked under my hat."

Lexan hugged her, and Joe slapped her back, then heard something outside and left the room.

"That's strange," he said as he returned. "I'm sure I heard someone."

Bob looked up. "Let me take a look." The men returned to the porch and found it empty, lit dimly by the single bulb in the ceiling fixture. The taillights of a car receded into the dark. "You get a lot of people ringing your bell at 11:00 pm?"

"Mr. Popular. I have to repel them with a cattle prod."

"Hey," Bob said and pointed.

"Why is this open?" Joe reached into the mailbox. "A cell phone!"

They hurried into the living room, Joe holding the phone in the air. "Look familiar?"

"Yes! Marie must have given it to Juan," Chelsea squealed. "Det. Kramer let me call her to bring my purse, and she figured out what I meant."

She looked at the screen, then at them. "You will never believe what is on it!" After she recounted the scene in the Mayor's room, their joy was tempered.

"She is a pig," Lexan said

"We caught the bastards red-handed." Joe looked at Bob expectantly, but the counselor said, "No joke this time."

"Come on," Joe said, and they followed him into his office, a small room facing the deck in the rear of the house. Chelsea plopped into the desk chair and began tapping keys. Lexan and Bob crowded around the screen.

"The video is of the Mayor and Governor Stanic. I got a few pictures of the girls, but most of those were on the phone they took away."

"You did fine, Chelsea," Joe said.

Moments later their elation turned to disgust. "I can't look at this," Lexan said as she played the video. "It makes me puke."

Bob laid his hand on the girl's shoulder. It was rock hard. "Sorry to make you go through this."

"I have to," she said, and took a deep, shuddering breath.

Joe swiveled her chair away from the screen. "Where should we send them, Lex?"

"The *Plain Dealer*, Channel 3 and Fox News."

"I got another idea," he said. "How about their website?"

"The Inaugural Ball site," Lexan said. "Great. They can't hide from it then."

Chelsea rotated back to the screen. "I know the address." An election night picture of the beaming Mayor appeared as the web page loaded.

"Wait, I got a title for it. A new title," Bob said. Chelsea stopped typing. "We change it from 'Inaugural Ball,' to 'Balling at the Inaugural.' What do you think?"

Bob watched them laugh, together, and knew they had succeeded. "You guys got this under control. I'll go get some more beer." He was whistling as he left.

Parked outside across the street, Peter Weigel sat slouched behind the steering wheel. He watched Bob pull away from the house, and got out of the car.

Three houses away on the other side of the street, a man reached for the door handle of a different car. Another man said, "Wait, *mi amigo*. Just a little longer."

Inside the house, Lexan laid her hand on Chelsea's shoulder as the girl's fingers danced across the keyboard. "Once we get these uploaded, we can send them to the local papers, and just to be safe, to each of our own email accounts as well."

"Think Mel would like his own set?" Joe said.

"It's not funny, Joe," Lexan said. Her other hand lay on his arm.

"I know," he said, then turned with her as they heard a voice in the hallway calling, "Where's the party?"

Weigel entered the room in the rumpled suit he had been wearing at the Ball. "The door was open and the lights on. I hope it was OK to come on back."

Joe stood and extended his hand to the assistant principal. "Sure, no problem. I don't think you've ever been here." A warning bell went off inside his head.

"Never had the pleasure," he said, his eyes moving rapidly around the room. "Good evening, Ms. Warner, and I know you, you're Chelsea Larkin, aren't you?" Joe returned Lexan's quizzical look as Weigel stepped toward the girl.

She tapped several more keys, and stood up keeping her body in front of the screen. "Yes, sir."

"Don't get up, keep doing what you're doing." Weigel motioned the girl to sit back down. "I don't want to get in your way." As he looked at Joe, the girl slid Maria's cell phone into her pocket.

"Can I get you something to drink? Water?" Joe said.

"No, thank you." He rubbed his stomach and grinned. "Anyway, the reason why I'm here, is I just wanted to thank all the volunteers who worked tonight. The Mayor and the School Board are so happy about the effort you and all the others made."

"You could tell us Monday at school." Lexan stifled a yawn. "Sorry."

"That's the old way, the way things used to work." Joe noticed the shine in Weigel's eyes and how his voice rose and fell in animated tones unlike his normal drone. He must have been drinking. "Now that the city and the schools are working together, we don't want to wait to thank the people who help us."

Joe watched the man bring his open hands together and intertwine his fingers, facing each of them in turn with his symbolically united fist. Lexan tried to stifle another yawn and failed.

"A brave new world, is that it?" she said.

"Better than that, a more streamlined way of doing business. No competition. Both facets of government working together."

Joe edged closer to Chelsea, his hand on the top of her shoulder. He could smell the alcohol on the man's breath. "They didn't work together before?"

Weigel's hands shot apart. "No. You probably couldn't tell, but coming in from the outside I could see how things really worked. It was a mess." A spit bubble burst on his lip and a hand darted to wipe it away. "A bunch of shit."

Joe felt the girl beside him stiffen. "Hey, now," he said.

"Oh, sorry, I'm very sorry," Weigel said, bowing toward the girl. "No excuse for my language. Please, pardon me."

"It's OK," she said.

"No problem." Joe took a step toward him. "Thanks for coming by. You must have more teachers to thank."

"My pleasure." Weigel looked around him to the computer screen. "What is it you're doing on the computer? It's so late."

"Trying to download pictures from the Ball site, Mr. Weigel," Chelsea said. "We wanted to see the celebrities, but it hasn't been updated yet."

"You know how to do that?"

"I took a class in it. At school." Chelsea looked to Lexan with furrowed brows.

"I took some pictures on one of the cameras they gave us." The teacher patted the girl's shoulder. "I uploaded them on a kiosk and wanted to see how they came out."

"Lex says she got a great shot of Mr. Radburn dancing with the new Mayor."

"They were really busting some moves," Chelsea said.

As Weigel's eyes flicked from Lexan's face to the computer screen, Joe felt Chelsea tug on his pant leg. "You should be able to download them onto a disc. Maybe we could show them at a faculty meeting." The Assistant Principal's mouth smiled as he spoke, but his eyes didn't.

"That's right, you're a tech guy, we could have asked you," Lexan's hands waved across her face. "Sorry, but I can't hold it any longer."

Weigel watched Lexan leave the small room. "I should get going," he said and stepped into the hallway. "I've taken enough of your time."

Joe stood to follow, but stopped as Chelsea grabbed his arm. "It's him."

Weigel continued down the hall and Joe lowered his voice. "What do you mean?"

"He was the other man. When they questioned me. They called him Pedro."

"His first name is Peter. He was with the cops?"

"His voice, I knew I heard it somewhere. When he said 'a bunch of shit'. I remember him saying that."

Joe looked into the dimly lit hall and reached out his hand. "Give me the cell, and let's get you out of here." He quietly opened the door to the deck and handed her his car keys.

"I'm not leaving."

"I don't know what's going on here, but you have to get to a safe place. Take my car and go home. Now, Chelsea."

She started to speak, but he glared at her. She handed him Maria's cell and stepped out the backdoor onto the deck without a word. He watched her descend to the darkened lawn and wave stiffly as she crossed onto the driveway. Behind him he heard a thump and a muffled scream.

He hurried down the hall and stopped. Weigel held Lexan against the wall by her throat.

"Lexan!" He ran.

Weigel smashed her into the wall and turned around. A wavy red smear trailed Lexan's head as it slid down.

Joe threw himself at Weigel, his arms flailing wildly. Peter checked him, stepped aside and calmly smashed a fist against his head.

Joe staggered back, his head ringing, his eyes losing focus.

><{+ +}><

Outside the living room window, Karl had his hand on Oskar's shoulder. "This won't take long."

The fat man struggled. "I want to kill him. You promised."

"Patience. The teacher won't last a minute unless he gets lucky. Then you can kill Pedro."

><{+ +}><

Weigel drove a fist into Joe's stomach, then spun him around with a blow to the face. Joe backed away, trying to get between Weigel and Lexan. She stared glassily at the ceiling.

"Leave her alone!" he managed, his voice cracking.

Weigel took a breath and shook his head. He cocked his arm and stepped forward.

Joe hunched his shoulders and raised his fists over his face.

Weigel landed on Lexan's leg and lost his balance. Joe shouldered him down as he stumbled past. Joe shook his head and tried to catch his breath. His vision cleared a bit, and he kicked the side of the man's head.

Weigel groaned once and settled on the floor. Joe stood hunched over him, panting, blood in his eyes, dripping from his mouth. He dropped to the floor next to Lexan.

He couldn't wake her. Frantic, he looked for something, water, a cloth, anything. His eyes found Weigel next to her, his suit coat open. He snatched the handgun from his belt. A Colt 1911 like his father's.

Joe rocked from his knees to his heels. He racked the .45 and stuck it into his waistband. Lexan's breathing was steady. She moaned as he pulled her away from Weigel. He got a sofa cushion and a chair from the living room, and slid the cushion under her head.

The pistol clattered onto the floor. He set the little table upright and laid the weapon onn it. He sat down on the chair between Lex and Weigel, drawing an arm across his face. He spit blood onto the floor. He flexed his fingers to keep them from shaking.

Some minutes later, Weigel stirred and tried to get up.

"Don't move," Joe said and picked up the gun.

"Fuck you--"

Joe fired into the floor, the shot much closer than he intended. Weigel's hands flew to his head.

"Yeah, I'm serious," Joe said. "Now sit up slowly."

Weigel leaned his back against the front door. To Joe's right, Lexan mumbled something, but he didn't look at her.

"Why are you here?" Joe said.

"You gonna kill me?"

"I might. I can barely see you. What do you want?"

"Fuck. The pictures, what else?"

"You took the pictures from the girl."

"The other pictures. You must have got them from Juan. Followed the little spic on a hunch."

The gun wavered in Joe's hand. "No."

"When I get up, you're gonna kill me or I'm gonna kill you." Weigel started to move.

Joe fired again. The bullet blew out the narrow window beside the front door. Glass shards showered Weigel's left side. He reached his hand to his elbow and saw it covered in blood. "You shot me," he said, his eyes wide.

"Not where I was aiming, but close enough." Joe carefully stood up and reached for his cell phone. Weigel gathered himself again and Joe stepped back. "I'm not going to kill you, I'm calling the police."

"I'd kill you if the positions were reversed."

"I'm not you."

"No, you're a better man than me. St. Fucking Joe." Weigel coughed a laugh and tried to straighten his arm. "First you screw things up with the strike, now this with Mayor Kim."

Joe thought a moment. "You must have been around last spring."

"Wait, you missed something? Shit. I told Karl we were wasting our time warning you. You never got the message."

"No, I guess I missed that."

"You have no idea how this town works." Weigel flexed the fingers beneath his bleeding wound. "I can't use my arm. You don't have one fucking clue. But you think you're better than everybody else."

Joe nodded. "I didn't kill anybody," he said and thumbed 9-1 on the phone.

"You would if you knew I killed your wife."

It was like looking through a tube. Joe saw only the clear center of Weigel's face, the rest was black. He pocketed the phone and aimed the gun at the eyes.

"There you go, now we're getting somewhere."

"What do you know about Cathy?"

"I know that piece of concrete hitting your car was no accident. I know how the car rolled over after we dropped it. I know how your face looked when she died."

The gun shuddered in Joe's hand. He braced it with his left.

"I watched you try to put her face back together as she bled out. So sad."

Joe's eyes filled. He lowered his aim to the killer's leering mouth.

"You cried like a baby." Weigel coughed. "You sensitive bastard."

Kill him, the voice screamed inside Joe's head. "No, I'm not like you," he managed to say.

"Yeah you are. We all are. Pull the fucking trigger."

The Colt clattered as Joe laid it down. He set his feet and clenched both his fists. The man who killed his wife grinned.

"You weren't even smart enough to get the message."

Joe kicked Weigel in the crotch, then jumped on him. Smashing his fists into his face, a right, a left, another right. Blood and mucous spattered the floor and the wall behind. His hands ached as he tried to erase the satisfied smirk.

"That's it, Joe, now finish the job." Weigel's words were garbled by the blood and barely audible over Joe's tortured breathing.

"No. That's what you want."

"That's what Karl wants." Weigel managed a broken grin. "You do. Too. Get the gun."

⚔

"He gets rid of him for us, and we keep it contained." Karl nodded, his eyes on the scene inside.

"He killed my Laurel Ann." Oskar pulled away.

Karl yanked him down by the collar. "She's gone, we can't help that."

Oskar swallowed a sob and pounded his fist on the side of the house.

⚔

Joe rocked back on his knees, and looked at his hands. Bloody, knuckles scraped, a fingernail missing. They hurt. "No, I'm not like that."

"Bullshit. Everybody is."

Joe wrenched himself away from the gore. I'm an animal with his kill, no better than that.

"You like the feeling, don't you?" Weigel hissed. "I do too. I really got off on killing the Larkin girl."

"You killed Amber." Joe grabbed Weigel by the throat and squeezed his thumbs into his windpipe. Weigel gurgled a laugh. His face reddened, his eyes bulged. Joe banged his head against the floor and squeezed harder.

"What did he say?" a voice said behind him.

Chelsea Larkin.

Joe's hands jerked open. Weigel's head thumped onto the floor. He twisted himself away from Weigel to look up at her. "Why are you here?"

She looked past him to the man on the floor. "What did he say about Amber?"

"Nothing, he's crazy." Joe heaved himself to his feet.

"Are you OK? You're all bloody." She looked around the room. "And Ms. Warner--"

"I'm fine. She will be. I checked her," Joe panted. "Get around behind me. Get away from him."

"Yeah, stay away from me, or I'll kill you, too." Weigel pulled himself up on his good elbow, his face a plump pumpkin, his nose bent to one side and bleeding.

Sea's voice cracked. "Did, did you kill Amber?"

"I did," Weigel gasped. "How does that make you feel?"

Joe struggled to hold the girl back with one arm and fish the phone from his pocket with the torn fingers of his other. "No, Sea, we're calling the police." She flailed at him, crying, then released his arm with a heart-wrenching sigh. He finished the 9-1-1 and pushed the call button without turning his face from Weigel's.

The phone rang and somebody answered. A gunshot exploded behind Joe's ear. He dropped the phone. Sea's arm flew upward. She sobbed something he couldn't hear. Red blossomed on Weigel's chest. Splashed onto the baseboard behind him. He thudded back onto the floor. The smirk still on his lips.

"--ford Police. Was that a gun shot?" The voice in the phone tinny, disjointed.

Joe tried to gather the girl in his arms, the web of her hand bleeding onto the gun, her eyes on Weigel. "No, no!" she cried and pushed him away.

"This is Stradford 911! What is the nature of your problem?"

Joe took the weapon from the stunned girl. He stepped in front of her and fired into the dead man's body, holding the Colt with both hands. He laid the gun on the table and picked up his phone. He held up Chelsea's hand to slow the bleeding and said, "There has been a shooting at this address. Send a squad and an ambulance. Call Kramer." He ended the call and wrapped both arms around the girl.

CHAPTER SIXTEEN

J oe was a few minutes early and stood for a moment to watch the turkeys spin around the inside of the Gazebo. Grouped in fours, they rotated like spokes on a wheel inside the white gingerbread structure. "Turkey in the Straw" played from hidden speakers.

He'd been here so many times he knew the way through the maze to Detective Kramer's office, and the officer behind the thick glass buzzed him through with only a cursory wave. It was convenient, but not particularly inspiring. The brass "Stephen Michalik, Chief of Police" plate was missing from the waiting room wall.

Joe didn't want to be here. He wasn't on probation, but it felt like it. Charges hadn't been filed and he hoped they wouldn't, but there was that possibility. Superintendent Metcalf had suggested that he cooperate with the police, 'as a good citizen,' and Joe didn't want to upset any more people than he already had.

He sat down as Kramer pushed a cup of coffee across the gray steel desk. "I feel like one of the family," Joe said.

"You're here often enough."

"My civic duty." He watched Kramer eye him closely, no emotion visible on his face. He's trying to look like that, Joe thought. Part of his job.

"Something funny?"

"No, it's like being called into the Principal's office." He reminded himself to be quiet. They wanted him to talk.

"The school folks are pretty happy with you, too?"

"I'm not exactly on the teacher-of-the-year short list."

"Neither is Weigel."

Joe held his breath and counted to five. "What do you want to know?"

"Are you going to stick to your self-defense story?"

"Yes."

Kramer looked up from the file folder. "That's it?"

"I've told you seven times."

"Make it eight."

"He was trying to kill me. We fought. He wouldn't stay down. I thought he was, so I called you guys, the police." He reached for the coffee to slow himself. "Then he jumped up and came at me again."

"You shot him four times."

"I shot five times." Joe held the officer's gaze. "Hit him three."

"Not twice."

"I tried to hit him all five, Detective."

"No one else fired the gun."

"You have the fingerprints, mine, don't you? On the gun?"

"There are other prints."

"It was his gun, his must be there." Joe shielded his mouth with the cup.

"Other prints, too. Smudged." Kramer stared across the desk.

"Is that a question?"

"No, this is. Did anyone else fire the gun?"

Joe set the cup down, willing his pulse to slow. "No, I shot him."

"There was a gap on the 9-1-1 tape between one shot and the two others. More than one person had time to fire."

"That's when I called. We've been through this."

"Humor me."

"Bob was gone. Buying beer. Lexan was unconscious. She couldn't move."

"How convenient."

Joe bristled. "Who else could have done it?"

"The girl. You could be protecting her."

"Why would I do that?"

"I don't know, Mr. Lehrer. Maybe to keep her out of it."

Joe wanted to pick up the cup again, but knew his hands would betray him. "Oh, wait, now I remember, there was a masked gunman on the grassy knoll. Or was he up in the book depository?"

The muscles in Kramer's jaw bunched. "That's all you're going to say?"

Joe nodded carefully.

Kramer closed the file and folded his hands on top of it. "Because if what you're doing is protecting the girl, that's really not such a bad thing." The detective bored his eyes into Joe's.

"In fact, it's an honorable thing. She's a minor. She doesn't need a record. And if she knew about her sister, she had a legitimate motive."

Joe counted again. At fifteen he said, "Do you have anything else?"

Kramer shook his head but didn't move his eyes.

"Then maybe you can answer something for me."

Kramer glanced to the closed door behind Joe's head. "Like what?"

"You getting Michalik's job?"

Kramer's gaze broke away. "They want to bring somebody in from outside. Somebody new."

"Odd that he would take a job in Cleveland, don't you think?"

"I have no thoughts about that at all, Mr. Lehrer."

"Kind of a lateral move," Joe said. "I heard he's taking a pay cut."

"We'll be in touch," Kramer said.

"OK. Anyone else want to speak, or should we get back to grammarland?"

"My weekend was very interesting," Chelsea said in German, and the second year class quieted. She was dressed in jeans, Lehrer noticed, and a striped V-neck sweater. Her hair was neither stark black nor blonde, maybe her natural color.

"Oh, what did you do?" he said, wondering what the girl would wish to share.

"I saw a very large pumpkin," she said in German.

Joe looked expectantly around the room. "Where was it?" Jodi asked.

"It was in front of the, um, police station,"

Joe spelled the word for them on the projector and waited.

TJ looked to him, then to Sea. "Why were you at the police station?"

Lehrer cursed himself for putting the girl in this position. Rumors of the fight at his house and her role in Weigel's death had swirled through the building. If he had lectured or drilled them on grammar, or almost anything else, she would not be facing them now.

"*Ich habe Kuerbisse gern*," she said.

"She likes pumpkins," he repeated and exhaled. She will get through this. He marked the clipboard and stood up. "And that makes an excellent transition to our grammar assignment, as well as your upcoming composition." They groaned collectively as he moved to the front of the classroom.

He wrote what Chelsea and Jodi had said on the whiteboard. "Copy this into your notebooks, please." He turned to watch them. "Welcome back to personal pronoun land."

"A very large pumpkin," he said, "look, this is masculine. *Ein Kuerbis* becomes <u>einen</u> here, a direct object."

"No, TJ, we can't speak all the time. This is a skill, too." He waited for the boy to lower his arm and copy the words.

"So when Jodi said 'Where was it', she was referring back to the masculine gourd, and she should have said *er,* not *es.*"

"Should Jodi have said *er,* Herr?" Chelsea asked with an innocent grin.

"Unfair," he said making the three words rhyme. He grinned back at her.

"You can't just substitute any pronoun for any noun, anymore than you can substitute a person for any other person. As I may have mentioned before." He tossed the marker at the tray and sat back down in the circle.

The bell rang and he watched them file out of the room. They'll be fine if they keep this up. He confirmed that thought with a glance at the marks for speaking he had made on the clipboard.

Chelsea patted his shoulder as she passed, and he noticed the Flintstones Band-Aid on her hand where the Colt's slide had caught her. She'll be fine, too. There's no rubric to measure her progress, but I'll keep my eye on her. Bob and Lexan will, too.

"You don't have to do that, Jodi," he said. "Get to class. I'll straighten the chairs."

The class mother. She thanked him and scurried away and he smiled to himself. Trying so hard to find out who they are. Defining themselves against every other 16-year-old in town. Like Chelsea's hair, black, blond, somewhere in between. They're all so different and they're all the same pronoun. He picked up the marker from the floor, replaced its cap, and laid it on the tray.

⊱⊰

Lexan was sitting alone at her desk as he entered the Language Department office and Joe could only see the back of her head. Curly blond tendrils reached out from the red scarf that tried to contain them. He had talked her out of having all her hair cut off when the gash was stitched up in the emergency room. He had been the reasonable one that night, convincing her that the bare patch would grow in and even out. The scarf was one of several he had bought her.

He leaned against the door jamb and watched her fingers on the keyboard. She typed like she spoke, like she did everything, quickly and forcefully. He wondered how she managed with her long, carefully painted nails.

"It's not an art museum," she said, neither stopping nor turning. "You can talk to the exhibit."

"You are pretty as a picture."

"Liar. You were staring at the hole in my head." She spun her chair around. "Admit it."

He walked toward her and sat on the edge of his desk. "I was imagining the vast crater beneath the scarf, how massive it must be."

"I hate you," she said, the gleam in her eyes a contrast to the words.

She had looked at him the same way across the Thanksgiving table at Bob's. Separated by the turkey carcass and a bowl of congealed yams, the combination of mirth and happiness and something else had touched him. Amid the din of one of Bob's endless stories and the kids arguing over the gravy boat, Joe had seen that look, but hadn't appreciated it. Her eyes found his now, and held them.

"Lexan, it would--" he began and saw a tear on her cheek. His throat seized up.

"Don't, not here," she said and turned away.

"Let me look at you," he managed to say.

"I'm a mess, I'm crying."

"You're beautiful." He gently turned her chin toward him. "Even if you are prematurely balding."

She snorted a laugh, and he did too. "I really, really hate you."

"Then you probably want to make me dinner tonight."

She dabbed a Kleenex under her nose. "Why on earth would I want to do that?"

"Well, I did fight a guy for you."

"Not before he punched me into a wall."

"I was a little late on that, but our bruises have healed. Mostly."

"So I owe you a meal?"

"No, but we should probably do some things together besides fight." His brows gathered as he focused on her. "I can't explain how we've gotten to this point any better than I know if we even are a couple. But I need to find out. We need to find out."

The tears carried the look from her eyes down the side of her face. "I don't really hate you," she said.

"I know. It just took me a while to figure it out."

"Typical, dumb male." She tried to pull away to wipe her eyes but he held her face in his hands.

"It's one of the many things I'm working on." Joe dropped his hands to her shoulders.

"You think we should give this a chance?" she said.

"I think we should," Joe said.

CHAPTER SEVENTEEN

From a block away it looked like a furry orange bowling ball and a phalanx of black-tipped pins, but it was hard to see through the misty rain. Joe turned the defroster fan up another notch as the traffic in front of him lurched forward. Somehow the pins moved aside and the ball passed through without knocking any of them down. He wiped the condensation off the side window. I hate bowling, he thought.

A worker in blue coveralls holding the turkey cut-out continued on his way to the storage shed behind City Hall. It looked to Joe to be made of some kind of weather- proofed fiberboard, and the large man controlled it easily enough in the swirling wind. Those returning from the shed with the taller toy soldiers were having more trouble.

As he inched closer to the intersection, Joe realized they were changing the Gazebo decorations from Thanksgiving to Christmas. When the light finally flashed green, he sped around the corner away from the Cleveland-bound commuters, and the traffic thinned out. The increased air flow enlarged the clear spot on the windshield, and he adjusted his bruised back against the seat.

Through the clear windshield he could see that the shops along Stradford's main street were celebrating the holiday season as well. Red and white striped candy canes and enormous reindeer heads alternated atop the electric poles; boughs of sparkly green connected them in a garland that stretched ahead as far as he could see. Store fronts were festooned with Santas, sleighs and goody-stuffed stockings, and little white lights outlined nearly every window. Family Video proclaimed 'Joy to the World' with its collection of holiday DVDs, and Taco Bell touted its 'North Pole Cocoa with Cinnamon Snowmen' as the perfect way to take the chill off the little elves at home. A revolving light in the window of the Auto Zone store reflected red and blue and green and orange off the crèche made from chrome exhaust parts.

Brummelberger's Farm looked more depressing than usual in the gray overcast. The green foliage was gone, and the bare trees and stunted bushes glistened black against the dirty white barn and rusted, unwanted machinery. The hayloft door still gaped open, the blackness inside only a deeper shade of gray. Oskar waddled across the muddy yard, a cloud of breath obscuring his fat, round head.

Joe watched the traffic light cycle through Thanksgiving amber on its way from Xmas green to Xmas red as the junk man opened the wooden door and disappeared inside. He flexed his right hand as he waited. The bruises had faded from a deep purple to a more festive holiday green, but it still hurt when he made a fist.

Stradford Way was a black ribbon against the slate November sky. Without their leaves, the trees in the suburban front yards revealed themselves to be imposters, twigs standing on former farmland, forlorn sentinels guarding dormant sod. The only thing that's changed around here is the calendar, he thought while lightly tapping his fist on the wheel. And me.

⚞┼┼⚟

Joe took a guess as she approached his table in the back of Competitors Sports Bar. "Karl lurking somewhere in the shadows?"

"I don't know any Karl." Mayor Hellauer paused to un-button her coat before sitting down in the booth opposite Joe. "But I do have friends in high places."

Joe checked the dark corners of the bar over her shoul-der and nodded. "You do."

Kimberly released part of the smirk she had been hold-ing back. "You thought you could beat us."

"Almost did."

"Second place is almost first." The rest of the smirk bloomed on her face. "I think the expression you people use is, 'you can't fight city hall'."

"We had city hall--"

"--but you didn't have the statehouse, now did you." The smirk was now a full blown derisive sneer. "As you know, the Governor and I are old friends."

"Close, personal friends." Joe nodded. "With enough pull to keep the pictures off the web."

"Now if you'd managed to upload them to a TV station or a newspaper first, we might have had to work a little harder." Kimberly used her expansive, talking-to-the-good-citizens-of-Stradford voice.

"But your other best friend, Peter, Pedro whatever his name is. Was."

"You could have uploaded the pictures to a safe site, but you killed him instead."

"I did." Joe bored his eyes into her face until she blinked.

"To protect the girl." Her laugh the aural version of her smile. "You're the hero. Congratulations."

Joe kept his eyes on her face.

"So do you have something for me? I can't imagine why you wanted this meeting." She gathered her purse onto her lap and opened her eyes wide.

"I wanted to hear you gloat."

Kimberly laughed, the sound demeaning and loud at first, then fading. "You must think you have something."

"I do." Joe laid Maria's phone on the table and covered it with his hand.

Kimberly's face feigned indifference; her eyes searched for a place to land.

"What's that?"

"What video is on it is the better question."

"You're bluffing."

"Try me."

"Show me what you have."

"No."

Kimberly looked around the nearly empty bar. "Why should I act like you have something on me, without knowing what it is?"

"But you do know what it is, Mayor." He gave her another few seconds to think about it. "The Honorable Governor Stanic does, too."

"You wouldn't dare." Her voice was icy and hard.

"Of course not, I'm a teacher. A role model for the impressionable youth of our fair city. I would never stoop to blackmail the Mayor." Joe dropped his arms and leaned across the table. "But then I wouldn't kill Weigel, either."

Her face looked to Joe as if she were doing a story problem with three variables. He waited nearly a minute.

She pursed her lips and let out a barely audible sigh. "What do you want?"

≈‡†≈

"Quit futzing with the line and relax, Karl, you're scaring the tourists."

"The tourists are back up north working, you old goat. These are natives." Karl finished untangling the line and cast it neatly into the deeper water away from the pilings of the pier.

Alfred carefully re-folded the sports section. "I thought you told me Florida didn't have an indigenous population." He turned on the bench to keep the morning sun over his shoulder. "Wasn't that your word?"

Karl watched the bobber dip under the clear water and felt a tug a second later. He quickly wound the reel. "It's not my word, Alfie, it's not anybody's word."

Hellauer watched him step away from the railing and brace his legs. The muscles of his upper arms bunched as he furiously reeled in the line. "Your words used to be *hakuna matata,* but it seems you may have forgotten what they mean."

"I never forget a word," Karl grunted, "or a phrase." He yanked the rod to his left, then his right, and cursed.

"Blasphemy is something else the tourists don't like, my friend."

Karl turned abruptly, stopping as he saw the smile on the old man's face. He tapped the butt of the pole onto the wooden deck and let out a sigh. "That's a fact. God had nothing to do with my line snapping. Maybe I should relax more."

The former mayor of Stradford put the paper in his lap and pointed his gnarled finger at the empty spot next to him.

Karl dropped down onto the bench. "I gotta keep moving, you know. I don't like feeling like this. Un-busy or something."

"We're un-busy, whatever that may mean, because our work is done. This is our reward for working all those years." Alfred removed his Chief Wahoo cap and leaned his face into the sun. "Our marvelous, warm, reward."

Karl looked at Hellauer. "I have to admit, this is beautiful. The water's clear enough to see the bottom."

"Water you don't have to shovel or cover with rock salt."

"You're right, it's warm and blue, and this is where the money is. It's a great place. Sure it is."

"Then relax, you big, dumb, bastard." Hellauer's face was tilted back against the railing, his eyes closed.

"I can't, that's just it. I mean it's great down here, but I didn't think I'd mind leaving as much as I do." He looked down the long pier then back to the palms along the beach. "We had it set up great, and they ran us out of town."

Alfred sat up. "You can't look at it that way. We did our job. Now it's over."

"It feels like we lost. Like we gave up. You even resigned the service director job."

"You said it yourself, Karl, we're out of town. They got nothing on us."

"Not now they don't, Alfie, but we're not there to make sure. If they start looking--" Karl pounded the butt of the fishing rod onto the wooden pier.

"Kimmy worked a deal. She'll cover us like we covered her all those years. If it comes up, we handle it then. For now, re-lax."

"Is Karl still not unwinding?" a cheery voice called. "Alfred, I gave you one job to do. One little job."

They turned to see Ursula standing over them, a straw hat covering her head and shopping bags tugging both arms. "Karl, what have we been telling you?"

The men stood up. "Sorry, Uschi," Karl said. "I'll try to be happier." He took the bags from her.

"That's more like it. Now then, it's time for lunch. There's this cute place back up 13th Ave. They have a lovely quiche on the menu, Gloria told me about."

She looped her arm through Alfred's and steered him down the dock. Several people nodded as the trio passed, most of them their age, some with grandchildren. Naples lay before them, dozing beneath a dome of cloudless blue. They stepped off the wooden planking onto the soft white sand and made their way to lunch. Karl walked alone behind them carrying Ursula's shopping bags..

Fr. Jon Hastings removed the stole he used for hearing confessions, folded the purple garment, and laid it on the end table in his rectory office. On the sofa opposite, Joe sat with his elbows on his knees and his hands clasped. The priest let out a long breath and removed his Roman collar.

"You were holding that in a long time, my friend. Must be good to get rid of it."

"It is," Joe said.

"I'm glad you let me help." Hastings looked at him closely, then continued, "You know, it only means you're human."

Joe looked at him and nodded.

"We all get tempted." Hastings smiled and pointed at himself. "Even we do." Joe remained silent. "The point is, it was a minor thing, a sin of course, but you didn't act on it."

"I didn't realize I was capable of that." Joe didn't look at him as he spoke, his voice distant and controlled. "She's only been gone six months."

"But you do see now that you're forgiven, right?"

"How long ago did you notice?" Joe didn't look at him.

Hastings leaned back in his chair and wondered why Joe hadn't answered his question. "We've known each other a long time. What, twenty years?"

"Back to grade school," Joe said and nodded briefly.

"I didn't know what was bothering you exactly, but I knew something was. When you were ready, you confessed. That's how it's supposed to work." He stood up and slapped his hands together. "Now, how about a cup of coffee?"

Joe waved his hand, "I'm fine."

The priest crossed to the shelf on the other side of his office where he kept the coffee pot, cream and cups. He glanced out the window. "Gets dark so early in the winter."

Joe hadn't moved when Hastings sat back down. "Something still bothering you?" He held the cup halfway to his lips.

"What do you mean?"

"You still seem a little tense." He gestured at his collar and stole. "We're off the clock here."

"I'm fine," Joe said.

Hastings took another sip and waited. "You used to say that word a lot."

Joe looked up. He wasn't agitated like he had been so often in the fall, but Hastings could tell he wasn't relaxed either. "I'm just saying, if you want to talk--" He let his voice fade off and set the cup on the table.

"Damn it Jerry, I'm fine, I mean, good. OK? Shit. Why do you do this to me?"

"I'm not doing anything." The priest paused. "I was just thinking, maybe if you and Lexan took another run at it, you'd feel better." He held up his hands. "But it's none of my business."

Joe laughed abruptly. "You sound like Bob."

"You have a lot of people who care about you, Joe."

Joe turned away and looked through the window to the darkness outside. He looked back at his friend, let out a long breath and began to speak. "Thing of it is, I didn't know who I was. Inside. I knew I was capable of both good and evil, but, you know, I never really believed the evil part."

Hastings nodded. "You've always held yourself to a ridiculously high standard."

"Probably not going to change," Joe said. "Part of who I am." He rose and walked to the widow. "I'm not entirely over Cathy's death."

Joe was facing the darkness outside and it was hard for Hastings to hear. He rose and stood at Joe's side. "You may never be, totally."

"There's still a hole," Joe continued. "A place where she should be. She isn't there." He shrugged. "I guess you know."

Jerry laid a hand on his shoulder. "I do, and I also know you're in a lot better place than you were."

"I guess. I never realized the violence around here either. The evil." He turned to the priest. "They killed her. I got in their way, and they killed her."

"You stopped them," Hastings said. "You and your friends."

"You don't know how." He stared outside. "Now I'm like them."

"Stop right there, Joe," Hastings said sharply. "You are not like them. You did the right thing."

"You sure? It's all black and white to you?" He faced the priest. "The only thing I'm sure of is, I didn't do enough. Certainly not soon enough. They were selling their children, Father. Making them prostitutes. Right in front of me, right here in Stradford."

"Come on, I agree the level is higher, but there's always been--"

"No," Joe said sharply. He tapped the window pane. "See the statue of St. Michael?"

The priest knitted his brows. "In the parish garden with the other statues. What about it?"

"St. Michael is an Archangel."

"Where you going with this? I thought we were talking about you."

Joe tapped the glass again. "He has a sword."

"It's an artist's rendering, Joe. He's also standing on a dragon. A mythical beast."

Joe kept his eyes focused outside. When he spoke, his voice was low and clear. "The dragon is a symbol of evil. He's killing it with the sword."

Hastings' mind raced, hoping his thoughts were wrong. "He has wings, man--"

"--armor, a shield and a helmet. He's a warrior."

The priest looked into the darkened garden with him. The reflection of Joe's face replaced the Archangel's statue. "For God's sake."

"That, for sure," Joe said. "And maybe I just can't let them win."

The End

ACKNOWLEDGEMENTS
AND THANKS

I am indebted to a number of people for their help and support in getting *Personal Pronouns* into print. First of all, my parents, who were writers and readers. They instilled in me their love for both sides of that coin.

Jimmy Brogan and Tommy Ehrbar, my first writing partners. Dr. Neal Chandler and the Public Workshop in Fiction/Nonfiction Writing at Cleveland State University. The All-Ladies-Except-For-Me Book Club. My current writing colleagues, Dory Stewart and the Medina County Writers' Club.

The professional writers whose lectures inspired me, Mary Doria Russell, Tim O'Brien and Les Roberts.

Photographer Judi Terrell Linden and cover designer Julie Bayer. The former made me look good, the latter made the book look good.

The good folks at CreateSpace, Kindle Direct Publishing, Goodreads, MailChimp and Bluehost: there is a special place in heaven for those who work with the digitally illiterate.

Lastly, I am especially indebted to my editor, Jeff Gabel. A man of great talent and even greater patience, he reversed the teacher/student paradigm with kindness and skill.

ABOUT THE AUTHOR

Author David Allen Edmonds began by writing **The Faculty Lounge Stories**, based on his career as a high school teacher. **Personal Pronouns** is his first novel, featuring several of the same characters. Now retired from the classroom, he lives in NE Ohio with his wife, Marie Mirro Edmonds, babysitting their grandchildren, working on a sequel, and ruing the inevitable demise of the adverb. Really. Visit him at www.davidallenedmonds. com

BOOK CLUB DISCUSSION QUESTIONS

1. Knowing that the author was a high school German teacher like Joe Lehrer is, do you suppose any of the events in the novel are true? If so, which? Does it matter to you as a reader, whether events in a novel actually happened or not?

2. What is Joe Lehrer's major character flaw? What is in him that prevents him from being happy or satisfied? Does his character change over the course of the book?

3. Did it bother you that Joe and Lexan became involved so soon after Cathy's death? Did it bother Joe? Lexan? Did it change them in any way?

4. Do teachers have the right to be involved in local politics, or as public employees should they stay in their classrooms and teach the children? How do Joe's Teachers Association activities affect his life?

5. Is there a standard, either real or perceived, for how teachers should act or speak? If so, what is it and is it fair for everyone? Is this norm specific to locality?

6. What role does religion play in Joe Lehrer's life? Is he a church-goer? Does he believe in God? Why does he choose a priest, Fr. Jon Hastings, as his counselor?

7. What leads Joe to make a deal with the devil herself, Kimberly? Does this jive with Joe's fundamental values? What will happen next?

8. Does it satisfy Joe that he and his friends succeeded in breaking up the prostitution ring? Did they win or lose? Why do you think so?

9. Did you study a foreign language in school? What are your recollections of the experience? Did your teacher approach the class as Joe does?

10. Joe and Bob's sense of humor is similar in some ways to Karl's: they are smart-asses. Does this get in the way of the good guy/bad guy dynamic? Are Stradforders similar in other regards? Does this point to a central theme?

11. Why do you suppose the author chose the title? Do you think it's effective: does anybody want to read a book about grammar? Does the book fit with the cover?

12. Knowing this book is self-published, did you have any preconceived notions of its quality? Did *Personal Pronouns* meet, exceed, or fall short? Is the bar for Indie Pubs lower than for 'real' books?

Made in the USA
Columbia, SC
08 June 2019